*V*ictor took m
trembled. I v
up but my b

I swallowed back tears. I was ashamed. I'd been stupid. I couldn't help Gabriel even when I wanted to. I'd made it worse.

Victor pressed me close to his body, his cheek meeting mine.

"Victor," I whispered, my lips near his ear and tracing over his skin. I was unable to speak louder. Now that it was over, I was a wreck.

He shuddered against me. He bent down, his arm going under my thighs and picked me up off the floor. My face buried into his shoulder. I was worried about the others, but too afraid to look at them.

He held me, not asking, not judging. He simply held on, his cheek pressed to my forehead.

"Sang," Gabriel whispered. I opened my eyes and turned my face toward his voice. Blood trickled from his nose and his cheek was puffy. His hand sought out mine and he squeezed it.

Kota was next to him, looking over his shoulder. Blood stained his white shirt. His tie was flung over his shoulder. His lips were taut, his eyes dark. "Let's get her to Dr. Green."

The Academy

The Ghost Bird Series

First Days

♥

Book Two

♥

Written by C. L. Stone
Published by
Arcato Publishing

From The Academy

***

Other Books by C. L. Stone

For the real "Mike", who asked me repeatedly to marry
him before knowing my name.

.

♥

MONDAY

♥

♥

FOLLOWING THE LEADER

That Monday morning in August in South Carolina was scorching. I was grateful for the shade of the front porch and the sweet coolness of the concrete on my bare legs. I stared down the mailbox, urging the postman to hurry.

It was the day before the beginning of school. I had an unusual affinity for classrooms and homework and being among other people my own age. It meant I could watch how they interacted and try to understand reality, normalcy.

This year would be different.

A wasp hovered in the hydrangea bushes along the front of the porch. I ducked my head as it flew past my ear and beyond, toward the neighbor's yard.

The mailman's truck meandered up to the box. The moments ticked by and I could see him fiddling with a collection of envelopes through the window. I crouched below the barrier of the porch and out of sight. I prepped my knees to get ready to run.

The glass door swung open behind me. "Is that the mail?" Marie asked. My older sister stepped out on to the porch. Her angular eyes squinted at the crisp morning sunlight. Her brown hair was pulled back into a ponytail that hung at her neck, the strands reaching down midway on her back. Her t-shirt advertised a marathon she'd never participated in. Her jeans were long, covering most of her feet except for her toes.

I couldn't understand how she could wear so much clothing, but I didn't really expect her to stay outside for long. I thought of how different we looked. I had dirty blond hair, or chameleon hair as Gabriel liked to remind me. He said it changed color depending on the lighting. With my cut off blue jean shorts and a thin pink blouse, I was barely tolerating the humidity.

I turned again to refocus on the mailman. I could still make it.

In that instant, the mailman pulled away from the mailbox for the next one down the street.

I flew off the top of the porch stairs, landing hard on the small sidewalk path that wound around the house and sprinted across the yard. I was halfway across before Marie managed to make it off the porch. When it was clear I was going to get there first, she stopped her pursuit.

I pulled out all the mail, shuffling through bills and junk mail to find an envelope with my name on it. The orange emblem of Ashley Waters High School was printed in the corner. I held on to it, crossing the yard at a slower pace. My heart was pounding from both the running and the thrill of what I held in my hands. A new school, a fresh start, and this time I had an advantage. This year, I wouldn't be alone.

"Hand it over," Marie said, meeting me halfway in the yard.

I removed my envelope out of the pile and gave her the rest. She took the cluster of mail and headed back into the house. If she had gotten to it first, she would have kept my envelope and, more than likely, given it to our mother and I would have had to fight with her to get it back.

I remained in the yard, waiting for my sister to disappear. When the front door closed behind her, I spun on my bare feet and sprinted down the street to Kota's house.

I couldn't let my sister know where I was going. My family couldn't learn my secret. Not yet.

The boys were waiting for me.

♥♥♥

Kota's black rimmed glasses were sliding down his nose a little as he was checking the mail. I called to him from up the road. He looked up and waved to me, pushing his glasses up his nose with his forefinger, masking his exquisite green eyes. "Did you get it?" he asked.

Dakota Lee and I have a tender friendship. Randomly a week ago he brought me into his circle of friends. It was how I came to learn about the Academy, the secret school they held loyalties to. The only problem was, I didn't know a thing about it, and I wasn't allowed to ask questions. I was going to keep this promise for the sake of our friendship, and for what Kota said was my own safety. There were dangers around them that I wasn't privy to. I simply had to have faith when they told me to trust them. It seemed surreal to me, but I kept my mouth shut and my eyes open, hoping to glean, over time, the answers to the questions that buzzed through my head every time they shared a glance or whispered something around me. They were my first friends. My only friends. What else could I do?

I held up my envelope. "Anyone else?" I asked.

"I'm still waiting to hear from Victor and Gabriel. They're heading over as soon as Victor confirms." He flicked through the mail in his hands, pulling out an envelope similar to the one I held on my hands.

"Hey!" There was a shout from up the street. Nathan jogged toward us. He was wearing dark running pants and a red tank shirt with a Nike swoosh on the front. I admired the way his biceps flexed as he held up his envelope. "Let's check them out."

Kota tilted his head toward the house, inviting us to follow. We entered through the side door in the garage. Kota dropped the rest of the mail off in a bin near the kitchen. Nathan held open a door in the hallway, revealing a set of blue carpeted stairs. Nathan held his hand out, ushering me to enter. I padded my way up the steps to the room over the garage, Kota's bedroom.

Nathan dropped onto his knees on the blue carpet and started to rip open his envelope. I sat cross-legged next to him, doing the same. Kota went to his desk, grabbing a silver letter opener and cut through his envelope, unfolding the printout inside. I swallowed as I read my schedule for the upcoming year.

> Homeroom Room 135
> AP English - Trailer 10 - Ms. Johnson
> AP Geometry - Room 220 - Ms. Smith
> Violin - Music Room B - Mr. Blackbourne
> AP World History - Trailer 32 - Mr. Morris
> Lunch
> AP Biology - Room 107B - Mr. Gerald
> Japanese - Room 212 - Dr. Green
> Gym - Gymnasium - Mrs. French

Seven classes. Barely room to breathe. Now looking at it and thinking ahead to the upcoming year, it seemed overwhelming. Maybe it had been a mistake to be so enthusiastic about this.

"What's wrong, Sang?" Nathan asked. His head tilted in my direction, a rusty brown eyebrow arching.

I pursed my lips, twisting them slightly. "I was just wondering if this was a good idea."

Kota looked up from his paper, coming over to kneel next to me and sitting back on his heels on the floor. "May I see?"

I handed it to him. Our fingers brushed as he took it from my hands, but he didn't seem to notice. None of them ever seemed to notice touching as much as I did. If they grabbed my hand or bumped my hip, they passed it off as if it were nothing. Coming from a family that never touched, there was a lot to get used to around my new friends.

Kota's eyes scanned my schedule, reading off the list under his breath.

Nathan got up, peering over Kota's shoulder. "Holy shit," he said. "How'd you get seven?"

"She doesn't have a study hall." Kota pointed to the paper, lifted a brow and then looked up at me. "How did you get into the Japanese class? When did you meet Mr. Blackbourne?"

Nathan's eyes widened in surprise and looked at me, waiting for me to respond.

I blushed. After everything that happened, I'd forgotten to tell them. "I... well when Dr. Green stopped me in the hall at registration, he brought me to his office. Mr. Blackbourne was in there. They adjusted my schedule."

Nathan and Kota shared a look between them. The only thing I caught was Nathan's eyes narrowing. Did they not like this? It was hard to understand their expressions.

"What?" I asked. "I know it's a lot but you said they were there to help out the school. Is it bad they changed it?"

"No, it isn't bad," Kota said, maybe a little too quickly. "Did you happen to mention us at the time?"

I pushed my forefinger to my lower lip, pushing it toward my teeth. "I might have said something like I knew you, Kota. I didn't say anything about the others. Dr. Green recognized your handwriting on my paper."

"I didn't know Mr. Blackbourne was teaching a class," Nathan said.

"I don't think it was pre-planned," Kota said. He hooked a couple of fingers into the collar of his shirt and tugged.

"What's wrong?" I asked. The way they were reacting to this made my heart shiver. "Mr. Blackbourne asked if I was interested and he offered to teach me. Should I drop the class?"

"It's just odd that he'd take an interest," Nathan said.

"Not fully," Kota said, relaxing into a smile. He handed my schedule back to me. "It's fine. He knows what he's doing. If he wants to teach you, you're in good hands."

Last time Mr. Blackbourne was mentioned, they diverted. Now they seemed nervous. They may not have voiced their opinion, but I got the feeling they didn't want Mr. Blackbourne to know about me, or me about Mr. Blackbourne. Academy secrets. I scanned my schedule. "I'll still share classes with you all, right?

"You're in my English class," Kota said.

Nathan moved closer to me and held his paper next to mine. He was close enough that I was breathing in the scent of cypress and leather. I tried to focus and compare.

"Just geometry and gym," I said. "But in gym the boys and girls are separated aren't they?"

"We'll mix up sometimes, I bet. Besides, we're all in the same gym. I'll wave to you. Maybe."

Kota's phone rang on his desk and he answered it. After a few minutes he hung up. "All schedules are accounted for. They're heading in now."

Nathan's blue eyes locked with mine. His reddish brown hair was a little mussed but I found it to be charming. He grumbled. "And so it starts..."

I used Kota's restroom as the guys went downstairs to wait on the others. I adjusted my cut offs a little lower on my hips and pressed my hands to smooth out my blouse, pulling out the lower hem so the length fell over the pockets of my shorts. I kept readjusting the buttons on my blouse, buttoning and unbuttoning the collar to figure out what looked better. There were thin spots in the material and I was sure my father bought it at a used clothing shop. The guys always looked so good. I simply couldn't compare. I was combing my fingers quickly through my hair, when I heard a car rolling into the drive. I threw my hair into a twist and clipped it. No time to fiddle with it. The boys were here.

I ran downstairs and out into the living room. Kota held open the front door, pushing his glasses up his nose. In a line came Victor, Luke, Gabriel, North and Silas. While they were all dressed casually, casual for the guys was a different level. Polo shirts, clean slacks, button up shirts with collars. Everything looked new and I spied Hilfiger and Abercrombie logos. It made me feel like a complete slob in my old things. I shifted on my feet on the blue carpet of the living room, my hands going behind my hips to hide any nervous shaking.

The others greeted Kota and Nathan in the hallway. Silas was the first to spot me. Locks of his black hair hung around his eyes and he brushed it aside, smiling at me. He came close, towering over me and pulled from his envelope from his back pocket. "Hey look, they let me in."

I giggled. His smile widened, his clean white teeth a contrast to his olive skin.

We congregated in Kota's living room. I sat in the middle of the couch. North, dressed in black with a single gold hoop earring, sat to my left, Gabriel wearing a bright orange shirt and blue crystal studs in his ears, sat to my right. Their contrasting styles had me glancing from one to the other, pondering how they managed to stay friends when they seemed so different. The others sat on the floor in a circle facing us. It felt strange to be higher up than everyone else but they didn't seem to notice.

I blushed as North casually put an arm behind my shoulders against the couch cushions. I peeked up at his tan face. His dark eyes caught mine quickly and I glanced away. While I knew he wouldn't hurt me, his eyes were so intense, it had my insides vibrating.

"I vote we get bean bag chairs," Luke said. He might have been North's step-brother, but Luke's long, blond hair loosely hung around his shoulders, and his smile was warm and always ready to laugh. He leaned back on his hands as he sat with his legs crossed on the floor. "If we're going to have meetings here, we need something besides the floor."

"We're working on that," Kota said.

North's fingers traced small circles at my shoulder. I glanced at the others to see if they noticed, but they were watching Kota. I tried not to blush. This was normal, right? I told myself he was just being friendly, and willed my heart to still.

"Now that we have schedules, let's start at the beginning," Kota said, getting the attention of everyone in the room quickly. "Or rather, let's start with getting there."

"I've got Gabriel," said Victor, fiddling with the silver medallion at his neck.

"We're good," North said. "Luke and I can grab Silas."

"Good. Logically, I'll take Nathan and Sang," Kota said.

"You mean on the bus?" I asked. They all looked at me. I

felt my cheeks radiating heat. "I mean, I don't think I could get away with riding to school with anyone. If I'm not getting on the bus, my sister will know and she'd tell my parents."

"Aw, shit," Nathan said. "I didn't think about that. Don't tell me we're riding this year."

I held up my hand toward him. "You don't have to. I mean, I can ride the bus. You guys can ride together. It's no big deal. I'll just see you when I get there."

The group exchanged glances. I caught Luke's gaze as he stared at me, his blond hair falling in front of his dark eyes. I wasn't sure if he realized he was doing it, or maybe he was just staring out into space but happened to be looking in my direction. When he came back, he started blinking his brown eyes and held a dazzling smile. His striking face had distracted me from watching the others. Did he do that on purpose?

"It's not a big deal," Nathan said, falling back on the carpet, putting his hands behind his head to prop it up. "We'll do it."

"But," I started to say. It just seemed too unfair. It wasn't a big deal to me. It was just a bus ride.

Kota cut me off. "No, it's fine. My car isn't totally reliable anyway. We'll ride."

I pursed my lips. His easy excuse to make me feel better left me feeling uneasy. The others simply nodded, taking Kota's lead. When Kota finalized a plan, everyone went through with it. It was hard for me to believe the guy who appeared to be one of the least aggressive; the least likely leader had come to the role he had developed.

"But that brings us to another issue," Kota said. His fingers brushed away the neatly-trimmed brown hair against his forehead. "We need to work on getting your parents used to us. It'll be difficult, but the sooner we find a way, it'll make it easier on all of us."

I bit my tongue to keep from saying something. I'd told him before I liked the way things were working now. My father didn't come home until very late in the evening, often well after eight when I was already up in my room and I didn't see him at all. My mother, who was ill, kept mostly to her room. I checked in once a day, and for the most part, I could escape outside. If she did ask where I had gone, I would rattle off different things; in the woods, the garage, taking a walk to the empty church down the road. In our old neighborhood, back in Illinois, I often took walks outside. Since the closest kid lived a couple of miles away, my mother eventually relaxed to let me walk in the woods near the house. Marie told me they bought our new house here on Sunnyvale Court because it was the least crowded street within an hour's drive of where my dad worked. It was a last minute purchase and my mother wasn't happy about it, but it did have a lot of wooded areas. So far, she hadn't questioned my going for walks. She only reminded me that I shouldn't talk to anyone. My mom would eventually realize how many kids were on this street. I didn't want to think about the restrictions she would impose once she found out. I needed to be more careful, though. I had to show up more around the house on occasion.

Gabriel reached out to my head, rubbing at my hair. I held back from cringing out of fear. I enjoyed their touches but they were always so unexpected and when they did it quickly, my first reaction was usually to back up as I was always sure they didn't mean to or it was an accident. "Don't worry," he said, his thin fingers massaging my scalp. "We've got a plan." He let go of me and turned his head to Kota. "We've got a plan, right?"

Kota brushed his own fingers through his hair "I still think we ought to call on Danielle. If we can get them to be friends, she could invite Danielle over. Her mother might get used to another girl being over there easier and we could slowly start showing up."

There was a collective groan.

"Is she that bad?" I asked.

"Yup," North said, his voice deep. His fingers stopped the gentle motion at my shoulder and simply rested against me. It wasn't exactly that he had his arm around me. It just felt like two fingers touching me. I kept telling myself to cool

9

off. Would my heart always pound so much around them?

"She's a typical girl," Nathan tried to explain. "She thinks we're all a bunch of nerds."

Gabriel nudged my arm with his and leaned into me to stage whisper near my ear, "Nathan used to have a crush on her."

"Fuck, no, I didn't."

"She used to go over to his house," Gabriel continued. "One day she tried to get him to skinny dip in the pool. When he refused, she got pissed and told everyone he was gay for a while."

"Like I give a shit what she thinks," he said, but he frowned and rolled onto his side on the carpet, covering his eyes with an arm. "Can we not talk about this right now?"

Kota cleared his throat. "Well, maybe something else will come up." He pulled out his schedule and unfolded the paper. "Are we ready?"

It took a good hour between us to get organized. Most of that time was taken up by general talking among the guys and Kota had to remind them what they were trying to do. Kota kept notes on a sheet of paper. In the end, my own schedule was marked up with his writing.

Homeroom Room 135
Luke, North
AP English - Trailer 10 - Ms. Johnson
Kota, Gabriel, Luke
AP Geometry - Room 220 - Ms. Smith
Nathan, North
Violin - Music Room B - Mr. Blackbourne
None
AP World History - Trailer 32 - Mr. Morris
Victor, North
Lunch
AP Biology - Room 107B - Mr. Gerald
Silas
Japanese - Room 212 - Dr. Green
Victor

Gym - Gymnasium - Mrs. French
Gabriel, Nathan

It seemed everyone was in each other's classes, except for their special electives and Kota's advanced science and math classes. I considered it unreal but I wondered if part of the reason was because they were from the Academy. Did Mr. Blackbourne and Dr. Green fix their schedules, too?

By the time we had it sorted out, I was sitting on the floor, leaning against the couch. Gabriel moved across the room and was talking to Luke. North stretched out on the couch. I was quietly reviewing my schedule again, when, out of the corner of my eye, I caught Victor scooting over to sit next to me.

"I already know a little Japanese," Victor said. He sat with his legs crossed and his knee grazed mine. The fire in his eyes flickered. "It's actually pretty easy to speak it."

I tilted my head as I looked at him, trying to ignore his knee pressing against mine. "How did you get in this class? I thought it was for upperclassmen? I had to get special permission from Dr. Green."

"Who do you think let me into his class?" He smiled at me. "He'd let anyone in if they asked, actually."

That confirmed things. If Victor's schedule was altered, the others were most likely done as well. Did that mean Mr. Blackbourne and Dr. Green wanted me in the same classes as the boys? "Where did you learn Japanese?"

"My parents travel a lot. They like to stop in Japan."

My eyes widened. "I'm jealous," I said. "Can you say something in Japanese?" It wasn't a challenge, but genuine curiosity in his ability.

A smile touched his lips. "*Kirei-na hitomidane.*" The way he said it in his baritone voice made it almost sound like a song lyric.

"Kirei..." My lips moved to try to mimic what he said but I lost it half way through. "What does it mean?"

That fire lit up in his eyes and his cheeks tinged red. "I'll tell you later."

I smoothed my fingers over the lower hem of my shorts in a nervous reflex. Did I ask something embarrassing? Did it sound like I didn't believe him? I went with changing the topic since I didn't want to say anything else wrong. "At least we've all got classes together or similar classes. Studying should be easy. Except for Kota."

"Are you going to be okay, Kota?" North asked from behind me. He was on his side, a cushion pillow propped up under his head. He looked half asleep. "There's periods where we won't see you for several hours."

Kota shrugged and waved his hand in the air, dismissing his words. "Most of these classes are close together on the second floor. I won't be in the hallways for very long."

Silas had been completely quiet for a long time, concentrating on his schedule. While the others were busy talking about how to get from one class to another with the trailers being a problem, I crawled over to him. He caught my eye and he patted the spot next to him, indicating I could move in closer.

"We've only got one class together," I said, sitting next to him, holding my paper near his.

He inched over, putting an arm behind me with his palm to the floor. He was close enough that his arm touched my back. "At least I get you to myself," he said, the corner of his mouth lifted up.

My fingers shook because of his touch. I put my paper down so I could hide my hands in my lap. "In a class full of people," I said.

He put his paper in his lap and leaned back on his hands. "It won't matter if they're there. I don't really talk much."

"Why?"

"Not a lot to say."

"You talk to me."

He reached over, moving a lock of my hair that had slipped away from my clip, tucking it behind my ear. His big fingers brushed across my cheek and against the lobe of my ear. "You talk to me, too."

My heart did flips in my chest.

There was a knock at Kota's door. All of us looked up at the same time toward one another.

"It can't be the mailman," Kota said, his brows creasing. He got up off the floor. As he walked around me toward the door, he dropped a palm on top of my head, pushing slightly to make my head bob down. I looked up just in time to catch his grin before he left the living room. I grinned back. It was nice to feel wanted. I tried to tell myself again that touching was normal among friends. They might be friends with a lot of secrets, but they were normal in their behavior, right? Having missed out on this for so long, I was simply unused to the attention. Did anyone ever get over this feeling or was this fluttering nervousness something they felt all the time?

It was only a minute before Kota returned, we all looked up at him expectantly. He looked pale.

"Kota?" Luke said. "What? Who was it?"

"It's your sister," Kota said, turning to me. "Your older sister. She's asking for you."

My heart stopped. How did she find out? How did she know I was here? My hand fluttered to the base of my throat and I leapt up. I didn't want her coming in. It would be bad enough she knew I was at Kota's. It would be worse if she knew there were seven guys here.

Silas caught my other hand, looking up at me from the floor. "Are you going to be okay?" he asked, giving my hand a gentle squeeze.

I shrugged my shoulders and tried to keep my expression calm. I squeezed his hand back. "Don't worry. It'll be fine." After the last time when my mother had reacted badly when Silas called, I didn't want to scare him with my worry over what she would do to me. I was too terrified now to be nervous that he was holding my hand.

"Would your sister say you were here?" Kota asked, pushing his glasses up on his face again even after they were already adjusted. I had the feeling it was what he did when he was thinking.

"Maybe," I said. "It might require negotiations." They all looked confused and I waved my hand to them, taking the paper that had my schedule and putting it in my pocket. "I have to go calm the waters. I might not be back today."

"Be careful," Silas said. He squeezed my hand again before letting go. The others looked like they wanted to say something, but no one did. North was sitting up on the couch, his hands clenched. Nathan stared at the floor. Gabriel, Luke and Victor looked between Kota and I, as if waiting for either of us to tell them what to do.

Kota walked with me to the door and the others stayed behind. I wanted to say something more to them, but there wasn't much else to say. This was far beyond what I was prepared to handle at the moment.

Outside, Marie was waiting on the steps. Her hands were in her jean pockets and she was looking impatient and sweating. I stepped out onto the porch. Kota had his hand gently rubbing my back on the way out and pulled it away before Marie could catch it. The instant his hand moved, I felt a loss. His touch was helping me to feel brave.

I stepped away from the door and gave Kota a small wave. He waved back, looking sympathetic. He said nothing but gave me a look that for once I understood. He wanted a word from me the moment I could find a way.

"Mom wants you to go home," Marie said after Kota closed the front door. "She's been asking for you for a couple of hours now."

"How did you know I was here?"

"I took a guess," she said.

I was fuming inside, angry at myself for being so reckless. She must have seen me from the house. "Does mom know I was here?"

Marie shrugged. That didn't mean she didn't know. It was her way of saying she wasn't going to tell me. This was bad. If Marie had gotten into trouble with something, she could have used her knowledge of where I was to try to get herself out of a punishment. It often worked.

We got back to the house and entered through the side garage door. As soon as we were standing in the living room, I heard my mom's voice ringing through the house.

"Sang! Come here now!" The anger and power radiated through her tone and it felt like the house was shaking around me. It was all I needed to hear. She knew everything.

Marie filed off past me and headed toward the stairs. She was getting out of the way. I was going to face this part alone.

♥

$\mathcal{M}$ISERY $\mathcal{L}$OVES

$\mathcal{I}$ huddled in the doorway of my parents' bedroom. It was colder than the rest of the house. A chill traveled up my spine, despite coming in from the hot of the day. "Oh, were you calling?" I said, trying to sound surprised.

"Come in here and close the door," she said with a cool severity that made my bones rattle. My mom was sitting up in her large four poster bed. Her head was propped up on three plump pillows. Her face was flushed and her eyes blazed.

Death would have been gentler.

I swallowed and tried to still my heart. There was nothing she could really do to me. She would yell at me, or make me sit on my knees for a few hours, or make me drink vinegar again and take my voice. I knew it wouldn't keep me away from Kota and the others.

I closed the door and stepped further into the room. I used the cherry wood post from her bed to stand behind, letting it partially shield me. It was as close as I dared to go.

"Where have you been this morning?" she asked, each word spoken with precision and that same suppressed rage.

"I was here."

"No you weren't." The words flew from her mouth. "You've been gone for hours."

"I was on the front porch."

"Your sister had to walk by herself up to a man's house," she spat. "How dare you leave here without permission."

I cringed. "I didn't go in for him," I said quickly,

16

coming up with something that could be easier for her to take. "There's a girl."

"Who?"

"Jessica," I said, thinking of Kota's sister. "She was there and she asked me to come in. We were talking about school."

"I do not care what you were talking about," she said, her eyes drifted to the television on a dresser across the room. The news was on, but the sound was muted. My mother shifted, sitting up further on the bed. Here it comes. "There were men at that house, too."

"I wasn't talking to them," I insisted. How did she know there were multiple? Or was she just assuming? Lying wasn't my strong suit as it was, but over the years it had become a necessity. I needed this to work now.

"They were there!" She shouted. "You deliberately broke the rules. I won't allow my daughter to run around like a whore in this neighborhood. You could have been raped."

"They won't rape people," I said. "You think everyone will do that."

"It happens all the time!" Her voice rose. She pointed to the television. "Everyday someone is raped or killed. You could have humiliated this family. I've done all this work to keep you in this house and you just waltz out there not even thinking about what we would have to go through if something happened to you."

"But," I gasped. My knees started shaking and my voice cracked. Why did she have to sound like she was more worried about what *she* would have to go through than for my safety? It was bad enough that she constantly reminded us of terrible things. Was she more worried about us, or exposing herself?

"There's no excuse." Her hands clenched into fists, gripping at the edge of her worn green blanket. "I've told you over and over again not to go into a strange place where I haven't met..."

The words slipped from my lips before I could stop them. "You can't meet any of them if you never leave your

C. L. Stone

room."

"I don't need to. I'm telling you not to leave this yard. Don't step a toe out of this house unless you have my explicit instructions to do so. I don't care if the house is on fire. Not a toe. Not a hair. You're probably lucky you haven't been kidnapped. I've seen the boys in this neighborhood walking by the house. First they trick you into going home with them, and the next minute you're tied up in the closet. Men are horrible and disgusting; they'll trick you if they can."

"What do I have to do, Mom?" I asked. Tears filled my eyes and I swallowed thickly. I hadn't meant to start this. I wanted only to get myself through her yelling so I could get up to my room. I couldn't stand to hear her say such nasty things about Kota and the others. I may not have known them long, but I knew in my heart they wouldn't hurt me. "We're not allowed to invite people over so you can meet them. We can't get you to go see anyone because you won't meet anyone you don't know. There are nice people out there."

"You don't know--"

"How could I? We're prisoners here!"

"Stop it!" she screamed. She slapped her hand against the bed. "I won't have you yelling at me and telling me what to do. *I'm* the mother. *I'm* in charge. You'll do as *I* say." She pounded her hand against the bed repeatedly with every point she made. She heaved herself to stand up, her breath ragged as if she'd been running. She marched to the door of her bedroom. "Follow me."

I trailed behind her. She stopped in the foyer, her bare feet smacking against the hard wood. Here it was. I would be spending hours on my knees again. I could deal with that.

"Stand right there and don't move," she said, pointing to the floor. She disappeared down the hallway. I flexed my knees in preparation, wondering what she was doing. Why didn't she ask me to kneel?

She came back from the kitchen with a bag of rice in her hands. I was confused. Did she expect me to eat it?

She opened the bag and she sprinkled the rice on to the floor near the corner. "Now, kneel on the rice."

What was this? Out of habit over the years, I sank to my knees. The rice bit into my skin as I knelt against the ground. I understood then. It was much worse than a bare floor. Each grain felt like a tiny cut, only it didn't break the skin. I performed a kowtow, trying to look humble.

"Stay," she spat at me. "Don't you move or breathe or even think. When your father gets home, we'll discuss an appropriate punishment."

I turned my face from her to stare off at the bare, white walls.

"I can't believe you would start this right before school." Her voice came down from her screeching, turning into a seething smolder of disgust. "It's hard enough on me. Now I have to deal with you."

I bit my tongue. Nothing I could say would help. I swallowed back tears. I wouldn't allow her to make me cry over this. My knees hurt, and every moment I was on that rice, it felt like near glass cutting into my skin. I would take it, though. She couldn't keep me there forever.

The boys never needed to know about this. They wouldn't let me come over if they knew this would happen every time. There was no way I could prove to her that the boys were nice. I would forever have to sneak around. I simply had to be more cautious when I did. If I planned it carefully enough, I was sure I could almost disappear from this house and my family would never miss me. Invisible, inside and out.

And I could never tell the guys what she said. Despite it all, I was protecting them from her. I was protecting her from them, too. What she didn't know wouldn't make her so angry. She could live in her small world. I would keep her from mine.

Hours passed before my mother left her room to go to

the kitchen and found me still kneeling on the floor. She blinked at me, as if she'd forgotten why I was there and ordered me to my room.

I wobbled back upstairs. It wasn't the longest amount of time I'd spent on my knees, but it was one of the most painful. My knees were bruised as I had spent a lot of time readjusting myself on the floor to try to ease the bite from the rice. I flicked out the rice embedded into my skin in the upstairs bathroom, collecting them to toss them into the trash.

Back in my room, I collapsed onto my bed. I flexed my legs, stretching the stiff muscles. I turned up the volume on the stereo to drown out the noises my mom made from the kitchen. When I felt I could, I crossed the room to look out at Kota's house, noting the cars parked out front. I was glad they were all still there. I thought of running back, but couldn't stand the thought of letting them see my knees and asking questions. I wasn't sure how I would hide it tomorrow for school.

A familiar buzzing noise came from the half-size attic door. I smiled. Despite everything, I still had the secret phone the boys had gotten for me.

I double checked my bedroom door to make sure it was locked, pulled a blanket from my bed, grabbed a book from my bookshelf, and collected the phone from the attic. I curled up on the floor near the window. I didn't expect to be interrupted. It was rare if my mother ever asked for me in the first place. Since she'd already punished me today, she wasn't likely to ask for me again and wouldn't come upstairs. Maybe I was being paranoid, but the secret cell phone was the only way the guys could talk to me if I was stuck inside. I would do anything to make sure it was never discovered.

I opened the book to a random middle page, putting it face down on the floor and within quick reach. I flicked on the phone and swiped at the screen.

There were three messages.

Luke: *"You okay?"*
North: *"Call me."*
Nathan: *"How bad? Text someone, damn it. We're worried."*

I felt lighter and curled up into a tighter ball on the floor, holding the phone to my chest as I took a deep breath. Despite what had just happened, despite my mom's warnings, seven guys out there proved that she was completely wrong. They were safe to be around. They thought about me while I was gone. I started typing a message back to Nathan.

Sang: *"I'm fine. I just need to hang out here for the day. I'm sorry if I worried you."*

I was just replying to North to say I couldn't call right now, but would try to do it soon, when the phone exploded with messages. I fumbled with it, unable to complete a message because it would vibrate and the screen would change for every incoming message.

Gabriel: *"Did she yell? Was it bad?"*
North: *"When are you coming back?"*
Silas: *"Do you need anything?"*
Kota: *"What happened?"*
Luke: *"Did you die? Are you grounded?"*
Silas: *"How long do you have to stay there for?"*
Victor: *"Can you sneak back out tonight?"*
Nathan: *"Why are you apologizing? Just tell us what happened."*
North: *"Goddamn it, call me."*

I dropped the phone onto the carpet, pulling my knees up and resting my face in my hands. My heart was beating too hard on too many levels. It was too much to still be angry at my mother and be so excited by the guys. I needed to calm down and find a place to call them from where I wouldn't be overheard and I couldn't leave the house.

I crawled to the other side of the room to turn down the volume of the music, listening for the sounds of my family. A radio advertisement floated from my sister's room. My mom's television was turned up again. That was a good thing.

I turned the music up on my radio again, this time raising the volume a couple of notches higher. I waited to hear again to see if my mother or my sister would yell at me that it was too loud.

Silence. I scrambled with the phone to the attic door and peered inside. The space was the area between the wall and the slant of the roof. There was a nook in the back that had a flat piece of plywood board, almost like a platform. Once I was inside there, I would be mostly surrounded by insulation in the most remote spot in the house.

I got down and crouched inside the attic door. The air was thick, dry, and hot and smelled like raw wood and insulation. I closed the door behind me. Technically I wasn't leaving the house but I didn't want them to know I was using this space. It was the last place I had left that they wouldn't think to look for me.

Sinking into darkness, I turned on the phone, using the glow to guide me as I crawled on my hands and feet deeper into the tunnel, ducking my head under beams to get to the platform nook. When I was there, I angled myself around a four-by-four beam that partially blocked the opening and climbed in. The nook was wide enough that I could sit cross-legged comfortably and the space above my head was tall enough that I wouldn't hit my head if I tried to stand.

I was still nervous about being heard, but I pushed the buttons on the phone, dialing Kota's number.

He answered before the first ring ended. "Sang?"

"It's me," I said in a quiet voice. "There were too many texts to answer at once."

Questions from six other male voices floated through from the background. I smiled. It was soothing to hear them all.

"Hang on a second, Sang," he said. There was a beeping noise and the clack of the phone being put on a wood surface. "Okay," he said. "I put you on speaker. Tell us what's going on."

I wasn't ready for that. I sucked in a breath, trying not to sound so small and lonely. "I'm fine. It's over with. She told me I had to stay in the house."

A mesh of voices started at once but it was Kota's that stood out. "How much trouble are we talking about? Does she know about us?"

"She doesn't know specifics," I said. "It was just in general for being in someone's house. It's the usual stuff."

"Sang," Nathan said, sounding distant from the phone. "Do you want us to try to come over and talk to her?"

"No," I said, probably a little too loudly and I calmed myself, putting a hand on my heart. "Just let her cool off. School starts tomorrow. We'll be busy anyway. I'll be able to get back but not today. I just have to be more careful with how."

Kota spoke, "We won't be able to hide this forever."

"We'll figure it out," I said, trying to sound hopeful. There wasn't an option for me other than getting better at sneaking out. "One thing at a time. Don't worry. I'll keep my head down."

I wasn't sure how long I could risk being gone from my room so I told the guys I would text. I just wanted to let them know all at once what was happening.

I got off the phone and leaned against one of the wood beams. A trickle of sweat started at my brow and slid down my face. Maybe I wasn't so important to them. It didn't matter. I needed them and much more than I could ever tell them out loud. None of them knew how much I'd needed to feel like I belonged.

And they were all just out of reach.

I curled up on my side, my face pressed to the wood of the platform. Tears dripped from my cheeks. I was lonely from years without being close to anyone. I'd tasted their kindness and I was starving for more. I would do whatever it took to keep this a secret.

Friendship was hard work.

♥

ℐOLARIS

hat night, I tucked the phone away into the attic space. I'd gotten more text messages, but everyone soon had to go home and deal with their own stuff. Tomorrow was the first day.

When my dad got home, my mom talked to him but they didn't call me down. I had been forgotten again.

It was after eleven. I slipped into a pair of soft cotton shorts and a black tank top that was almost too small for me. The house was asleep. I was trying to sleep, but my mind kept wandering to what would happen tomorrow. Instead, I wrote in a small, brown cloth bound diary my father gave me last Christmas.

Diaries were hard to keep in my family. For one thing, Marie was prone to snooping, as was my mother. I tried to keep a regular notebook diary when I was younger but I often got into trouble when I bothered, because I wrote about how angry I was many times. Marie would use it as evidence if she got into trouble, putting me in the middle of the latest argument with my mother.

To combat this, I found another language to borrow. I used Korean lettering in a slightly different format. I made lines and circles that made up the Korean alphabet, writing my thoughts in a language they couldn't read. I didn't know any Korean, the words were in English. The Korean alphabet was simply a code. If Marie tried to use a translation tool from the Internet, it wouldn't work. If she bothered to decode, it would take some work. I knew Marie tried to read it once, because she wrote in the front of my diary in black Sharpie how I was stupid. I might have been stupid, but it stopped her from using my diary and my mother stopped looking at it, too.

It was exciting to know I would be around the guys all day and my parents couldn't do anything about it. For once when I was around them, I could almost relax and not worry about getting caught. I wrote the guy's names into my diary, admiring how they looked in my secret language.

A soft tapping started at the window.

I sat up from the bed. A human figure shadowed the glass. Shivers ran through me and my breath caught in my throat, but I dismissed it. I dropped the diary on the bed, and crossed the room, expecting Nathan to be there. He'd climbed my roof before.

Instead, it was North, crouching and looking in. In his black t-shirt, black jeans and boots, if I hadn't known him, I would have been screaming.

I waved and unlocked the window.

"What are you doing?" I asked as I pushed the window up.

He held his hand out, palm up and fingers spread out. "Come see."

My mouth popped open. "North..."

"We won't go far."

My heart thudded hard in my chest. My hand disappeared into his as he closed his fingers around mine. He tugged me out onto the roof.

I angled my body and stepped out. The air was sticky warm. The half-moon shed a gentle glow against North's tall frame.

North kept my hand, his grip strong, and started to step up the incline to the apex.

"Where?" I asked.

"Up." He motioned and continued to climb.

My legs wobbled as they still ached from kneeling for so long. I hoped they wouldn't cause me to misstep.

Once we made it to the top, he pointed to a flat section of the roof that covered the back porch. He let go of me to slide down and when he got to the flat part, he held out his hand to me again as a support.

"Right here," he whispered, his deep voice carrying to me.

I slid down and he caught me by the legs. He half picked me up and positioned me until I was standing beside him. We were protected on one side by the edge of the chimney. He pointed to the corner, and I sat with the bricks to my right and he sat next to me.

In front of us was the view of the yard and the woods behind it and the stars above our heads.

"Sit back," he said.

My heart flipped in my chest. Why was he doing this with me? I pushed my hand to feel where the roof made a gentle incline. When I sat back, it was like resting on a hill.

He nestled himself next to me and so close that I could feel the warmth of his arm near mine. There in the dark, we looked up at the stars above our heads. While my heart was still pumping and my body shivered at how unexpected it was, North remained quiet. His silence made me nervous but I didn't know what to say to break this tension. I clamped my lips shut, gazing at the stars.

At some point I finally relaxed and the skin of my arm touched his. He didn't move. I left my arm as still as possible. The touch was casual enough. I wasn't directly reaching for him. It was just nice to feel him there in the dark and without being embarrassed or awkward.

My mind was totally not focused on the stars.

About a half hour passed before North spoke. "What happened today, Sang?"

My eyebrows arched in surprise at his question. "What do you mean?"

He turned until he was on his right side, his head propped up with his hand. His dark eyes were in shadow. I caught the gentle outline of his thick eyebrows and his dark hair brushed back away from his face, all but one strand which hung over his forehead. "I want to know what happened the moment you got back to this house after you left today. You weren't fully honest with us."

How could he know? "I was--."

"You were protecting us." He used his free hand to grasp my arm, his fingers wrapping around my elbow. "I know what softening the truth sounds like. The others might be willing to buy it, but I want to know."

I twisted my lips. "It's not really that bad."

"I don't want your opinion," he said. "Tell me what happened. I'll make the decision. Tell me exactly what your mother said."

I pressed my fingers to my cheek, unsure of where to start. Eventually I did tell him. He listened quietly as I described what she said, my eventual defiant replies, and, with my lips trembling, I told him about kneeling in rice.

When I finished, I heard him swallowing. "Let me see," he whispered.

"See what?"

He sat up, stuffing his hand into his pocket. Keys rattled. A light broke through the dark. He swung the flashlight toward me and the glow washed over my knees. His hand moved to my thigh as he pulled one of my legs closer. He bent over me, his eyes lit up from the LED bulb. His thumb traced over the crest of my knee. When he did it, I winced, feeling sensitive to both his touch and the pain.

"Baby," he whispered. "How long were you there for?"

I pushed my finger to my lower lip, "I don't remember. I wasn't watching the clock."

"Did it start right after you left Kota's?"

"About, yes."

He looked up from my knee, flicking the light off again and casting us into shadow. My eyes blacked out as they adjusted. His hand found mine against my mouth and he pulled it away to hold it. "And you called us right after?"

"Yes," I said.

"That had to be over three hours," he said. "At least." He let go of me and rolled to lean back against the roof, putting his arms under his head to prop it up. "Trouble, trouble, trouble..." he said.

"I'm sorry," I said softly.

"Stop apologizing for shit that isn't your fault."

"I'm the one that left the house."

He turned onto his side again. He cupped my chin in his hand. "Listen to me, Sang," he said. "Your mother has issues. I get that. She can't keep you locked up like this. You're not a bad girl. You're not drinking or smoking or selling your body." He let go of my face and brushed a strand of my hair away from my cheek. "I don't like to think of you being holed up here because your mother can't handle reality. You shouldn't be on your knees or swallowing vinegar or any of that shit. It's not healthy for you."

"What can I do?" I asked. "She's my mother."

His face twisted and he looked pained. "I know she is," he said quietly. "I'm surprised she lets you go to school. From what you've told me, it sounds like she'd try to home school both of you."

"My dad won't let her," I said. "She used to say she would, but he insisted that we go to school like everyone else. He said if she did home school, the state would be way more interested in us. Besides, she was sick so much, he thought she couldn't keep up. If she failed to report to the state, they'd come around and investigate. She didn't like that."

He sighed, let go and sat back again. We gazed back into the sky.

I tried to come up with something else to talk about. I was tired of my problems being the center of attention. "North? Are you and Luke going to start the diner with your uncle sometime soon?"

"We already purchased the property, so we better."

"Is that what you want to do when you graduate? Work with your uncle?"

"No," he said.

"What would you rather do?"

"Travel."

"On your bike?"

"Or a better one. Or in a plane. Depends on where I'm going."

"Where would you go?"

He turned his head toward me. "Where would you?"

I thought about it. "To the beach. A nice one with bright blue water and white sand."

"We're not far from the beach," he said. "We'll go one day."

Butterflies did flips in my stomach. "With the guys?"

He paused and I wasn't sure he was going to answer. "We'll see."

While we sat together in the dark, staring up at the stars, his musk mixed with the salt breeze that drifted from the east. I breathed in deeply, letting it fill my lungs. I fingered the grit of the tile below us. Stars twinkled and shifted across the sky.

North knew exactly what I needed. Somehow, amid all the other things going on, he sought me out in the darkness. He knew I needed that escape. I needed to know that somewhere out there someone could come for me. I needed to know I wasn't alone any more.

How he knew I needed it, or if that was what he was thinking, I don't know. I felt better simply knowing he came for me. Someone out there cared enough about how I felt to comfort me. I could deal with my parents. I could deal with anything they wanted. If North, Kota and the others could be patient with me, I would find a way.

We were only out there a few more minutes before North insisted I get some sleep. He helped me climb over the roof. Once I was inside again, I leaned out the window. If it were up to me, I would have stayed out there with him all night. I was sorry he needed to go but he was right. We had school and other things to do. "Goodnight, North," I said.

He leaned down and brought his face close to mine. His coarse fingers swept across my cheek. I steeled myself to not pull away. "Goodnight, Sang," he whispered.

With that, he moved back the way we had come, climbing the roof and dropping out further than I could see.

A little later, the sound of a motorcycle started up in the distance and faded away. I did my best to listen, trying to memorize the sound. I wanted to always know when he came near.

Next time I wouldn't hesitate to open the window.

♥

TUESDAY

♥

♥

$\mathscr{F}$IRST $\mathscr{D}$AY

I dreamed about a frost sweeping over a field. I was running to stay ahead of it. The frost froze animals and plants solid. If it touched me, I would freeze to the spot forever.

woke two hours before I needed to get ready. I wrote in my diary about my dream. Most of my diary consisted of a record of the dreams I had. I tried looking for patterns sometimes, but after a while, I stopped trying to analyze so much. It was now just a habit to occupy my time. There was rarely anything else for me to do in the house.

When it was time, I put on a simple short green skirt and a light pink blouse. I buttoned the blouse up to the top, thinking of Dr. Green and his opinion on fashion. I brushed and twisted my hair and clipped it, the end strands tracing my neck. I strapped some sandals on and picked up my book bag, which had a couple of notebooks and a few pens and pencils. I wasn't sure if we would pick up books today, but I wanted to be ready.

I also found some very old makeup compacts in a box underneath the sink of the bathroom. Marie often picked up odds and ends leftovers from her friends at school like that. I used the closest color on my knees, hoping to mask the bruising. When I was done, the area looked dark, but it managed to hide the purple splotches. I tucked the compact into my book bag just in case I needed to redo it later.

I couldn't make myself eat breakfast. I was thinking of how I would be spending the entire day with the guys. Plus with it being a new school year, I didn't want to have a nervous stomach after eating something.

I walked outside into the already sticky morning air. Marie stood at the end of our driveway. She was wearing jeans and a dark blue t-shirt that looked too big for her, even on her tall frame.

"Why are you bringing that?" she asked, pointing a long finger at my book bag. "You don't show up for the first day of school looking like a complete nerd. And why are you wearing a skirt?"

"Everyone at our last school wore skirts. I wanted to look nice."

"Your shirt's buttoned up all the way. You look stupid."

I pursed my lips. This wasn't the type of fight I wanted to deal with this morning.

"Just stand away from me. I don't want to look like we're related."

"We are related."

"We can pretend we're not," she said, flustered and taking a few steps away from me until she was on the other side of the wide driveway.

I blew out a sigh, wrapping my fingers around the straps of my book bag. I scanned the street. Kota stood alone in his driveway. I couldn't see Nathan out in front of his house. I hoped he wouldn't miss it and be late.

The bus appeared from around the bend and stopped in front of our house. Marie got on first. The brown seats were ripped in places and patched with duct tape in others. Five other kids clustered together in seats toward the front. Marie went for the very back seat. I picked something in the middle.

Kota got on next. I slid further into the seat to give him room.

"Morning," he said, smiling and sitting next to me.

A happy warmth swept through me. He wasn't ashamed to sit next to me on the bus like my sister. He wore a blue striped Ralph Lauren collared shirt with a blue tie at his neck and tan slacks. "I like the shirt you're wearing," I said, forcing myself to say something nice despite being unsure and shy.

His cheeks tinged. "You're looking pretty good, too."

I blushed but I caught sight of his green messenger bag. "Are you using that to carry books around?"

He picked it up and put it in his lap to look it over. "What's wrong with it?"

"Aren't you in really smart classes?"

He laughed. "Yeah."

"Then won't your books be really heavy?"

"Ah," he said. He opened the flap and looked inside. "It's pretty sturdy."

"I was worried it might hurt your shoulder. You know, putting so much weight on it all the time."

The smile on his lips softened. I wasn't sure if I said something stupid. "Well if it does, I'll switch shoulders."

Nathan ran out from his house an instant before the bus arrived. The bus driver motioned to him and Nathan bent over to hear what he had to say before nodding and heading to the seat near us on the other side of the isle. He wore a red dress shirt, subduing the red in his hair.

"The bus driver said we should probably gather at one house," he said. "He says we're close enough that he shouldn't have to stop three times like that."

Kota looked at me. "Will your mom let you do that?"

I shrugged. "If the bus driver says we have to." It made me nervous to figure out how to mention it. I'd have to consult with Marie, which didn't seem like a good thing to do right now. I thought I would just make sure to let her know after school and we would have to both agree not to tell our mother about it.

The bus turned the bend in our neighborhood and stopped at a house in the middle of the other side. Derrick was standing at the end of the drive and he turned to face the bus. I remembered him as the boy who had once tried to play basketball with Marie at my house until my mom dismissed him. He was standing with a girl who looked just like him.

"Is that Danielle?"

"Yeah," Nathan said.

Danielle was as tall as her brother, with brown hair cut in an even bob around her chin. She had high cheekbones and a wide forehead. Her big brown eyes glared critically at the bus. She turned to her brother, snapping something at him. He frowned but got on the bus.

They both headed for the back seats. After a few moments, I heard my sister talking and Danielle responding.

"She didn't look too mean, I guess," I said. I wasn't really sure about that, but didn't want to sound rude. "We could be friends."

Nathan shook his head, smirking at me. "Just wait."

The rest of the bus ride took thirty minutes. We sat in silence together as we watched students get on and off. When the bus arrived at the school, we followed the crowd into the building.

"I told the others to meet us in the cafeteria," Kota said. "We'll pick out a table."

At first the school seemed to echo with our footsteps. The smaller hallways were empty. As we drew closer to the main hallway though, students clustered together along the walls, making it difficult to navigate. Nathan switched from being on Kota's other side to walking along beside me. They closed in around me until our arms were touching as we headed toward the cafeteria. Nathan stuffed his hands in his pockets and looked uncomfortable.

"Don't be nervous," I whispered to him. I knew the school's reputation was a bad one. It was why Academy students were there in the first place, right? Still, I couldn't imagine anyone wanting to pick a fight with Nathan. His collared shirt only slightly masked his muscles. He wasn't someone to be taken lightly.

His eyes shifted from the groups of kids. "I don't know why they have to stand around like that."

"It's the first day," Kota said. "They're not going to be interested in trouble right now." As he said this, his eyes started to glance to different groups as well.

I pressed my fingertips into my palms. I focused on the

path ahead of us. I didn't want to catch someone's eyes and draw attention to myself. Invisible was something I could handle. The guys, however, were making me nervous.

In the cafeteria, we found an empty table close to the large windows overlooking the courtyard. There was no sign of North or Victor or the other guys. Nathan sat next to me and Kota took a spot on the other side of the table. We dropped our bags onto the table to spread out and claim the space.

"Should I text them?" Nathan asked, glancing around at some of the students at the other tables.

Kota turned in his seat, looking down some of the connecting hallways. "They should be here soon," he said.

"Is this seat taken?" A familiar smooth baritone spoke next to my ear. My hand fluttered to the base of my throat, my breath caught as I turned around. Victor stood there, his wavy hair was brushed back from his angular face and he was wearing a white button up shirt and black slacks. He kept a couple of buttons undone at his neck. The sunlight through the window caught in his silver medallion resting against his collarbone. He took the seat next to me, his fire eyes subdued.

Gabriel had followed him. He hovered over me and snuck a hand toward my head. Confused, I twisted away but he was quick. I felt the clip loosening and my hair falling around my shoulders.

Gabriel smirked. "I'm keeping this," he said, holding my hair clip between his long fingers. His two locks of blond hair blended with the rest of his brown hair behind his ears. He wore a thin red tie and his collared white shirt was untucked from his tan slacks. He wore ruby studs in his earlobes today. The three rings along the crest of his right ear were the usual black.

"I should keep it for gym," I said. I half stood up, reaching for the clip, but he easily grabbed my wrist to hold it back and held the clip out of my reach. I pouted a little, trying to get some sympathy. I didn't want to have to sit around with hair in my face all day. I was so used to having it all pulled back out of my face that it felt strange to have it down.

"You aren't going to be running today," he said. "You can have it back at lunch. Maybe." He moved around to Kota's side of the table, tucking my clip into his pocket. "And don't pout that sweet lip. That shit never works on me."

"It really does look better down," Victor said. His fingers stretched toward my face and I forced myself to remain still. He slipped one of the locks of my hair behind my ear. The edge of his fingernail traced delicately across my cheek. My breath caught as the fire in his eyes fixed on me.

The school day hadn't officially started yet, and I was already overwhelmed by their attention.

More students filtered into the cafeteria. Familiar friends collected and huddled together in groups. Some stood alone along the edges, waiting to be invited or noticed. Most of the kids wore loose jeans and t-shirts. Compared to everyone else, the boys and I stood out quite a bit. I sighed about this. This wasn't like my old school. Blending in would require a different strategy.

If I had been alone, I would have worried more. With Kota and the others, it felt like they were my shield against being too different.

The boys seemed intent on checking out what was going on, too. We sat quietly and kept an eye out for the others. Sometimes a large group of students filed in from off a bus. The cafeteria filled up quickly and there were people hanging around the edges against the wall. There simply wasn't enough space for all the students.

Students were checking us out, too. I was paranoid about what I was wearing and how I looked. What are the other students thinking of a girl sitting with a group of guys like this? The guys were better looking, in my opinion, than a lot of the kids around us. In the past, I was that forgettable girl in the corner, reading and lost in my own head. What did they think of this mismatched, plain girl with these incredibly attractive guys? I reached into the pocket of my bag for the schedule and checked it over once more. I was feeling a little uncomfortable.

"Where are they?" Kota asked, cutting through our silence.

Nathan fished out his cell phone and typed something in. He sat it on the table and we all hovered, waiting for the response.

Silas: *"Traffic was backed up on the interstate. Should get there soon."*

I chewed my cheek, checking the clock on the wall. "They're cutting it really close."

My eyes focused on a table across the cafeteria and I recognized Danielle and my sister. A couple other girls sat around them, giggling.

Nathan followed my gaze out into the crowd of students. "That's your sister, isn't it?"

I nodded and everyone else at the table turned to look. I was leaning to see around Kota's head and I ended up almost cheek to cheek with Victor. I pulled away but he didn't flinch.

"It looks like they're getting along," Victor said.

"This might be good for us," Kota said. "If she gets friendly with Danielle, it'll save us some trouble." He turned to me. "You should get your sister to invite Danielle over. Can you go talk to her?"

"My sister warned me this morning that she wanted to pretend we weren't related."

"What?" Gabriel said, pulling his head back around to look at me.

I shrugged. "I'm not cool enough."

They all laughed loud enough to draw attention from others at another table.

My cheeks warmed. "Is that funny?"

"No," said Nathan. "It's just ironic."

The bell rang before I could ask what he meant. Silas,

40

North and Luke were going to be late. I lifted a finger to my lower lip, worried that they might get into trouble.

Nathan checked his phone. "No update," he said. "Come on." Nathan took my hand from my face and pulled at it to get me to stand. "I'll walk you to class."

I looked back at the others but they had homerooms on the opposite side of the building. I waved to them. They waved back, disappearing into the crowd.

Nathan held on to my hand while we were walking through the hallway. His fingers enveloped mine, a little too tightly but I didn't want to say anything. It was hard enough to not want to pull away from his grip from nervousness. I glanced at other students around us, but everyone was in such a hurry that no one appeared to be interested in what we did. My heart fluttered in my chest from the excitement of first day at a new school and from his palm pressed to mine.

The hallway narrowed and the crowds closed in as they crawled forward, making it impossible to stand side by side. I slipped behind Nathan, letting go of his hand and pressed my palm to his back so he knew I was right behind him.

The crowd halted and he stopped short. I bumped into him. I stood on my tiptoes to look over his shoulder.

He looked back at me and his cheek almost met with my lips, bumping my nose. I blushed and rocked back on my heels.

"If this is what the rest of the day is like, it'll be a miracle if anyone can get into their classes on time," he said.

When it thinned out on the other side, we were almost to my homeroom. He walked me to the door and stood by it, looking inside, noting the people.

"I thought maybe North and Luke might have made it," he said.

"They're going to be late," I said. "But you are, too, if you don't get going."

He nodded. "If they don't make it, just head straight for your next class. Don't stop in the hallway."

I was waving goodbye to him when a voice cut through behind me in the classroom.

"Hey Sing Sang Song."

I spun around, recognizing the voice but not remembering the face. Leaning up against the frame of the door to the homeroom class was Greg, his goateed chin tilted in my direction. I took a half step back in surprise. What was he doing here? I recalled when I first met him at the mall and how he'd gotten into a fight with Kota and Silas. My heart leapt into my throat, and my hand fluttered up to the base of my neck.

"Who's that?" Nathan asked, his blue eyes darkening.

"Long story," I said. I swallowed back the desire to ask him to stay near me. "Get to class." There was no point in trying to stall him. Besides, Greg couldn't do anything to me now. We were in school.

I hoped I was right about that.

Nathan shot Greg a look and turned, walking off. I raced into the classroom, ignoring Greg and sat at a seat close to the door. There were two empty chairs, one in front of me and one behind me and I tucked my book bag in the one in front to hopefully save it for one of the guys if they showed up.

"So where's your other boyfriends?" Greg asked as he sat behind me. He leaned over the top of his desk. Menthol cigarette smoke wafted toward my nose.

I faced the front, folding my arms and focusing on the chalkboard. My heart was thudding loudly in my ears. Would ignoring him work?

"You know, I never got that kiss," Greg said. He started making kissy noises behind me.

My nose crinkled at his smell, but I pressed my lips together, trying my best not to say anything.

"Hey Greg!" Someone across the classroom called to him.

"I'll catch you in a minute," Greg told me and he got up. He tugged at a lock of my hair and walked away to sit near his friend who was waving to him. I trembled, grateful he had a distraction. This was terrible. It was the last person I wanted to see and he was right there in my homeroom. What were the chances?

The bell rang and the class stilled. From a side office, the teacher walked in. He was short, pudgy with graying dark hair and wore a maroon shirt and black slacks. "Welcome to homeroom," he said. "I'm Mr. Ferguson. Check your schedules. It should say room 135. If not, you're in the wrong class."

The door opened, shifting the air in the room. North and Luke walked in. I removed my book bag from the seat in front. Luke took that one and North collapsed into the seat behind me.

Mr. Ferguson looked expectantly at them. "Did you get lost?"

"The parking lot is backed up," Luke said, rubbing a palm over his forehead. "All these parents are trying to drop their kids off."

"Next time get here early and it won't be a problem," he said. He started calling roll.

"We were worried," I whispered to them.

"Don't be," North said.

Luke grinned. "The bell was early. We were right on time."

I side glanced at Greg. He was immersed in a conversation with another guy.

"Something wrong?" North asked, checking out where I was looking.

I shook my head and smiled. "No." I caught Greg taking glances my way and whispering to his friend but I turned away from them. I didn't want to worry North or Luke.

North wore a black collared, short sleeve dress shirt, unbuttoned all the way with a black tank shirt underneath. It accented the muscles in his chest. Luke's collared shirt was white and the top three buttons were undone with nothing underneath, so I got a good look at part of his chest and the angle of his collarbone. Luke messed with his blond hair, trying to push it back behind his ears but it kept falling away into his eyes. The girls across the room were whispering and watching.

43

"Do you have a hair tie?" Luke turned in his chair to face me.

"Gabriel stole my clip this morning."

Luke laughed. "We'll have to bring extras. He doesn't understand hair in the face. He just started growing his out." He let go of his hair, letting it fall. The tips traced along his neck.

I took two pencils out of my book bag and put them on the desk. "I didn't want to show him this," I said. I fingered my hair, combing it back and then twisting it into a small bun behind my head. I stuffed the two pencils into my hair like hair sticks. A couple of strands close to my face fell out but I pulled them behind my ears.

Luke beamed, his wide lips curling up. "Hey. I want that."

I dug two more pencils out of my bag. I held them out to him but he twisted in his chair. Did he expect me to do it? I bit my lower lip and combed my fingers through his hair. He sighed. I did a quick twist, stabbing the pencils into the bun. A lock of hair fell away but he tucked it behind his ear. His appearance was different. It was like I was finally seeing him with short hair. His brown eyes looked bigger, and his smile was brighter.

The girls across the classroom narrowed their eyes at us but I ignored it.

North was slumping in his seat, tracing his fingertip on the edge of the desk. I glanced at him but he was looking at the other students.

The door opened again. A tall, lean man with a tight-set jaw and hollow cheeks walked in. He was wearing thick, brown-rimmed glasses and his head was shaved clean. The muscles under his light gray suit looked bulky.

"Principal Hendricks," Mr. Ferguson said. "What are you doing here?"

"I'm just making rounds today. Saying hello," he said. He smiled at the rest of us. "Don't let me interrupt."

Mr. Ferguson stood straighter and everyone in the room was quiet as he finished up roll call. There were school announcements over the loudspeaker but my focus was on the principal. His gaze settling on Luke and North.

After the announcements were over, the room started a low hum of chatting. Principal Hendricks walked over to us, standing over my desk. "Aren't you boys from the Academy?"

He knew? I glanced at Luke.

"Yes, sir," Luke said. "Although I thought we weren't supposed to mention..."

"Where are your uniforms?"

Luke blinked at him.

"Uniforms?" North asked.

"I thought your school had uniforms."

Luke and North exchanged glances over my head. What was going on?

"Well," Luke said, scratching the back of his neck. "We do have a dress code, I guess."

"Hm," the principal touched the knot of his pale gray tie. "I believe there may have been a misunderstanding."

The principal thanked them and walked out of the room. Was he really only there to talk to Luke and North?

"What was that about? Did he expect you all to wear uniforms here?" I asked.

North frowned. "I don't think so. I thought our job was to blend in as much as possible. We weren't supposed to stick out."

"It'd be too dangerous for us to start wearing something like that," Luke agreed. "We'd be isolated quickly."

North mumbled something even I couldn't hear, folded his arms and put his head down on the desk.

When the bell rang again, we all stood up. We found a hallway that led outside. North's first class was at trailer thirty, almost all the way at the end of the row. I walked between him and Luke, following the sidewalk that lead away from the main building.

"Who was that guy?" North asked. "The one that kept looking at you?"

My face heated. I didn't have to ask which one. I knew

exactly who he meant. "I bumped into him at the mall one day."

"You mean that day with Silas and Victor?" he asked. His eyes widened and hands clenched. "Why didn't you say something?"

"North," I said, my fingers brushed his arm to get his attention "He backed off when you two showed up." It surprised me he heard about that. How much did the boys tell each other about me? Did he tell the others about what happened yesterday?

"Yeah," Luke said. "We don't have to worry. Sang's schedule is covered and he didn't seem that interested in her."

North's lips pursed. He walked us to our trailer.

"I'll wait for you," I said to North, "so we can walk to the next class."

He nodded and turned away. I kept an eye on him until I lost him among the other students.

Luke put a hand on my shoulder, urging me inside. "He'll be fine," he said. "You might not have noticed, but he's pretty scary looking. No one's going to mess with him."

I widened my eyes at him. "I'm supposed to be worried he was going to get messed with? I was just thinking he was walking too slow and he might be late to his next class."

Luke's eyes lit up and he grinned like he wanted to laugh.

"What's so funny?" I asked.

He said nothing and opened the door for me.

♥

*U*NUSUAL *C*LASSMATES

*L*uke and I found seats near the back of the room together. Kota entered a minute later, fell into the seat in front of me and adjusted his glasses. "Oh good," he said, looking at Luke behind me. "I was worried you wouldn't make it."

"Traffic was crazy," Luke said.

Kota glanced at our seats and the others that were still available in the room. "Let's change this."

Luke shrugged. "You're the boss."

"He is?" I asked. Kota's orders were strange to me and it was weird to hear Luke acknowledge them.

They exchanged glances and Luke laughed. "We've been friends for so long, we're just used to him bossing us around."

"I don't boss you around," Kota said. "I make suggestions."

"We're too nice to say no."

The looks that passed between them told me there was more to this. Was Kota really in charge in some official way from the Academy? I pursed my lips, biting back the questions.

Kota pointed to three seats. Luke sat in the last one near the back. I sat in front of him and Kota sat in front of me.

"I'm always in the middle," I said. I wasn't really complaining, just making an observation.

"How can you say that?" Kota said, turning around. "We just started."

The bell rang as Gabriel rushed in the door. He collapsed into a seat to my left. "Walking from the second floor is a

47

bitch," he said.

"Gabe," Kota's tone was warning enough.

Gabriel shrugged, putting his hand on his chest as he breathed heavily. His red tie was flipped over, revealing the Gucci brand label. He smoothed his hand over his chest to straighten it. "You try getting down those stairs. You'd let one slip, too." His head twisted and his crystal blue eyes narrowed at me. "Nuh uh," he said. "Hand them over." He snapped his fingers and pointed to my hair.

"Kota," I whispered.

Kota turned to look at me and the pencils in my hair. His green eyes lit up. "It's cute."

"Nope," Gabriel said. "I'll take all your pencils if you don't get it out of your hair right now. I want it down."

I twisted my lips, tempted to ignore him. I felt a hand near my hair and the bun loosened. Luke handed back my two pencils. He kept the ones in his own hair. I dropped the two pencils on the desk. Luke ran his fingers through my hair to undo the twist.

Gabriel grinned, satisfied.

The class started and we were handed an agenda. On it was a list of books we were to read outside of class and instructions to take special tests that were in the library.

Ms. Johnson stood in front of the room. The trailer walls were a faux wood panel and with her brown dress, she almost blended in. She was thin, pale, with curly dark hair cut short around her ears. "I know you don't have your books yet, but that doesn't mean we have time to slack off. I need everyone to take out some paper."

There was a subtle collective groan and a lot of shuffling. I reached for my bag, pulling out two of the notebooks and two pens, handing a set to Luke behind me before he finished poking me in the shoulder to ask.

He blinked as I handed it to him. "I guess we did need to bring stuff."

"You can keep it," I said, "if you want."

He smiled at me in a way that made me shiver. I turned around as I didn't know how to respond.

Ms. Johnson put her hands in the air in an effort to quiet the class. "I don't have a loud voice so I can't talk over you." She paused to allow the class to quiet down. "Today, I want a poem. We'll be starting with poetry and I want you to write a poem for me."

Another wave of groans swept through the room.

"I know kids don't like poems, but I know you've heard of at least one in your life. I want one original poem from each of you by tomorrow morning on my desk. You can start now."

I stared at the blank page in front of me. A poem. I tried to think of the last one I had read and couldn't remember. They all had to rhyme, didn't they? I wished I could read a few first to get an idea of what I wanted to go for. How long of a poem did it have to be?

The sound of scratching filled the room as pens and pencils were applied to paper. I managed to write my name on my page and started with writing pretty words that I liked in a curly cursive lettering.

I felt a nudge at my arm. I glanced up to see Gabriel holding up his notebook. He'd drawn the word "poem" into a rose unfolding into bloom. It was so lifelike that if it wasn't for the fact that it was in pencil, I would have thought it was real.

My mouth popped open in surprise. I wrote something quickly on my paper and held it up for him to read.

I thought you said you weren't good at art?

He smiled and then wrote something back on his page, holding it up. *It isn't good.*

I wrote back. *You're crazy. It's beautiful. You belong in art class.*

He beamed. I admired his smile and the way his ears turned red, almost matching the ruby studs in his lobes.

"Unless you're willing to read what you have to the class, I want eyes on your own paper," Ms. Johnson said. While she was smiling, she clearly meant her threat.

We both tucked our heads down, grinning. Gabriel wasn't too bad. He might have stolen my hair clip and was

49

demanding, but he was fun.

Sometime during the writing session, I felt Luke touching my hair. I wanted to check to see what it was but I felt Ms. Johnson's eyes on me and after getting caught with Gabriel, I didn't want to risk having to stand up in class.

When the bell rang, Kota got up, said a quick goodbye to all of us and dashed out the door. I looked to Luke and Gabriel. They both shrugged.

Outside the trailer, Luke went on to his next class and Gabriel stood with me as I waited for North.

"You don't have to wait," I told him. "I should be okay standing here, right?"

"I know," he said, grinning. "I'd feel better though."

I reached up to tug my hair behind my ears. Part of me hoped he would get the hint and give my clip back but he didn't seem to notice. "Will you be late?"

"Will you stop worrying about me?"

"But if your class..."

He reached out with a straight hand and gave me a light chop on top of my head. "Stop it. I'm not going to be late."

"Late for what?" North said, approaching. Being so much taller, he stood out among the rest of the students. He had his hands in his pockets and walked up to us. He looked at Gabriel. "What are you doing to her?"

"Nothing!" Gabriel hiked up his book bag and waved to us. "See you at lunch." He started off alone toward the trailers.

I watched him leave. Maybe I didn't have to worry about North, but did I have to worry about Gabriel?

"He'll be fine," North said as if reading my worries on my face. He wrapped an arm around my neck and pulled me around until we were walking together toward the building.

"How was class?" I asked him, trying to ignore the sensation to shiver at his touch.

"Nathan's right. Public school is a pain in the ass."

We ran up to the second floor together. Nathan was waiting for us in our next class, sitting in the back with two empty seats in front of him.

"It's about time," Nathan said. "I about gave up holding these seats."

"Switch places with me, Nate," North said.

"I want the back, though."

They both stared at each other. Faces became stern. I hesitated to sit down, not sure how to handle this.

"I could... I could sit in the back," I said. I tried to give a cheesy smile, hoping they'd settle down. Would humor bring their tempers down or just irritate them more? Where was Kota when I needed him?

Their eyes slid to me and they seemed to relax. North took the front seat. I sat in the middle again with Nathan behind me.

"What happened to your hair?" Nathan asked me as we waited for the geometry teacher to finish passing out some papers.

I reached for the back of my head, feeling something like braids or twists. "Luke happened." I tried pulling one around but the lock of hair I grabbed was too short for me to stretch where I could see.

Nathan laughed.

"Let me see," North said.

I turned myself around, showing him the back of my head. He laughed, too.

"Is it bad? It's purple or something, isn't it?"

"It's loops." North pulled a strand around to show me how Luke had twisted it so much at the tips that it made a natural loop and held together.

I smirked at it, taking the strand from him. I used my fingernails to comb through the lock to brush the loop out.

The teacher started talking so I had to sit back. Nathan started pulling the other loops, trying to untwist my hair. "You've got to watch out for Luke," he whispered to me. "He does this shit all the time."

The geometry teacher had passed out some worksheet

homework for us to get started on that night and gave us our book assignments for the week.

North slumped very low in his chair and leaned back. His head was almost back against my desk.

I leaned, looking over his face. His eyes were closed. "Tired, North?"

"Mmm."

"You stayed up too late."

He grinned. "Yup. There's this girl named Sang, and she's a terrible influence on me."

I giggled loud enough that it caught the attention of some of the others around us. I blushed and pretended to focus on the worksheets we were supposed to be doing. Luke and North might have been step-brothers, but they were so different, and not in a bad way.

♥♥♥

After geometry ended, Nathan walked with me to the music room.

"What's Mr. Blackbourne like as a teacher?" I asked him. My heart was thudding as I remembered Mr. Blackbourne and his A-perfect face and stern, steel eyes. It was exciting that I would finally get to learn to play something, but I wondered how I could possibly focus on music when someone like Mr. Blackbourne would narrow his critical gaze on me.

"He's fair," Nathan said. He walked close to me in the corridors. His arm brushed against mine and on occasion the backs of our hands touched, but he never reached for it again like he did that morning. Why was I thinking I wanted him to? "He can be very strict. Just remember: he yells because he cares."

My mouth popped open. Yelling? I wasn't so sure how I would handle someone like that trying to teach me a musical instrument. In the past, I had a few teachers who liked to yell when students weren't paying attention and I always felt so numb when they did. I couldn't focus on the rest of class when it happened.

Nathan held the door to Music Room B open for me but released it to let it swing shut when I was inside, saying goodbye. I missed him instantly, wishing he could have stayed a moment or two.

Music Room B was smaller than I expected. It held a single upright brown piano on the far side of the room and had a couple of rows of chairs surrounding a dark green chalk board against the wall. Mr. Blackbourne sat at the piano bench. He was playing a jazz piece. I stepped further into the room, my fingers twisting around the straps of my book bag as I listened to him play.

He seemed to be lost in the music for the moment. His fingers flowed over the keys with an artistry that I was awestruck to witness. Even with the clunky upright piano, he seemed to pull off magic.

He stopped playing, as if sensing someone watching, and turned to face me, his eyes meeting mine. The corners of his mouth dipped softly. He stood and walked around the piano, straightening his red tie. His striking features gave me the urge to stare, but I was terrified to do so. As he looked at me, my spine stiffened as I willed myself to remember my posture.

"Miss Sorenson," he said in greeting, touching the corner of his dark-rimmed glasses. It was hard to think of him as a teacher. He looked barely nineteen. It was his stern expression that made him seem older.

"Mr. Blackbourne," I replied. I put my bag down on one of the chairs. The bell rang and the room was still empty. I felt my throat closing but I swallowed. "Where is everyone else?"

A brown eyebrow rose. "Else?"

"The other students."

"There aren't any others. I can't teach a classroom to play. Just one."

My face radiated heat and my finger touched at my lower lip, pushing toward my teeth. I was going to be his only student this year?

He stood at the front of the room. I wasn't sure what to do. I froze, my hands clasped behind my back.

"You didn't bring a violin," he said. It was almost a question, but he asked as if he knew what my response would be.

"I'm sorry," I offered. There wasn't much more for me to say. The truth was I hadn't approached my parents about this class. I had been waiting for a good time, but with the recent argument with my mother, I wasn't sure when this would happen. Part of me had thought the school would have one for me, like my sister could borrow one of the extra flutes from our old school when she didn't bring hers. He couldn't have expected me to get one so soon, could he?

Mr. Blackbourne didn't seem fazed by this. He crossed the room to the bench of the piano again and brought out a black case. He positioned it on top of the piano and opened it to reveal a beautiful ebony violin. The tuning pegs were encased in gold plating. The fingerboard and the chin rest was a lighter shade of gray. Elegant perfection.

"Come," he said. "Take this."

I slinked forward but kept my hands behind my back. "I don't want to break it."

"You won't break it unless you're careless."

I sucked in a breath and held it, reaching delicately to take the violin from him. I cradled it between my hands, my fingers smoothing over the wood, feeling the cool material with my fingertips. Even the smell of the wood and polish and resin made me tremble with nervousness.

"We're here to play, not to look at it." His steel gaze settled on my face. He held out the bow.

I nodded, bringing the violin to my neck like I had seen countless times in videos and pictures. The violin was lighter than I expected it to be and yet the length of it made me feel clumsy just holding it. Taking the bow from him, I held it loosely between my fingers and I waited for instructions.

Mr. Blackbourne inclined his head. His fingertips traced my elbow and I lifted the violin higher. He repositioned the violin at my neck until the very center of it was pointed at the middle of my throat. He stepped around behind me, checking the angle from next to my head. "Do you see the strings? Do you see how I've positioned it?"

I looked, catching the straight line down the neck of the violin.

"This is how it should look every time you pick up your violin. You need to get used to this now. Keeping good habits from the beginning will make this more comfortable for you. Posture and balance are important." His breath teased the back of my hair as he spoke. I smothered my trembling. He was so close, only he was so focused on my posture, I wasn't sure he noticed.

"I understand," I said. I elevated the bow, settling the horsehair strings on a spot against the violin's bridge, ready to be directed to the next step.

Mr. Blackbourne straightened immediately, and snatched the bow from my hands. "Not yet," he said, the sharpness of his voice returning.

I lifted my eyebrows in surprise. "No?"

"No." He wrapped his hand around my wrist, moving the violin from my neck. "Now put it back where I placed it.

I did what he instructed, pushing the end of the violin to my neck.

"Check the strings."

I looked and he was right. I adjusted the neck to hold it up straighter.

"Put your chin against the rest."

I did.

"Let go of the violin."

I blinked at him, shocked. Would he have me wreck his beautiful instrument? "I'll drop it."

"If you're holding the violin right between your chin and your shoulder, you won't drop it. Let go of the violin," he instructed, his voice rising.

I hesitated. I couldn't afford to pay for another one. Visions of the violin crashing to the floor and splintering into a million pieces floated past my eyes. He had to be crazy to trust me to hold on to it. "I don't think I should."

He seized my hand from the neck of the violin and pulling it away in a sharp motion. It jarred me forward and the violin nearly slid away, but I pushed my chin down on the rest, hiking up my shoulder to hold to it. The violin dangled precariously.

He frowned, letting go of my hand. "Put the violin back into position."

My fingers shook. I picked the violin up and put it back against my neck, checking the lines of the strings to make it straight.

"Now let go, this time without scrunching your neck." His steel gaze penetrated through to my own heart, as if he knew exactly how fast it was beating.

"I almost lost it last time."

"Now!" His voice intensified, echoing throughout the music room.

I closed my eyes. My hand slid away from the neck of the violin. I did my best not to move my chin or shoulder to try to compensate.

The violin rocked forward but remained balanced.

"Good," Mr. Blackbourne said, softer this time.

I opened my eyes to gaze down the violin, noting how badly it shook as my body shivered.

He crossed his arms, circling me. I kept my hand down, fearing he would smack it away again. He stopped behind me. I looked out toward the opposite wall, holding my breath.

"You did well, Miss Sorenson," he said softly. "It's important for a young lady to speak up and ask questions, or even resist an order when a situation seems dangerous." He treaded around again until he was facing me. He grasped the violin by the neck, taking it from my shoulder.

I gazed at the floor. He was testing me. Did he need to do this to teach me music?

His hand touched my chin. The tender fingertips lifted my head until I was looking back into those gray eyes.

"I also need you to trust me," he said softly. "Beyond doubt. Beyond probably what you've ever been comfortable with in your life. If you'll allow me the chance..." His lips pursed as he scrutinized my eyes.

My cheeks radiated with heat. My throat felt dry and I wanted to swallow but I was too afraid to move. He held me captivated by his command and confidence.

His eyebrow lifted and he let go of my chin, stepping back. "I expect you to have your own instrument by tomorrow."

I felt my mouth drop open. "I..." There was nothing to say. Was he expecting me to just magically create one? How could I convince my parents to rush out and pay for a violin by that evening?

"Tomorrow." His voice rose to that sharp severity. "Don't come to class unless you have one."

When the bell rang, I collected my bag and ran out into the hallway. There was no way I could get a violin by tomorrow. I felt my chest grow heavy with anticipation of the argument I would have to face with my mom that afternoon. I wondered if I would be back at all.

♥

*H*UNGRY

*O*ut in the hallway, I realized that for the first time since that morning I was walking without the boys around me. I slowed to a nervous pace. I had gotten used to their company. Without them there, I felt a little lost.

Now that I was alone, however, I wasn't so distracted by the guys that I was able to check out some of the other students. As I tugged my book bag tighter to my body, I spotted how some people would cluster along the walls of the hallways, talking with friends, holding hands. I even spotted a couple kissing in the shadows near a doorway. I blushed at catching someone in such an intimate moment and turned away.

As I walked, I couldn't help but notice how people reacted whenever I was within view. They seemed curious about every face they didn't recognize. I wondered, too: would this girl like me? Would he make fun of my clothes?

A sharp whistle cut through the hall, a catcall. I twisted my head in reaction at the first tone. A group of boys leaned against the wall. They laughed together and I wasn't quite sure if their whistling was meant for me or for one of the other girls around me.

"Sang!" Victor's voice sounded from behind me. I turned in time to spot him trying to hustle past some other students to get to me. "You should have waited by the door," he said. His cheeks were flushed. His white shirt looked rumpled. He smoothed some of his wavy brown hair back away from his forehead. "I was coming for you."

"I'm sorry," I said. "Mr. Blackbourne..."

"Oh. Yeah," he said, smiling. "No need to say more. But next time wait for me. I'll come get you." He moved next to me so we were walking together.

"Sticking together?" I asked.

His slender frame moved so elegantly next to me that I felt clumsy even though I was just walking. "It's what we do."

I smiled. "How was your morning so far?"

He shrugged. "It's not the Academy."

I blinked at him, surprised that he would say it out loud. "Isn't that supposed to be a secret?"

"No one's listening," he said.

What he said confused me. I couldn't figure out what this secret school must be like. I imagined dark hallways and masks and other students who were just as intelligent and beautiful as the boys were. Compared to the cracked tiles of the floor, the lack of variety in the classes, and the rambunctious students of Ashley Waters High School, what would inspire nine people to bother with trying to make it better?

"So how was Mr. Blackbourne?" he asked.

"I need to get a violin by tomorrow," I said. "Or I can't go back."

He smiled. "Yeah, he's strict. Can you get one?"

"It's kind of short notice but I'll have to ask my parents. My mom isn't too happy with me right now."

His fire eyes flickered. "I can get you one."

I shook my head. "Victor, you can't..."

"Is this the right way?" he asked. He turned his head, looking for the right door. I had a feeling he knew it was the correct way, but he had wanted to change the subject.

We had to walk outside and down the long sidewalk to the trailer furthest away from the school, number thirty-two. While the crowd thinned out considerably the further out we went, Victor still walked close beside me so that his arm was slightly in front of mine. Anyone who gave us a glance might have thought we were holding hands. Was this how other friends walked together?

He opened the door of the trailer for me. North was already inside, sitting in the back row. I grabbed the seat in front of him and Victor sat in front of me.

"I'm in the middle again," I said. "If I didn't know any better, I'd assume you guys planned this."

North playfully tugged at a strand of hair hanging in my face. "Baby, we plan everything."

I didn't doubt this. Now their plans involved me, dictating where I was sitting or who walked with me to class. Strange but I found some comfort in it. I only wished I knew what they knew so I didn't feel like I was in the dark. Maybe it only took getting used to.

Victor sat back in his chair. I admired the way his wavy hair hung around his ears. The clasp to the cord at his neck looked to be hanging by the edge.

"Hold still, Victor," I said, reaching to his neck.

At my touch, he jumped, rubbing where my fingers brushed his neck as if I had pinched him. "What is it?" His eyebrows creased together.

"Sorry," I said. "Your necklace. The clasp didn't look like it was holding on very well."

His cheeks went red. "I thought it was a bug or something."

I laughed, shaking my head. "I wouldn't have touched a bug."

"Well thanks."

"Turn around and I'll fix it."

He hesitated and he glanced at others in the room. With his face still red, he turned around. I adjusted the clasp so the chain was secure.

"You're going to lose it," I said. "Be more careful."

His fingertips smoothed over the surface of the medallion. I was about to ask him what the symbol meant but the teacher walked in.

Mr. Morris was a thin man, with small eyes and a closely cropped head of dark hair. He stood at the front of the room, his arms crossed over his chest and as straight as an arrow. "Good morning. I'm Mr. Morris. You can call me

Mr. Morris or sir. I respond to either." He moved to his desk and picked up a history book. "You'll need to pick this up at the book store. You should always bring it with you to class. We'll never have a day where we won't be using it."

The volume looked thick, even in his big hands. I sat back in my chair, my legs sliding a little under Victor's desk. I sensed North leaning forward as I could nearly feel his breath on my hair.

Mr. Morris dropped the book on his desk, and the corresponding slam caused me to jump. "We're starting with the Agricultural Revolution and moving quickly into Egypt and then the Persians. As such, I want a one page essay on my desk tomorrow about the Agricultural Revolution."

There was a chorus of muttering and a few groans.

"I'll make it two pages. It's no big deal to me how much you write."

The class quieted down quickly. I chewed on my lower lip. Mr. Morris was going to be tough.

After class was lunch. Everyone surged for the doors. Victor, North and I lingered back well behind everyone else as we headed to the main building.

"This being in the trailers is going to get old quick," North said. He stuffed his hands into his pockets as he walked.

"It might be nice," I said, readjusting my backpack. "I mean getting out of the building into some nice weather should be fun."

"It won't always be good weather," Victor said. "What about when it rains?"

I pushed my finger to my lower lip. "It's not so bad. I mean with an umbrella and everything."

Victor kicked a pebble off of the sidewalk. "We'll see what you say in the winter."

I had to smile at that. Did he not remember that I was from Illinois? I couldn't imagine South Carolina getting a few feet of snow or being any worse in the winter than that.

When we got to the cafeteria, the place was hectic with students in long lines that stretched out into the hallways. All of the tables were teeming with kids. People sat against the walls, too.

"I don't see any of the guys," I said.

"I found them," North said, pointing out the window to the outdoor courtyard in the middle of the building. In one of the corners, I could see Silas's head over the crowds.

When we got outside, I was relieved to see they were all there. They stood around one of the benches, a collection of book bags piled up on the concrete seat.

"The lines are crazy long," North said. "I don't know how they get everyone fed."

"I'm hungry," Gabriel complained, gripping his stomach. "I don't want to wait an hour for food. Tell me there's an open campus policy."

"Nope," Kota said. He opened his bag and pulled out a wrapped sandwich. He split it with Victor. "No going off campus once you're here."

"There's some vending machines in the front hallway," I said. I glanced at Gabriel. "I'll walk over with you if you want."

Gabriel nodded. "Yeah, I'll eat anything."

I dropped my bag on the ground near North's feet. "Keep an eye on it?"

"Grab some crackers for me, will you?" North asked. He dipped his hand into his pocket and found a couple of dollars.

I was beaming and I couldn't hide it. It made me happy to be somewhat useful to the group that was constantly doing things for me.

"And get me a candy bar," Luke said.

"Are you going to give her money for it?" North asked.

"You just did."

North shook his head. "Get him something a little healthier than candy, will you?"

Gabriel laughed and then grabbed my arm. "Come on."

The main hallway was even more crowded than it was that morning. The cafeteria wasn't big enough to accommodate over two thousand students at once. There was a line for the vending. We stood arm to arm at the back of the line for our turn.

"No wonder everyone here looks grumpy and gets into fights," I said. "Everyone's hungry."

Gabriel said nothing, seeming distracted by students leaning against the trophy cases, some sitting down on the floor. I felt their eyes on us. I realized that Gabriel and I were dressed a little nicer than everyone else. Most of the other students seemed to be wearing jeans and t-shirts. The girls wore jeans and low cut tops. Gabriel and I stood out more here without the others.

The line crept forward. Machines spit back out dollar bills more often than they accepted them.

"What are you getting?" Gabriel asked.

"I wasn't going to get anything," I said. "I didn't bring any money."

His eyebrows shot up. He brushed his fingers through the lock of blond hanging next to his eyes. "Then why did you say you'd come with me?"

I blinked at him. "So you wouldn't go alone. I thought that was what we were doing. Always sticking together like Kota said."

His crystal eyes lit up. "You dummy. Tell me what you want. I'll get it."

"It's okay, I don't..."

"Just pick something."

I hesitated. I had been so anxious that morning that eating hadn't really been a concern. My stomach was still rattling from nervousness now.

"Say something or I'll buy you one of everything," Gabriel warned. He poked at my arm with a lean finger. "Pick. Pick. Pick."

"Maybe some crackers, please," I said, relenting.

In the end, we returned with two packets of crackers, three packages of trail mix, a couple candy bars, and three bottles of water.

"What took you guys so long?" Luke said as we approached. He reached for a candy bar. "We were about send a rescue team."

"You're lucky we came back at all with stuff," Gabriel said, opening one of the trail mix packages. "Even the vending machines were nearly empty. I was going to get more but we were taking too long and the line behind us was grumbling."

I handed North some crackers and his change. He stuffed the money back into his pocket, ripping open the crackers.

I opened the crackers Gabriel bought for me. I noticed Silas eyeballing us. I smiled to him and pointed my package at him.

He started to wave his hand. "It's okay," he said.

"Eat one," I said.

He reached and took a cracker, smiling. "Thanks."

Gabriel handed some of the trail mix out to Nathan and Victor. "Welcome to fine dining at this fucking school."

Kota shook his head and pushed his glasses up his nose. "Look at us scraping for food. This is ridiculous." He reached into his bag and pulled out a package of chips. He opened it and offered it to the others.

"I guess the only answer is to bring stuff every day," I said. "We'll know better tomorrow."

Between us, we managed to share Kota's lunch and what we got from the vending machine including the bottles of water.

As we stood there together, I recognized a few geek groups and a cluster of hippies sitting on their book bags in the grass around the courtyard. Compared to the rest of the crowded halls of the school, the courtyard actually seemed peaceful. The weather was hot, but if it kept the courtyard from being crowded, I thought it would be nice to sit outside every day. A small corner of peace from the chaos inside.

"Well," Kota said, picking up his book bag and standing. "I want to check out the library. Anyone else going?"

"I will," I said. I had no idea where the library was and I was curious about it. "We should probably pick up at least one of those books for English, right?"

Kota brightened at the suggestion. "Might as well start now."

"Aw come on, it's the first day," Gabriel complained. "Stay here with us, Sang."

"You should get one, too," I said. "Come on. We'll all get the same book and then we can compare notes."

He seemed to like this idea and he picked up his book bag.

"I guess I should go, too," Luke said. He grabbed the notebook I had given him earlier. There were doodles on the front cover. At least he used it for something.

When his head tilted, I recognized my clip. His blond locks were pulled back and twisted similar to how I did mine.

I smirked at him. "Nice hair," I said.

He looked surprised and reached back, his fingers catching the curve of the clip. "Like it? It's a new thing I picked up."

"He threatened me in the hallway, Sang," Gabriel whined. "I didn't want to give it to him. I was going to give it back. Eventually."

I sighed. Luke was right. I'd need to bring reserve clips around Gabriel. Perhaps even additional spares for Luke.

We were headed out of the courtyard when I noticed Silas was following us. I paused so I could fall back and walk next to him.

"Do you have some required reading, too?"

"No," he said. "But we've got our class coming up. I thought I should stick with you so we could walk together."

It was so thoughtful and while I wanted to say so, I couldn't find the words. Instead, I smiled as warmly as I could. He dipped his hands into his pockets as we followed Kota up the main stairwell and through a set of hallways.

The second floor was empty.

"How come no one hangs out up here?" I asked.

"They probably aren't supposed to," Kota said. "There are lockers up here. I imagine they don't want to encourage theft or property damage."

Still, there was no one around to tell us to not be there. I wondered how well those upper hallways were monitored.

We found the library at the end of one long hallway, as if tucked away in the most distant corner of the school. Kota held the door open for us and we all stepped in.

The library appeared to be the same size as my garage at home. Shelves were lined up around the walls of the room. There were a handful of older computers in one corner with Windows 2000 screensavers. There was a small circulation desk, painted in orange and brown and two women with peach-tinted hair and glasses stood guard behind it.

We were the only students in the library. The librarians' eyes followed us as we moved toward the walls of shelves. It was hard to tell if we were unexpected or if they felt they needed to monitor us so we didn't damage or steal anything.

"Hm," Kota said, looking through the rows of books. "It appears to be only encyclopedias and all the required reading books. Not a lot of other options."

I picked up a copy of The Count of Monte Cristo, the cover was torn in half and the binding was a little loose. "Good thing we came today. There are only a handful of copies of each."

Everyone except Silas debated on which book to start with but it was Kota that decided to start with Dracula. "It's one of the only ones with four copies available. We'll go somewhere else for the next book. I feel guilty as it is just taking their last copies of this."

"I've read a few of these already," I said, checking out the reading list again.

"I know. Me, too," he said. "Save the ones you've already read just in case things get busy later. If not, we'll use things we've already read for the last couple of tests and have an easy time before finals."

That was pretty clever thinking. I was happy that Kota was there or I would have been tempted to reread something

I already knew.

We were at the circulation desk before I realized the others had pulled out cards.

"Do I need a library card?" I asked. "It hadn't occurred to me that there might be one. In my last school, the librarian just typed in your name."

"It's a school ID," Luke said. "You were supposed to go get one during study hall... oh wait, that's right. You didn't get a study hall."

I rubbed a fingertip over my eyebrow. "I didn't realize we needed one."

Kota took the book from me. "I'll get this. Silas, you go with her to get her ID."

"Are you sure?" I asked Kota.

He smiled at me and nodded. "Don't worry. If you forget to turn it in, I know where you live. I'll come by and get it."

My eyes widened and he laughed. He knew how to keep me in line.

I walked alongside Silas through the quiet hallways. It was starting to feel like a rush to get everything done today. I felt flustered trying to come up with something to talk about, but he seemed content to walk quietly beside me.

"You're going to join the baseball team here, right?" I asked, finally settling for sports. I knew he liked baseball.

"I'm considering changing my mind," he said. "I checked out the field and it looks pretty bad. Besides, the football coach was bugging me this morning about tryouts."

I looked up at him but he stared at the ground, his face unreadable. "Football isn't your favorite?"

"Not really."

"So why settle for football? Why not go with something you love?"

He shrugged. "Not everything works out the way you want it to."

"It should," I said. I felt it was true. There was so much fun stuff to do out there and it seemed silly to waste time with doing something you didn't want. I spent a lot of time at my parents' house when other kids were in dancing school or summer camps or going to the park to play. Even now my mind was turning as to what I could do, what my parents would allow for me to do, that involved more time away from the house. "Maybe the baseball team could use a player like you. Someone with talent and passion for the game. It might inspire others to play."

His lips curled up. "Perhaps. I might do both. Football for the fall, baseball in the spring. Mr. Blackbourne might want me to do it, anyway. I may try to convince North to go with me."

"Does North like sports?"

"Watching them," he said. "He hates playing. He doesn't really like being told what to do."

Silas lead the way to the offices downstairs and near the front of the building. We followed a small corridor near the nurses' office. A round wood table had been set up with a computer hooked to a camera and a printing station. A teacher sat by a machine. She asked my name, typed it in a computer and had me stand in front of a blue sheet of paper that had been taped to the wall.

I was waiting for the photo to flash when Silas got into my line of sight. "Smile," he said.

I blushed. "It's just a school photo."

He shrugged. "Do it anyway. Say cheese or fiddlesticks or San Francisco or whatever."

I felt my lips moving into a grin hearing him say fiddlesticks and the camera light flashed. Red and green spots washed over my eyes.

In five minutes, I had a photo ID where my cheeks were pink and I had a crazy smile. I couldn't remember the last time I'd had my picture taken, so my face looked strange to me.

"I look terrible," I said, holding my ID up and analyzing how my hair looked mangled on one side.

"Let me see," Silas said, reaching for the card. He tilted it toward his face, angling it away from a gleam of light reflected in it. "It's not bad. You're cute."

I rubbed my hands over my cheeks as they felt hot. "I only have to use it if they ask for it, right? And for the library?"

"I think they use it as your yearbook picture, too."

My eyes widened. He broke into a grin and started laughing.

"That's not funny," I said, reaching for the ID.

He held it up over my head. "I might keep this. I don't have a picture of you."

I leapt into almost an *en pointe* on my toes for it, but with Silas being so tall, he held it outside of my reach easily. I stumbled forward, and on instinct put out a hand to stop myself and ended up pushing into him. I let go quickly after I was stable. He jerked his chest forward, bending over a little, feigning being hurt. I stepped away from him, walking backward and laughing at the crazy face he was making. I backed up into something solid.

I turned and my heart dropped into my shoes in horror as I faced a bristling Mr. McCoy, the vice-principal.

"You have a nasty habit of running into people, Miss Sorenson," he said. He brushed at his brown suit coat as if I had soiled it. "You should watch where you're going." His chubby cheeks protruded and his watery eyes squinted at me.

My finger fluttered up to my lower lip. I receded. Silas came up behind me and I stopped so I wouldn't bump into him, too. "I'm so sorry, Mr. McCoy."

His small eyes slid down to my skirt. I snapped to attention, putting my hands to my thighs to show him my skirt was well within regulation. He scowled, looking back up at me. "Goofing off in the hallways is not permitted."

"We were getting our IDs," Silas said. "And now we're heading to our next class."

The bell rang and the hallway moved into action with students shuffling off in different directions.

Mr. McCoy cleared his throat. "Follow me, Miss Sorenson. I believe there's a detention slip with your name on it in my office."

"I don't believe an accident is a cause for a detention, sir," Silas replied.

I bit my lip, reaching back to touch Silas's arm, silently pleading with him to not press the issue. I didn't want him to get a detention, too.

Mr. McCoy turned to him, squinting into Silas's face. "You're one of Mr. Blackbourne's kids, aren't you?"

Silas glared back at him. "I'm from the Academy."

"Not now you aren't," he said, his lips curling into a sneer. "Don't think for one minute I won't give you detention, too. Or worse." He jerked is head back to me. "I'm going to let you go this time. The next time I see you, you better keep your head down. I'll be watching." He glanced once more at Silas and stalked down the hallway.

I let go of the breath I'd been holding. "Silas..."

He shook his head and grabbed my hand. "Come on," he said. "We're going to be late."

We slid into class at the last minute and took two seats near the back. I collapsed into the chair, panting. Mr. McCoy was going to be a problem.

"That was the vice-principal, right?" Silas asked, tilting over the top of his desk to talk to me.

"Yeah," I said. "I can't believe I ran into him twice."

"I don't think this was your fault. He was watching us from down the hall and when we got close, he leaned into you. He was waiting for this."

My mouth fell open. "He was looking to give me detention?"

Silas's lips pursed and he shook his head but didn't say anything. Whatever it was, I was sure I wanted to keep clear of Mr. McCoy. What stopped him this time? Was it Silas or the lingering name of the Academy that made Mr. McCoy recant his promise of a detention? Was he afraid of the Academy?

FLIRTING

While the teacher was going over the agenda, I shifted my feet under my desk. I stopped short, hitting what I thought was my book bag. I checked so I could move it. Silas snapped his feet from under my chair, his knee knocking into his desk top. He covered his knee with his hands and he sucked through his teeth once.

"Sorry," I whispered to him. "I didn't mean to scare you. I thought I hit my book bag."

"Don't worry about it," he said, and put his head to the desk. He let go of his knee, but I could tell he was uncomfortable. He had to tuck his legs in an odd angle. The desks weren't made for someone so tall.

"Hey," I said. "If you need to stretch your legs, go ahead and put them under my desk."

He sat up, his cheeks tinted red. With his black locks against his face and his olive skin, it was really handsome. "I don't want to be in your way."

"Don't sweat it. Stretch your legs out."

He did, leaning back in his seat until his feet were sticking out from under my desk. I moved my feet until I had one on each side of his legs.

"There," I said. "No big deal. I'll just know it's you down there. If I kick you, I'm sorry."

The corner of his mouth curled up. "Ditto."

We sat like that through class. On occasion I would rock my ankle, forgetting he was there. My heel would gently bump into his leg. He didn't jump like before. At some point I was unconsciously leaning my foot against him. When I realized I was doing it, I froze, unsure if I should move it quickly. I didn't want to spook him again.

He never said a word about it.

When the bell rang, he walked with me through the hallway. "My next class is near yours," he said. "Victor's on his way, right?"

I nodded. "He should be."

We ended up pushed together on our way up the main stairs. Silas moved me until I was standing in front of him. I didn't understand why until I noticed how squished we ended up being. I was standing so close to the girl in front of me that I could smell the shampoo in her hair. Silas kept himself so close, that when I had to stop suddenly, his chest bumped into my head.

The stairwell was going to be a problem. Too many students needed to get around it and everyone was in a hurry. Silas kept a hand on my shoulder the entire time and I was grateful for it as I felt unstable. I thought for sure at some point I'd trip and get trampled.

When we were on the second floor and close to my next class, Dr. Green appeared in the hallway right outside the door. "Oh!" he said, looking up and smiling. I relaxed as his gentle gaze caught my eyes. Out of all the teachers I had come across that day, I knew Dr. Green would be my favorite. I remembered how kind he was with me at registration. It seemed strange he would teach a class. He looked the same age as Mr. Blackbourne: nineteen at the most. His soft green eyes lit up with recognition. "Hello, Miss Sorenson. And Silas, you're not in my class, are you?"

Silas shook his head. "Not this time, doc."

"It's a shame," Dr. Green said. "Learning a third language would look good on a resume."

"What's the other language you know?" I asked Silas.

"Greek," he said, his dark eyes sparking.

"You've not said one word to me in Greek," I teased. I was embarrassed that I didn't know this. I knew he was from Europe but I never got the chance to ask where he was from and while on occasion he did carry an accent, his English was so fluent that I often forgot.

"*M'aresei o tropos pos gelas,*" he said, and he waved goodbye as he walked on toward his class.

I looked to Dr. Green. "Do you know what he said?"

"I'm afraid I don't know Greek," he said, a slight smile on his lips. "But it sounded romantic. Are you two dating?"

I flinched out of surprise. Are teachers supposed to take an interest in students like that? I blushed but shook my head. "Oh no, we're friends," I said.

He nodded and adjusted the green tie at his neck. "Ah well." Was he disappointed or pleased? It was difficult to tell.

I found a couple of desks near the back and took one, putting my bag in the seat behind me for Victor. I was tempted to take the back but the guys seemed to enjoy sitting behind me. I wasn't sure why, but I didn't mind.

He slipped in at the last minute. "I hate the trailers," he said, moving my book bag out of the seat and to the floor for me.

"Me, too," I whispered to him.

Dr. Green stood at the front of the class, writing his name in Japanese on the board and wrote it in English below that. "Good afternoon, class," he said.

I said a soft good afternoon, but no one else in the class joined me.

Dr. Green laughed. "I think my class is missing. Did no one show up today? I'll have to mark everyone as absent. I believe I said good afternoon."

The room chorused a low murmuring 'good afternoon' in reply.

"This won't do," Dr. Green said. "I'm here to teach you Japanese. I can't very well teach you English, too." He folded his arms behind his back and walked up through an aisle between two rows of desks. "We'll be taking a lot of time to discuss Japan and the culture and of course, the language. You'll be practicing with your classmates." He made a loop around behind the back row of desks and strolled toward the front of the class. "As such, I think right now is the time to select a partner. I want you to work on a project for me."

There was a collective groan. I glanced back at Victor, his fire eyes flickered at me. We already had our partners.

"Groaning is not a word," Dr. Green said. "In this class, we use our words to express ourselves. And get ready for it. A month from now, we won't be using English at all. If you can't say it in formal Japanese, you won't be able to do anything. That includes permission to leave my classroom." Dr. Green rocked on his feet in front of the room, a soft smile on his face. "Let's hope I remember to tell you what the phrase is first..." He shook his head. "But for now, pick a partner. I want you to prepare a list of things you both already know about Japan. I want to see how much my students know about the place we will be studying."

"What do you know about Japan?" I asked Victor, turning in the seat to face him.

He shook his head, a slight smile on his face. "They grow rice."

I reached for a notebook and a pen in my bag. "Do you want to write it down?"

"You write," he said. "Your handwriting is nicer."

"How would you know?"

"Girls always have nice handwriting."

I smirked at him, plopping the notebook on his desk. "I want to see yours."

He took the pen from my hand and wrote something in the notebook. He flipped over the notebook so I could read it.

Japan grows rice.

"It's not bad," I said, being honest. I'd read worse. His was legible.

"But you probably write all swirly and with hearts and stuff," he said, fiddling with the medallion at his neck.

"I don't use hearts," I said. "Unless you want me to." I took the notebook and wrote our names at the top of the page. I used my plainest writing for my own name and wrote his in a girly script, using a heart over the "i".

"He's going to know you did that," he said. "He knows my handwriting."

"Yeah but no one else will," I said. "And we have to pass it up at the end of class, right?"

His eyes went wide. "You wouldn't."

"I already did."

He rolled his eyes, reaching for the pen in my hands but I put it behind my back.

"What's wrong? I like your name in hearts." I was feeling good. I thought I would like this class and I was happy Victor was there with me to share it. It was the first time I wasn't feeling so nervous that day.

He smiled but his cheeks tinted red. He shook his head and crossed his arms over his chest. "Stop being so damn cute."

"Victor?" Dr. Green said.

Dr. Green approached my desk. I spun around to sit properly.

"Dr. Green." Victor sat up, pulling his shoulders back to face him.

"If you're going to flirt with Miss Sang in my class, it must be done in Japanese." Dr. Green brushed a lock of his sandy-colored hair from his forehead. "I believe you were saying she is cute? In Japanese, you say *kawa...*"

"I'm not doing that," Victor said, interrupting him, blushing again and turning his head away.

Other students listening in started to giggle.

"No?" Dr. Green looked at me. "Well in that case..." He picked up my hand. His warm fingers wrapped around mine delicately. "*Kimi ga ite shiawase. Koi ni ochite shimatta.*" He bowed his head, puckered his lips and hovered at the crest of my knuckles as if he were about to kiss my hand.

The whole class around us started to gasp.

He stopped a millimeter away and his breath teased the back of my hand. He gazed up, smiled at me and winked. "That is how you talk to a lady."

I felt my cheeks and ears getting hot. "What does it mean?" I asked, my voice catching.

"When you figure it out, I'll give you a free A on your next test." He let go of my hand. He stood fully, putting his hands behind his back again and headed to the front of the room. "Are we finished? I don't see pens and pencils moving. Please don't turn in a paper with just two or three things. I am hoping my class is brighter than the average student population."

Whispers filled the room. Eyes focused on me and I slid further into my seat, unsure how to respond. So many questions popped into my mind.

Academy teachers were very different.

♥♥♥

Victor escorted me to the gym for my next class. He was quiet, gazing at the floor and he bumped into other students as he walked.

"Victor?"

"Hm?"

"Is Dr. Green normally like that?"

His fire eyes met mine. He considered me, an eyebrow raised. "You mean kissing girls in the middle of the classroom?"

My cheeks warmed again. "He never did kiss my hand."

"He would have," Victor said, gazing down at his toes again. "And yes, he's like that."

"Do you know what he said to me? The kimi ga--"

"No," he said, his tone rising. His cheeks turned red. "I have no idea what he said."

Was he being honest or did he not want to tell me? And why was he snappy with me? I stopped walking, rewrapping my fingers around the straps of my bag. "Hey," I said. "I was just asking."

"Well stop asking me about him. Who the hell cares what he said?" he scoffed. His face changed and he reached into his pocket, pulling out his cell phone. He glanced at the messages and frowned. "I've got to go."

"Victor?" I asked but he was already walking away. He

76

wandered off into the crowd and I lost sight of him.

I couldn't understand him. Why would he be so angry with me? Was it because I basically started it and embarrassed us both in class? I sighed. Sometime later I needed to remind myself to apologize to him for it.

And where was he going?

♥♥♥

Since it was the first day of gym class, all of the students for that period gathered in the large gymnasium. The bleachers were closed and there was a wide area of the floor in front of the basketball court. The girls were directed to one half of the area and the guys to the other. We were told to sit on the ground. I knelt in my skirt, the wood felt rough against my already bruised knees. I slid onto my butt quickly for relief. It was awkward but my knees didn't hurt.

I found Gabriel right away across the room. I waved to him to catch his eye. His eyes brightened when he noticed and he waved back. I moved so I was sitting close to the outside of the group of girls and he did the same on his side, sitting on the edge of the boy's group. The gym teachers were clustered together under one of the basketball goals. They talked to themselves, hovering over their clipboards.

"Where's Nathan?" I asked him.

"I don't know," he said. He tucked fingers through his hair, combing the locks of blonde behind his ear to blend in with the brown. "I thought he would be here."

I twisted my lips. "You know, Victor got a message on his phone and ran off. Would they be together? Did something happen?"

Gabriel's eyebrows arched and his mouth opened in surprised. He fixed himself quickly, shrugged and shook his head. "It's probably nothing to worry about."

I couldn't be sure, but it seemed like Gabriel knew more than he was letting on. What were the boys doing that was so important they would miss a class on the first day of school? Kota would be furious. So would Mr. Blackbourne and Dr.

Green. I hoped whatever was going on, they wouldn't find themselves in trouble.

The gym instructors started to talk to all of us as a group, informing us about where to pay for gym uniforms, giving us sheets of paper as an insurance waiver for our parents to sign and a gym locker number with a lock combo. We would be given five minutes to be dressed and in the gym every day. Our grade depended on us being there on time and daily participation.

Coach French, the girl's instructor, barked at us. "We will also be requiring everyone to pass the physical exam. We're going to do that soon to get it out of the way. This includes the mile run, sit ups, push-ups... everything."

I made a face, squirming to find a comfortable way to sit that was modest in a skirt without sitting on my knees.

"Don't like the sound of exercising?" Gabriel asked.

I swallowed, trying to find a good distraction so he wouldn't notice. "I hate running."

He laughed. "You know what's the best part about running?"

"What?"

"The stopping."

I laughed with him. "Yes. I agree."

After this, there was nothing for us to do but wait until the end of class. They allowed us to talk together and the gym seemed to vibrate with the voices of our chatter echoing in the room.

The door of the gym opened and from the hallway walked in Mr. McCoy and Principal Hendricks. They crossed the basketball court together, talking to each other. Principal Hendricks folded his arms over his chest, his gaze searching the students. Mr. McCoy instantly spotted me, leaned in and whispered something to the Principal. My heart thudded. Was he going to give me detention for sitting incorrectly?

"Who are they?" Gabriel asked, catching where I was looking and my expression.

"It's the principal and the vice-principal."

"Why do you look like you're about to run out the door?" He smirked, poking at my arm. "Are you in trouble already?"

"I don't know yet," I said.

Gabriel's face turned solemn and he twisted around to watch with me. Mr. McCoy and Principal Hendricks crossed the gym toward us.

"Excuse me, kids. We'd hate to interrupt," Hendricks spoke to both of us. Gabriel and I stood up so we could address him. "You're one of Mr. Blackbourne's kids? Mr. Coleman, right?" he asked Gabriel.

He nodded, his crystal blue eyes darkened. He kept his hands behind his back. "Yes, sir. How can I help you?"

"Mr. Morgan didn't show up for his last class today. Would you have an idea as to why?"

Gabriel glanced at me quickly and shook his head. "I have no idea. Perhaps he felt ill and went to see the nurse?"

Mr. McCoy's eyes lingered on me for most of this conversation but he turned to look at the other students. "Wasn't there another one of you in this class? A Mr. Griffin?"

Were they keeping tabs on the guys? "He's not here," I said softly.

Principal Hendricks raised a bushy gray eyebrow. His bald head gleamed under the bright lights in the gym. "Is he sick, too?"

"I'm sure if you ask Mr. Blackbourne," Gabriel said, "he would know. We are required to report to him."

Principal Hendrick's friendly face turned serious. "I understand there might be some differences in how you handle things at your Academy. In the future, though, please report to either myself or Mr. McCoy if there are ever any more *incidences*." His eyes fell on me and his smile returned, but from the way his lips curled on his mouth, it was like staring into the face of a crocodile. "Keep these boys in line, won't you Miss Sorenson? Tell that professor of yours to call me."

I blushed, surprised he knew my name. He thought I was

from the Academy? "But I..."

"Don't worry," he said, patting my shoulder. "I'm helping our newest students to adjust. I know it's different than what you're used to."

He turned away. Mr. McCoy coughed shortly, shot a glare at me and sauntered away with the principal, heading back out of the gym.

My fingers trembled and I pressed my hands to my thighs to still them. I looked to Gabriel, who was shaking his head.

"Gabriel," I said. "What was that?"

His crystal blue eyes met mine. That crazy smile returned to his face, masking the worry he carried a moment ago. "Who knows? Those guys are weird."

The moment class was over, Gabriel strolled beside me toward the busses. The mass of students around us made it hard to walk together. Gabriel sought out my hand to keep me nearby. The suddenness and ease of him simply holding my hand had me blushing. Not that it mattered as other students held hands. It just mattered to me as my already overworked heart quivered at his touch.

He pulled his cell phone out with his free hand and was typing something in.

"If Victor's gone, does that mean you're stuck here?" I asked, knowing Victor had driven him there that morning.

Gabriel looked up for a moment and gave me another reassuring smile. "Oh don't worry. I'll probably just catch the bus with you."

"With me?"

"Yeah. I'll hang out at Kota's. It's okay."

I bit my lip. This felt like a pre-arranged plan. So Victor's sudden disappearance was expected to happen at some point. If that was the case, then Gabriel knew more than he was telling me. I couldn't think of the questions to ask to figure out the truth.

Gabriel's phone vibrated and beeped in his hand. He checked it. "Victor and Nathan have training. They're with Mr. Blackbourne now." He put his phone in his pocket. "See? They're fine."

"What kind of training?" I asked. "What does that mean? Is it for the Academy?"

He shrugged, squeezing my hand. "Don't worry about it, okay?"

How could he be so calm? They skipped a class on the first day and the administration knew about it. "They can't skip class like that," I said. "Why is the principal checking up on everyone? It's the second time I saw him today."

Gabriel blinked at me. "What do you mean?"

I told him what happened in homeroom with North and Luke and how the principal had asked about uniforms.

Gabriel rubbed the back of his head. "Now that's really weird."

We got onto my bus. Kota was already in a seat in the middle. I slid in next to him and Gabriel took the seat across the aisle.

"Good," Kota said. "You made it. In this mess, I was worried I would go home alone." His lips curled up and his green eyes brightened at seeing me. He didn't seem one bit fazed that Gabriel was on the bus, too. He appeared used to getting unexpected visitors.

"Do you know where Nathan is?" I asked Kota.

His smile faltered for a moment but he recovered it quickly. "He's at training?" he looked over my shoulder at Gabriel. I turned in time to see Gabriel expressing something to him but he quickly changed his face and flashed me a grin.

I sighed, sitting back with my arms folded over my chest. "What kind of training is this?"

"Probably jujitsu." Kota said.

"During the middle of school?"

"Uh..."

"With Victor and Mr. Blackbourne?"

His face turned pale. "Well..."

I pursed my lips and rubbed a palm over my forehead.

What kind of Academy was this school they went to? They would take their students out of class for surprise jujitsu training? I didn't need to ask. This was a lie to mask whatever secret the Academy made them swear to keep. I wasn't allowed to know. "Fine," I said. "You don't have to tell me." They both blinked at me in reply so I went on. "I mean you said it, Kota. There are some things you can't tell me. Just tell me that. It's something you can't tell me."

A smile crossed his lips. He leaned in to me so close I could feel his breath on my ear as he whispered. "It'll be fine," he said. "I promise."

It would have to do for now. There was no way I could make them tell me. But why did they make it sound so dangerous? Or was it they didn't want to put me in the middle in case they got into trouble? Plausible deniability? A secret school for unusual people. In my mind, the dark mystery school I envisioned the Academy being was full of ninjas all sparring in silence.

The bus was warm and as it filled up with students, I started sweating. There were nearly double the amount of kids from that morning. Eventually Kota and I moved over to make room for Gabriel. We were sitting with our thighs pressed against each other. All the students were like that.

"How many students can this bus hold?" I wondered out loud.

"Probably not this many," Gabriel said, squeezing in closer to me as another student passed us to get to the back. I wasn't quite sure, but it looked like in some seats there were at least four students.

It felt strangely exotic to be so close to the two of them. I considered them both very good looking and simply being friends with guys who were so handsome was still amazing to me. When it came to being snuggled between them, I found it difficult to deal with. The circumstances made it so we were forced into this, but I secretly looked forward to the long bus ride home and wondered if this would happen every day. I inhaled Kota's spicy scent and Gabriel's musky wood and they mixed together well. Gabriel's lean hip pressed against mine. Kota, in an effort to make more room, moved sideways, putting an arm on the seat over my head. His long fingers hung down over my shoulder, brushing against the collar of my shirt.

"I'm sorry, guys," I said. "If it wasn't for me, maybe you would be riding with North or in your own cars."

"Don't worry about it," Kota said.

"You worry about me. Isn't that why you're here?"

He smiled softly but said nothing.

"We stick together," Gabriel said. "It's what we do." He rubbed a palm on top of my head, messing up my hair. "You've got to get used to that, Sang. You're with us now."

I took in a deep breath. I'm with them. The only thing I wasn't totally sure about was what this was.

♥

PAINFUL SECRETS

We spent nearly forty minutes squished together on the bus; more students meant more places to stop and a longer wait as students had to rearrange themselves to get off.

When we got to Sunnyvale Court, the bus driver stopped in front of Kota's house. "Everyone on this street, this is your stop. I'll pick you up here in the morning," the driver said.

I shuffled out with Kota and Gabriel. My sister, Danielle and her brother were behind us.

I stood with Kota and Gabriel in the driveway. "I guess I've got to go. If my sister checks in and I'm not there..."

"Can you get back out?" Gabriel asked.

I glanced at my sister, who was talking to Danielle. "We'll have to see how this goes. I might have to negotiate."

"What does that mean?" Kota asked. He pushed his glasses up his nose. "You still haven't told me."

"It's too hard to explain right now."

Gabriel held out his forefinger with his thumb up like his hand was a gun. He jerked it, taking a shot at me. "Call us," he said. "Or run back over if you can."

I nodded. I started up the road toward the house. Marie soon followed me.

I walked alongside my sister. It felt strange to be standing next to her after spending the whole day with the guys. She looked strangely uncomfortable. I wondered how her first day was. I assumed she didn't talk to the principal at every turn.

"So, that was Danielle, wasn't it?" I asked her.

She scrutinized me, frowning. "How would you know?"

"The guys mentioned her and her brother," I said.

Her lips screwed up on her face. "Yeah, well, she told me about those *boys*," she emphasized as if to suggest they were toddlers rather than our own age.

"What did Danielle have to say?"

Marie shrugged. "I wouldn't hang out with them. They're snobs from some private school."

"They're not snobby," I said. "They're nice."

"They don't talk to anyone but themselves."

"They talk to me."

"Yeah, well, you're weird so go figure."

I let out a breath. There wasn't a point to talking with her. When she set her mind to how a person was, she pretty much kept that opinion. Still, I wondered how she managed to make friends as she seemed so negative. We were never really close but sometimes I wondered what it would have been like if we tried to get along. It wasn't that I was mean to her. We didn't really have a lot in common and with our parents being the way they were, instead of becoming closer, we'd grown apart. I partially blamed myself. I'd let it happen. When I tried to take an interest, it felt like we ended up fighting. I didn't know what to do.

When we got back to the house, I tiptoed through the hallway toward my mother's room. Putting my ear to the wall, I held my breath, waiting for signs of life. I needed to ask her about getting a violin. I knew how the conversation would go before I even started it, only I had a small hope the result would be she would call my dad at work and have him pick up a violin on his way back home.

The drone of the news on the television played and rustling noises came from the bed. I stepped into the open doorway, peering in.

She was perched on the bed, her arms crossed over her chest. I treaded forward, purposefully stepping in spots that creaked to get her attention.

Her head snapped around. Her blue eyes were glossy. It made me wonder if she'd been crying. "What do *you* want?" she asked. Her tone erased my previous assumption about her mood.

"I need to bring a violin to school," I said quietly. "I need to go get one."

Her eyebrows scrunched together. "Since when do you play the violin?"

"One of my classes is violin lessons."

"Shouldn't the school provide one if they're giving you the lessons?"

"They don't have one for me."

She frowned. "We can't buy a musical instrument every time you want to piddle with something."

"I need one for class tomorrow."

"Did your dad approve of this?"

"He signed the paper for my schedule." What I'd said was true, he did sign my paper. What I was implying wasn't true. He didn't really know about my violin lessons because Dr. Green and Mr. Blackbourne changed it after.

She sucked in a breath and slowly released it, scratching at a spot on her face. Her eyes focused in and out. Maybe the television was hurting her eyes. "I don't think you should take this class. You'll never keep up with it."

My heart plunged. *No, please. Don't do this now.* "But I'm already signed up," I said. "I'm sure it wouldn't be expensive. It can be something cheap from a pawn shop."

"If we buy one for you, you'll just quit."

"I can't quit," I urged. I was losing this. I had to come up with something. "I'm already signed up. I have to go for the whole year."

"You shouldn't have signed up for it. You don't know anything about music."

"Marie has her flute," I said, feeling terrible about using my sister for this. I always did my best to keep my sister out of the middle of any discussion with my parents, even if she didn't do the same for me. It felt like a betrayal of trust and I didn't want to be that type of person. Still, my argument was weak and I knew what my mother would say before she said it.

"Just go to the front office tomorrow and ask them to drop you. You don't have any business in a music class."

That was it. If I asked any more, she'd punish me for talking back, or worse, she'd call the school. If she did that, I'd be at the mercy of her whims. My whole schedule could get reworked if she wanted.

I swallowed and backed up to the door. It was a risk I didn't want to take. I plodded down the hallway. What else could I do? Tomorrow I'd have to admit to Mr. Blackbourne that my parents wouldn't allow me to get a violin. I didn't want to envision his steel eyes looking at me with pity or with resentment for wasting his time. The only student he took on the entire year was quitting.

I sucked in a breath and shook off the thoughts. There was nothing I could do about it. I would do what I had to do and get it over with. Maybe it was better this way. What did someone like me do to deserve any time and attention from a talented Academy professor?

I couldn't stand to be in the house anymore. I shivered, suppressing the anger at feeling trapped.

I climbed the stairs to the landing. I was about to enter my room when I noticed Marie's door was ajar. She never left it open and I edged over to it to take a peek.

Marie's bed was unmade. The black ceiling fan was on, the window's curtains were open. Clothes cluttered the floor, some spilling out from the closet. A diary sat haphazardly open on the floor. Papers from the day of school sat in a pile near her door. No Marie.

I quietly closed her door and backed away from it, thinking. I padded through the house. Marie wasn't around. My mom already saw me and dismissed me so she wouldn't likely ask for me again. My dad wouldn't be home for hours.

I grabbed my book bag and the cell phone and was out the door before I could second-guess myself. I wasn't going to waste a moment if I could get away.

♥♥♥

I took a longer route through the woods behind my house, coming out around Nathan's and out into the street. I didn't want to take the chance of anyone in my family paying attention and seeing me. It also gave me time to cool down from my mother's resounding rejection.

Max, Kota's Golden Retriever, padded over to me as I crossed the yard to Kota's drive. He panted happily and nosed at my hand. I pushed my fingers through the fur on his head. He followed me into the garage and sat next to me when I used the doorbell.

Jessica, Kota's little sister, answered the door. Her pink-rimmed glasses slid down her nose a little as she looked up at me and smiled. "Hi Sang."

"Hi Jessica. Are the boys still here?"

"Yeah," she said. She opened the door wider for me and I slipped inside. She unhooked Max's lead from his collar. Max raced through the house and disappeared into the living room, sniffing at the air. "They're up in Kota's room."

"Thanks," I said. I closed the door behind me. Jessica ran off back to her bedroom, Max followed behind her.

I opened the door to Kota's room and suddenly realized I probably should have knocked. It seemed awkward to simply run up the stairs. Would he even hear me if I tried knocking?

I opted for calling from the bottom of his stairs. "Kota?" I called up. "Gabriel?"

Creaking and paper shifting noises drifted to me. Kota and Gabriel poked their heads out from over the rail barrier.

"Hey!" Gabriel said. He'd removed his dress shirt and tie. He left on a white ribbed tank shirt that he had worn underneath. While he was lean, he had some definition to his chest and arms and the look was still stunning. "You made it. How did you escape?"

I finished climbing the stairs. "My sister ran off somewhere so I thought it'd be okay to come over."

Kota's collared shirt and tie had been replaced by a green t-shirt. He tilted his head toward me. "How long can you stay?"

"I don't know. If we spot her walking back, I'll go. Or before my dad gets home."

"Are you sure it's okay?"

"Aw, come on, Kota," Gabriel said. His slim fingers encircled my arm and he pulled me into the room. "If it were up to her parents, she'd never leave the house. If she doesn't break out, we'd never see her."

Kota shifted on his feet as if he was trying to decide if this was a good idea. It made me wonder if he felt guilty for the day before when I got into trouble. I searched for the words to help calm his worries, but nothing seemed right. I didn't want to go back so I tried my best to smile warmly at him, hoping he'd understand. He hesitated but took a step back, relenting.

I sat down at the foot of Kota's bed, dropping my book bag on the floor. Gabriel crawled onto the bed, crossing his legs, and pointed to the pile of papers that he had collected in the middle. "We've already got homework. Can you believe it?"

"I've got a lot, too," I said. "What are you doing for the English assignment?"

"I've already finished that," he said. He shuffled through the papers on the bed, picking one out. "It's more like song lyrics than a poem."

"Can I see?"

He passed the notebook paper to me. "It's not good."

His poem was about a lost princess in a tower and a prince pining for her from the ground. He threw apples up to her every day hoping she would eat them and think of him. One day he hit her in the head and she fell from the tower and she died. The prince felt so bad he took her to a mountaintop where he held on to her until he froze to death in the night, binding him and her together forever in ice.

"It's sad," I said. "Tragic."

He grinned. "Girls love that shit."

"I like happy endings."

He pulled a face, leaning back on his elbows against the bed. "Life isn't always happy."

"It should be." I moved to sit back on the bed far enough to where my ankles were hanging over the edge and my back was up against the wall. Kota huddled over his desk. "Did you finish yours, Kota?"

"Working on it now, actually."

"How's it going?"

He sat up, turning in his chair and holding up his notebook. "I don't know. What rhymes with formaldehyde?"

My eyes widened. Gabriel laughed, rubbing his fingers against his forehead. "Dude, what kind of poem are you writing?"

Kota blinked at us. "It's about a doctor."

"Does the doctor fall in love?" Gabriel asked.

"No."

"Does someone die?"

"Not in the story, technically."

"What does he do?"

"He performs an autopsy."

I glanced at Gabriel, sharing a smile with him. I held out a palm to Kota. "Can I see it?"

Kota's cheeks turned red but he handed the notebook to me. The poem had a lot of long words describing the procedures of cutting up a dead body. It was more like a set of instructions with every other line rhyming. The gruesome details made my stomach churn. Was this accurate? How did he know how to perform an autopsy?

"Kota..." I said, not sure exactly how to phrase it.

"I'm not very good at this," he said. He fiddled with the edge of the arm on his desk chair. "I'm not very creative."

I thought about the lines. It wasn't bad work. It was just too formal. "May I see your pen?"

He handed it to me. I replaced a handful of words and added in a few more phrases at the end. When I finished I handed it back to him.

He looked over my notes and smiled, shaking his head.

"It's a horror piece."

"You already had most of it. You just needed a change of perception. A live patient being operated on by a murderer."

He laughed, pushing his glasses up his nose with a forefinger. "You're going to make me sound smarter than I am."

"What are you talking about?" Gabriel said. "If anything, this school is going to dumb you down. I'm surprised you went along with this going into the public school thing."

Kota shrugged, sitting back in his chair and using his legs to rock himself back and forth. "You guys were going. What was I going to do?"

"Personally," Gabriel said, "I'm regretting we ever started. This school seems hopeless. I mean you saw the classrooms."

"The trailers are kind of unusual," I said, for a lack of a kinder word.

"And the library," Gabriel added.

Kota rubbed at his chin. "There isn't much to the library."

"And don't even get me started on lunchtime," Gabriel said. "I mean come on. You saw that. There were still kids in line for lunch when the bell rang."

"Something doesn't add up," Kota said, rubbing a palm over his cheek and folding his arms over his chest. "And with the problems from the principal today, I don't think Mr. Blackbourne and Mr. Hendricks are on the same page about what they want from us."

I hadn't thought about it before but now that they were talking about it, it did seem unreasonable to put such a thing on the shoulders of seven students. "Who made the arrangements?" I asked. "Who asked you all to come into the school?"

"The whole thing was designed by the school board and some of the administrators," Kota said. "Technically the principal had the final say, but he was under a lot of pressure to allow us in. It was basically do it or it meant his job. He claimed he couldn't guarantee the safety of 'spoiled students'. The school board thought if we could help improve the school overall, the state would develop a second school nearby to split the population. They won't bother to spend money on a school that looks like it might be a waste of time."

"But isn't that what they need?" I asked. I was surprised they were telling me about this. Then I realized it really wasn't about the Academy, but about my own school. It didn't count so much as an Academy secret. "Wouldn't you give money to a school that needed it?"

"You would think," Kota said. "The only way a school gets attention is by the quality of the grades and curriculum for the entire student body and financial interest from state officials in control of school spending. They'll only help a school that seems worth investing in, because that's what it comes down to. They focus more on middle and high income neighborhoods. It makes a bigger impact than these poorer districts. Not as many registered voters here. However, there was a deal struck by a state official. He's documented that if Ashley Waters can improve, he'll give the go ahead to start building another school."

"Which is why this is stupid. There's not a lot worth saving. They might as well build two new schools. And the mismanagement is terrible. I feel like we're wasting our time," Gabriel said. He stretched out a leg over his homework, tipping his foot to nudge my leg. "If it weren't for you, I'd be asking Mr. Blackbourne if we could drop this whole thing."

His attitude surprised me. They could leave if they wanted? Would they if they were pushed out at all or felt it was too much? "You don't have to stay for me," I said softly. "I mean, if you feel it's that bad." I didn't want to be so demure about it. They were my only friends in the school. Even so, it just seemed silly to stay because of me. If I had the choice, would I have stayed? I could only imagine what the Academy was like but I knew it had to be better than

Ashley Waters.

"We're in for the year," Kota said. "We promised we'd do our best for the school and that's what we'll do. We don't get to give up just because it's complicated. Mr. Blackbourne's plans weren't made lightly, so there must be something we can do."

So it was Mr. Blackbourne who was officially in charge. Mr. Blackbourne made the arrangements. Did he call Victor out of the class? I bit my lower lip; talking about Mr. Blackbourne only reminded me of secrets I couldn't ask about and what I had to do tomorrow. "Maybe we should make something for lunch tomorrow so we aren't stuck with vending food. There might not be anything left tomorrow."

"I think there's a loaf of bread downstairs," Kota said, standing up. He held out a hand to me. It took me a moment to realize he wanted me to take it. I sucked in a breath to summon some courage and put my hand in his. He grasped it as I stood up, letting go when I was standing. In the back of my mind, I was somewhat sorry he released me. "Unless you mean you want to cook something."

"I suppose I could," I said, putting a finger to my lower lip. It seemed kind of weird to make something in his house and I couldn't imagine what to fix.

"Hold up. Are you telling us you can cook?" Gabriel said. He swung his legs around and stood up next to me. "I have to see this."

"Who doesn't cook?" When it came to my family, unless I wanted dinner from a can every night, my sister and I had learned how to cook. I couldn't remember not being able to at least make scrambled eggs or spaghetti as needed.

"Luke and North can," Gabriel said. "It doesn't happen often."

"If you can read, you can cook." I crossed the floor, heading to the stairs. I glanced over my shoulder at them. "Ready?"

Kota shot a look at Gabriel. Gabriel smirked. "I might be able to use the can opener."

♥♥♥

Within a short amount of time, taco soup simmered in a pot on the stove. The boys had managed to cut onions and open cans. They stood back and watched as I cooked up ground beef, added beans and vegetables and different spices and put it all together.

"There," I said, wiping my brow with the back of my hand as I stirred the pot. "Kota, you've got dinner for tonight. What you don't eat, stick into a thermos. We'll take some plastic cups and spoons and bingo. Lunch."

Gabriel hovered over my shoulder. He stuck his finger into the mix and yanked it back to put into his mouth. "He might not have leftovers," he said, licking his finger. "I'm gonna stay for dinner."

He attempted to reach into the pot again and I playfully swatted at his hand. "You're going to eat it all before it's dinner time."

He pouted and the way the bottom lip curled melted my heart. It was adorable. "Don't be so cruel, Sang. You didn't tell us you could cook and now that you've made something and it smells really good, you won't let me taste it."

"You're going to burn your fingers," I said. "It's hot."

"I'll live. It's just a finger." He threaded his hand around my side with a pointed finger aimed at the pot. I pushed his arm in a panic, worried he really would burn himself. He grasped my wrist. I laughed, dropping the large wooden spoon into the pot. I tried to wrestle my arm away. He captured my other hand, and collected my wrists together against his chest. "You're in trouble now," he said, grinning.

"What?"

I heard the spoon getting picked up behind me. I twisted against Gabriel's hold in time to see Kota dip the spoon into the soup and taking a sip.

"Kota!"

He smiled, putting the spoon down into the pot again. "It smells good. It's making me hungry."

I groaned and wrenched my hands from Gabriel,

playfully pointing a finger in the direction of Kota's bedroom. "All right guys, out of the kitchen. Let's go get homework done before you eat it all."

It took more coaxing, but I managed to get the guys back up the stairs. I set the stove on low so the soup could simmer for a while.

We gathered back in Kota's room and got to work. I was on my stomach on the floor, writing in a notebook for the English assignment. Kota was at his computer desk and Gabriel was half asleep on Kota's bed.

Thudding footfalls came from the stairs. Victor popped his head up. His cheeks flushed when he spotted me on the floor, but it didn't distract me from the bright bruise on his face or the gash at this cheek.

"Victor!" I jumped up off the floor probably in an undignified manner. I crossed the room as he stood by the stairs. The closer I got, the worse his injuries looked. "What happened?"

"Training," he said quietly.

My fingers hovered in the air close to his face, only I was too afraid to touch him as it looked painful. The gash on his cheek had already started to crust over. The bruise was a purple mess, splotching across the side of his face and along the start of his jaw by his ear. "With what? A bear?"

He shook his head. He turned to Kota. "I didn't think she would be here."

Kota nodded, standing up. "It's not important. Are you okay?"

"Yeah," he said. His fire eyes settled on me, a quiet smolder. "I'm sorry, Sang."

I swallowed my heart in my throat and my eyebrows nearly popped off the top of my forehead. "Sorry? For what?"

"I yelled at you earlier before I left. I'm sorry about that. I didn't mean it."

My mouth fell open. I had nearly forgotten about it. "How could you think that? You get into a fight and the only thing you can think to say is you're sorry about something that doesn't matter?"

He flinched, sticking his hands in his pockets. "Fine. Next time I won't apolo--."

I realized I'd snapped and it broke my heart. I wrapped my arms around his neck, hugging him. I didn't say anything. I couldn't find the words as to why I did it or what I was feeling. He'd disappeared and I had been worried about him. Seeing him injured like that forced me to think of every bad thing that was out there and I kept picturing it all happening to him. It was everything my mother said would happen to me if I wandered away from home. Friends hug when they want to support one another, right?

"Ooof," Victor choked out. "Sang, I..." His hands settled on my back and he pressed himself to me. His fingers traced along my ribs. He pressed his cheek to mine and I wondered if that was the proper way to hug someone and I'd done it wrong. "I am sorry," he whispered in my ear, his warm breath teasing my lobe.

I sighed, regrouping myself and stepping back. I felt so awkward, and my face felt hot. I hid my shaking fingers behind my back as I looked over his injuries again. "We need to clean you up."

Kota disappeared into his bathroom and grabbed his medical kit. He brought it out to me. "Where's Nathan?" he asked as I took the medical kit and opened it up.

Victor looked at me and then lowered his gaze. "He's still training."

"Where?" I asked, pulling out the peroxide and a gob of cotton and knelt to the carpet. When my knees knocked against the floor, pain from the bruises radiated into my thighs. I steeled myself, and shifted to sitting on my heels to lessen the pressure. I hoped no one noticed.

Victor followed me, sitting cross legged on the floor next to me. Kota and Gabriel joined us on the floor.

"It's just at the Academy," Victor said.

I frowned. It was obviously not this simple or he would have said it before. "Did Nathan beat you up?" I asked.

Victor attempted a smile but he pursed his lips to stop

himself and shook his head. "No."

I applied some peroxide to a cotton swab and cupped his chin in my hand to steady him. I dabbed the cotton against his cheek. The liquid started to sizzle at the cut.

He thrust his head back, grabbing at my wrist that held the swab and yanked it away from his face. He sucked in a breath through his teeth. "Easy, Sang."

"I barely touched you." I fished out a clean swab of cotton, holding it to the bottle to absorb more peroxide.

I did my best to clean his cheek but Victor fought it at each step, sensitive to every touch. I kept waiting for Kota or Gabriel to start asking questions, but it felt like they already knew what they needed to know, or they couldn't ask because I was there. I chewed on my cheek as I applied bandages to Victor's face.

"Does this happen a lot?" I asked in a quiet voice. "To all of you? Do you get called out of school to go do 'training'?"

There was a lengthy silence before Kota spoke up. "One of the stipulations for us being there is that Mr. Blackbourne would have full control over our schedules. If we ever needed to be called up for something that was Academy business, we would be allowed to leave class to deal with it."

"Does it always involve fighting?"

Kota's lips lightly curled up at the corner. "No."

"Am I allowed to ask what kind of business at the Academy makes Victor's face look like he got mauled by a baseball bat?"

Looks were exchanged by all three of them but lips remained closed. I sighed, crumpling the wrappers from the bandages in my hand, putting the kit back together and standing, heading to Kota's bathroom to replace it all.

"It's better if you don't know, Sang," Kota said. "I don't want to keep you in the dark but if you knew..."

I tossed the wrappers in his trash and put the kit back in the drawer. "Are you worried that I'd be scared for you? I'm freaking out now. How is knowing worse than not knowing?"

They exchanged looks again. Their silent communication irked me.

"Do your parents know?" I asked. "I mean what if Kota walked in one day and his poor mom saw him with bruises all over his face?"

"She..." Gabriel started to say but I caught Kota shooting him a look. Gabriel blushed, looking down at the floor.

What else could I say? Who was I to say anything to them? I had just as many secrets, didn't I? I didn't tell them about my knees, about North on the roof, and so much more. I wanted to find out what they were up to, but asking them wasn't going to work. I sighed, biting back the questions. It might not be up to them to tell me about it. I thought of Mr. Blackbourne. He was in charge. Maybe I could ask him without revealing what I knew of Kota and the others. No, the truth was that I'd agreed to not ask questions. It was harder to do now that I saw Victor's bruised face.

I calmed myself and walked back out of the bathroom. The guys looked uncomfortable for a moment but I sat at the foot of Kota's bed, crossing my ankles.

"Are we done with homework yet?" I asked. I hoped the others understood. It was too frustrating talking to them about an Academy that was so full of secrets. I thought it was best that I kept listening and catching these hints when I could. Maybe next time I'd follow Victor and see where he disappeared to. Right now I knew for certain that the Academy was more than a secret. It was true what Kota had warned me about. It could be dangerous.

They exchanged another set of looks, but Kota gave the slightest shaking of his head to the others. He smiled weakly at me. "It's time for a break."

"What smells like tacos?" Victor asked.

DEEPER

I left Kota's house an hour later. I wanted to make sure I got back before Marie did to avoid any more trouble. Making an appearance at home was important. I was still sensitive to how my mom had reacted yesterday when she found out I was at Kota's. Before I met the guys, I could go for a couple of days without seeing anyone in my family, locked away in my room without any interaction from any of them. Right now seemed a critical time and I couldn't be too reckless. After I figured out how our lives would be different with the new school, I'd be better prepared to spend more time with the others. A routine would eventually settle in.

I was crossing through the woods, taking a path that lead behind Nathan's house. A voice bellowed, echoing from the otherwise quiet forest.

"Fuck... fuck, ouch, fuck me, fuck."

I recognized Nathan's voice and stopped, looking toward his house. It wasn't quite dark yet, but through the fence of his back yard, I could see the light was on in his shed.

I took the wood plank bridge across the ditch and opened up the gate to his fence. The door to the shed was open and I crept over to peek inside.

Nathan knelt on the wood floor, clutching at the ground. His shoulders shook. His shirt was off and he was wearing green camouflage shorts. His back was layered with bruises and cuts.

"Nathan!"

He straightened onto his knees and twisted to look at me.

There were more bruises along his arms and chest. One of his cheeks was swollen. His blue eyes squinted at me. "Sang?"

I climbed into the shed and crossed the room to him. I dropped down to sit on my heels to look closer at his back. "Victor made it sound like you were fine. Why did he lie to me?"

Nathan groaned. He slipped and crashed back against the cabinet. "You know you shouldn't trust boys," he said. He was breathing heavily and yet through it he grinned. "We're... um... something bad that I can't think of right now. Remind me to tell you about it later."

"You're all driving me crazy," I said. There was another medical kit on a tray nearby, the bandages and containers of creams spilled out around him. I reached for the creams that had rolled out on to the floor and checked the labels. "Which one did you want?"

He pointed to one. His ring finger on his right hand was in a splint and taped. I took his hand, pulling it to examine it closer and he winced.

"Hey!" he shouted.

"Is it broken? Why aren't you at the hospital?"

"I saw a doctor," he said. "That's where I got the bandage thing."

I reached for the tube he had pointed to and read the label, recognizing the bruising cream. "Is this all you need?"

He nodded.

"Come on," I said. I stood up and clutched his arm to help him up. "Let's get you to inside so you can lay down. You look terrible."

He laughed. "Are you calling me ugly?" He picked himself up and started limping for the door. I tucked myself under his arm. It wasn't that I could pick him up if he fell, but I could at least serve as a minor crutch. He looked a little relieved and he leaned against me as he moved forward.

It was slow progress back to his house. He kept stopping to take in a breath. I opened the door for him and he hobbled in.

"Where do you want to lay down?" I asked.

"In my bed," he said. "Once I'm down, I don't think I'm getting back up."

I gritted my teeth and got under his arm again, letting him guide the way through the living room and down a dim hallway until we faced a door at the end. I opened it and he hopped in.

There was a low dresser pressed up against the wall and a standard double bed in the middle of the room, no headboard. The bed was draped in a dark brown blanket, maroon sheets and two pillows stuffed in the middle, unmade. There were karate movie and jujitsu poses posters along the walls. There was a walk-in closet completely filled with clothes, boxes and some scattered workout equipment. A workout bench had been pushed to the corner, dumbbells sat on a box next to it. There was a window on the other side, the wood slat blinds were drawn.

Nathan plopped onto his stomach on the bed. He landed halfway, with his legs hanging off the edge. "Fuck."

I climbed up onto his bed. "Scoot up."

He did a push up and crawled further onto the bed until he smashed his face against the pillows and collapsed again. His broad shoulders shook as he took in a heavy breath.

I crawled on my knees next to him, opened the tube and squished the bottle in the middle to get the white cream onto my fingers. "I don't suppose you're going to tell me what happened," I said. I spread the cream over the bruises on his back.

"You don't want to know," he said, his words were half slurred by the pillow in his face.

I sighed. "Are you in trouble with the mob? Do you owe them money?"

He barked a laugh. "Not at the moment."

I used the cream over the bruises along his back, rubbing it in. I worked silently, not knowing what to ask, knowing there was nothing I could probably say to him to get the truth from him. When I was done with his back, I patted his arm. "Let me see the front."

When he flipped over, there was another layer of bruises along his ribs and down his stomach. I squeezed at the bottom of the tube to get more of the cream out. Touching his back had been one thing. Now that I was looking at his muscular bare chest, my fingers trembled. I pressed my fingers to the bruises, trying to calm myself as much as to help his injuries.

I felt his eyes on my face but I couldn't look at him when I was touching him in such a way. I focused only on rubbing the cream in. My cheeks started to heat up when I realized what I thought had been shorts were only a pair of boxers. I'd been too preoccupied that he was hurt to notice. I was in a bedroom with a half-naked boy.

"What were you doing out there?" he asked, punching at the pillows under his head to fluff them up.

"I was going home from Kota's."

"I didn't know you were allowed out yet. Aren't you grounded or something?"

"Weren't you supposed to be in gym class today?"

He smirked. "I had something to do."

"Huh." I finished rubbing the cream in and then replaced the cap on the tube.

He reached out to me, grabbing my wrist. "It had to be done," he said. His face was stern, getting that serious look I recognized, his blue eyes going dark. "If it wasn't important, I would have been there with you in class. I wouldn't leave you alone."

Why was I that important to him? It seemed ludicrous. "I'm not worried about being alone," I said softly. "I've been alone for a long time. I can handle myself. What I'm worried about is the next time you're gone from class and I'm wondering which hospital you may end up in."

Nathan's mouth opened as if he wanted to say something but he promptly closed his lips again. He held on to my hand, giving it a gentle squeeze, but said nothing.

I noticed the light in the window going dim. "I have to get going," I said. "Do you need anything?"

"I took a pain killer before you got here," he said. He let

go of my hand. "Don't worry about me. Go home before you get into more trouble." He turned slightly as if he wanted to move onto his stomach. Groans escaped his lips and he gave up, falling on his back again. "I might not get to school tomorrow."

"That's too bad," I said.

"Why?"

"You'll miss taco soup."

I crossed the room, flicked the light off and shut his door, ignoring the questions he was asking as I left.

♥♥♥

Victor: *"You need a violin for class tomorrow, right? Did you get one?"*

Sang: *"It's okay. I'll explain it to Mr. Blackbourne."*

Victor: *"I can go get you one."*

Sang: *"Don't do that!"*

Victor: *"Why not?"*

Sang: *"Don't spend money on me. It's bad enough you pay for this phone."*

Victor: *"Please?"*

Sang: *"Goodnight, Victor. Stop worrying about me."*

♥

Wednesday

♥

♥

No *Longer* *Invisible*

I dreamed I was trapped inside a car. I didn't know how to drive and I was turning the wheel, pushing the breaks. The car careened down a hill and the ground was tilting. Cars raced around me. I was going to crash.

I woke with a start, jumping out of bed and running for the bathroom. I ran the cold water in the sink, splashing it across my face to erase the nightmare. It didn't help. The memory stuck. When my heart settled, I stumbled back to my room, flicking on the light, grabbing my diary to write in until it was time to get going to school.

Marie and I walked the short distance between our house and Kota's before the bus came. Danielle and her brother were already there, standing on the very edge of Kota's driveway. Kota stood alone, his head down, scuffing his shoes at the concrete.

"Kota," I said, walking up to him.

His head lifted and his face lit up. "Hi."

"No Nathan?"

His lips pursed and he shook his head. Marie walked around us and headed straight to Danielle, waving to her. Danielle greeted her with a smirk and they tucked their heads together, talking.

"I saw him last night," I said quietly, not wanting the others to overhear. "I wouldn't blame him if he didn't show."

His eyebrows shot up. "How is he?"

He didn't know about this? Or was he surprised to hear I

went over there? "I think he broke one of his fingers. There were bruises all over his body."

He blanched. "I didn't know it was that bad."

Was that the truth? Did Nathan or Victor not keep him informed? Did he not go see him? "What's going to happen? The principal was asking about him yesterday when he didn't show up for gym class and now he's going to miss the second day of school."

"Mr. Blackbourne is telling us to redirect any questions from teachers to him."

"It sounds like that's implied to me, too?"

Kota's eyes looked toward the others across the driveway and he tilted his head toward me. "I'm sorry, Sang. I didn't want to involve you at all, but it looks like you still ended up being in the middle. They shouldn't be asking you but I guess they're associating you with us."

I brought a finger to push at my lower lip. Flashes of Victor's elegant face bruised and Nathan unable to pull himself out of bed crept through my mind. "Is this why you don't tell me anything about what happens? So I can honestly tell people I don't know?"

Kota's cheeks flushed and he nodded. "Yeah, that's pretty much it."

How strange was it that before I had met Kota, I wanted nothing more than to blend in with the other students, but here I was with the strangest set in the whole school.

At the school, Kota and I were the first of our group to arrive. We picked up our books at the school bookstore and waited for the others at the bench in the courtyard. Kota perused the textbooks, his and mine, inspecting the material. I was standing near the bench and leafing through a book when hands popped over my eyes and I felt a warm breath by my ear.

"I have something for you," Gabriel sang in my ear.

"Don't scare her, Gabe," I heard Victor say. There was an underlying command in Victor's voice. A warning?

Gabriel's hands fell away from my face. "What the fuck? I wasn't scaring her." He pulled out a sheet of paper and put it in my hands. "I fixed my stupid poem."

I blinked at him, blushing. Fixed it?

It was about the same princess in the tower, the prince throwing apples to her. A witch tried to make a bargain with him. She would give him the sweetest apple that would win over his love's heart if he traded his voice for it. He agreed, won over the princess, and together they tricked the witch to get his voice back.

I laughed when I got to the ending. "You changed it? What happened to winning the girls over with the sad part?"

"What? I don't want to make girls cry. Girls look all crazy when they cry."

"I like it," I said. "It still sounds like song lyrics."

"Right," he said. "It might make a good song." His lips pressed together and he hummed a few bars.

I glanced up at Victor, who only looked bemused. The bandage was blatant, but his bruise looked almost gone. I leaned closer to him, my eyes squinting.

Victor took a step back. "What?"

"What happened to your bruises?"

"Oh," he smirked. "Nothing."

They couldn't have healed already. I was sure by today they would look worse. My own bruises always looked worse the following day.

I floated a finger toward his cheek to trace where one of his bruises had been.

"Hey, hey," Gabriel said, poking at my hip. "Hands off. You'll smudge my work."

"Make up?" I asked.

Victor grinned at me. "Don't laugh, okay?"

"Yeah," Gabriel said. "I couldn't just let him walk around looking like a moving target all day."

I sighed. At least they were thoughtful. I handed the poem back to Gabriel. "You hang on to it." I dropped my book bag off my shoulders. "I'm going to the restroom. Would you watch my bag, please?"

Gabriel picked it up, pulling it closer to his own.

Victor dropped his bag, too, and started following me.

"Victor..." I said, gazing back at him. "It's okay. You don't have to walk me over there."

He paused, frowning and glimpsed over his shoulder at Kota.

"Do you guys have to follow me to bathroom?" I asked. That really seemed awkward.

"I suppose not," Victor said. He moped but he stuck his hands into his pockets and went to stand next to Kota.

I felt their eyes on me as I walked away.

I walked over to the main hallway and stopped short just inside the doors, hesitating. I wasn't really sure where the restrooms were. Walking alone down the hallway that was already getting crowded was making me feel less confident than I had been with the guys. It amazed me at how comfortable I had gotten at relying on the boys for something as simple as directions and their company. Last year at my old school, I was alone and had to rely on myself so much. It felt like a million years ago.

I found some bathrooms down a hallway. When I was finished, I checked my blouse and skirt in the mirror. I smoothed them out, taking my time. I wanted to prove to them it was okay for me to do something alone. In a way I guess I wanted them to worry less about me. They had so many problems as it was now.

Back out in the hallway, it was more crowded than before. Kids were sitting on the floor, their legs stretched out. I had to step over calves and shoes to get by as they refused to pull back and out of the way for people walking through.

A cat call sounded and echoed. I remembered the boys from the day before and this time I focused on the path ahead of me. They were just goofing off. I wanted to avoid eye contact to not draw attention to myself.

"Sing!"

I cringed when I recognized it as Greg, sorry that I had responded at all.

An arm plopped around my shoulders. Greg's big-lipped grin rocked close to my face. The smell of smoke was heavy as if he had just put out his cigarette. "Hey," he said. "Where are you going?"

My heart thundered. I had to get rid of him and get back to the courtyard before the guys came looking for me. I remembered the last time Greg and his friends ran into Kota, Victor and Silas while we were at the mall. The last thing I wanted was to lead him straight back to Kota and start another fight.

"I'm going to the cafeteria," I said. "I'll see you later."

He held on to me by my neck, tugging at me. "Don't go so soon. You're always so busy when I see you in the hallway." He towed me around until I was facing a group of guys. They were all dressed like him, baggy jeans, and oversized shirts. "Guys, this is Song."

"Sang," I said.

"Sang," he repeated.

The others bobbed their heads at me. One of them mumbled something, but his words were so mashed together I couldn't understand him. The others around him laughed. I couldn't help but blush and they laughed some more.

"I need to go," I said again.

"What? Is your boyfriend waiting on you?" Greg said, swiveling his head around to look. "That reminds me, I still owe him something."

"I don't..." I wanted to say I didn't have a boyfriend, but I wasn't sure exactly what to say. Saying no might encourage more attention and saying yes might make for additional trouble for Kota and the guys.

"Sang!" Luke's voice echoed through the hallway, drawing the attention of not only the group of boys around me, but everyone else in the hall. Luke and North stood together at the start of the hall. North shoved his fists into his thighs. Luke dropped a hand on his arm, like he was holding North back. Luke waved at me.

"I have to go," I told Greg again. I could see this getting ugly.

"What are you, his bitch?" He squared off his shoulders, sizing them up. "Why is he calling at you like that?"

I wanted to point out how he had called for me in a similar way, but I didn't want to get into that. I wrenched myself from under his arm and started backing off. "Don't worry about it." It was probably a stupid thing to say but at that point I just wanted to get out of there.

"Where you goin' girl?" he called after me as I hurried down the hall. "Greg's shortie doesn't just walk off without a kiss."

I shivered and didn't look back. Laughing echoed behind me.

"You okay, Sang?" Luke said. He had a few blond locks framing his face, but the rest of his hair was in the clip he had borrowed from me the day before. He reached out when I got close, putting an arm around my shoulder. "What's going on?"

"Apparently I can't go to the bathroom alone," I said, my heart thumping. I sought out North's eyes. He zeroed in on Greg and his friends, his hands pressed against his legs. I brushed my fingertips across his hand, tugging him in the opposite direction. "North..."

His grumbled and gazed at me with intense, dark eyes. "What did he say to you?"

"He was teasing me. I don't want a fight. Please? He's not following."

He glanced back at the kids. He turned around, dropping a hand on the back of my head, his fingers massaging at my scalp. "I hate this school."

To my relief, North and Luke didn't say anything about Greg when we got back to the courtyard and as we waited for the first bell to ring. Homeroom was quiet. Greg said nothing, completely ignoring us. Still, as we waited there for our first class, I got the feeling things were bubbling under the surface. I noticed how the other students looked at us. Were we really that different? Some part of me wished we blended in more than we did. Whispers with our names hovered around us like mosquitoes.

Hiding in the shadows seemed so much easier. With the boys, I stood out so much more and drew so much attention.

I was no longer invisible.

♥

WHATEVER YOU NEED

s. Johnson's pleasant, smiling eyes sought out our attention during first period English class. "Hand in your poems."

I bent over my desk, pulling my notebook from my book bag. I tore out the pages that had my poem. Kota caught that I had more than one page. He reached into his bag and fished out a mini stapler. I smiled to him as he held the edge for me and stapled my pages together.

"You're always so thoughtful," I told him.

His cheeks tinted.

Gabriel leaned over the isle and snatched the paper from my hands. "You didn't show us yours," he said.

My eyes widened and my face heated up. I grasped for the pages to take them back. Gabriel leaned far over the opposite side of his desk, and out of my reach. His eyes scanned the page, reading quickly.

"We have to turn it in," I said. "It's nothing. Just a stupid poem."

My poem was about hidden hearts being everywhere in the world, and a little girl who was the only one who could see them. Her parents thought she was crazy, and they locked her up in an asylum. She was released only when she promised never to talk about hidden hearts again. It was sad, and I didn't think it was really finished, but I didn't have an ending.

"What's it say, Gabriel?" Luke asked behind me.

"It says Luke's a nerd." He stuck his tongue out at him.

"Gabe," Kota said. "You can read it later. Turn it in."

Gabriel made a grunting noise and pouted, but handed it

to Kota, who collected ours and passed them along.

I put my elbow on my desk, leaning my face in my hand, grateful for Kota.

♥♥♥

I walked into Mr. Blackbourne's music class without a violin. I know he said not to, but if I wasn't going to get a violin for the class, I wanted to tell him myself why I had to quit. It felt wrong to go behind his back and cancel the class after he went through all the trouble of making the arrangements in the first place.

I hadn't said a word to the others about this. Somewhere in my mind I assumed I would simply get put into one of the study hall classes. It couldn't be helped. They would figure it out after I changed my schedule.

As I entered music room B, the space seemed to become infinitely smaller. Mr. Blackbourne waited for me next to the piano, his arms crossed over his chest. His steel eyes studied me as I entered, scrutinizing me so much that my hand instinctively touched the collar of my blouse to ensure all the buttons were closed.

All morning, I had envisioned the things I would say about how sorry I was to have wasted his time. I wanted to encourage him to pick someone else. I thought there had to be other students here who would relish such an opportunity like I did.

As he stood there looking back at me across the room, I felt my heart tripping in my chest and the words I had worked on escaped my mind. The coolness of his gaze settling on me was enough to solidify my muscles and make my mind melt into nothing.

"Miss Sorenson." His voice was so smooth and confident, commanding without asking anything of me.

I opened my mouth and felt the words escape me but the voice sounded different than my own. Soft. Weak. "Mr. Blackbourne."

He stepped away from the piano. His arms dropped from

his chest and he closed the distance between us. I didn't move a muscle. Would he yell?

"Are you not coming in?" he asked.

"I..." I felt my face heating up and my shoulders started to shake. "I'm sorry. I just came to tell you..." My tongue darted across the roof of my mouth, finding it parched. With my eyes on the floor, released from his penetrating stare, I tried again. "I can't take your class."

A gentle finger traced my chin, lifting my face until I could see the spark of almost silver in his eyes, shimmering in the light through his glasses. "Didn't you tell me a week ago this was what you wanted?" While his voice had the same power, his tone had softened considerably.

"Yes," I said, pressing a hand to my chest to quell the shaking as his gaze sought out answers I wasn't able to offer.

"Are you suggesting you don't want to study with me now?" His eyes demanded my answer, unrelenting.

"My mother won't allow me to play. I won't be able to get a violin." My tongue felt rough against the dryness of my mouth. "I know you said not to come to your class without one, but I didn't want to leave without thanking you first for at least giving me a chance."

His lips were pursed for a moment as he looked over my face. His finger released my chin. "Tell me what your mother said to you."

My face radiated. Why couldn't he just tell me to go? Why wasn't he yelling at me for wasting his time? "She... she wanted me to drop the lessons. She said I had no business in a music class."

His eyebrow raised a fraction. "Isn't your elder sister in the school band?"

I nodded.

"Hmm." His hand went to his chin. He turned around and headed toward the piano.

I thought that would be it. I turned around, ready to leave the room.

"Where are you going?" his stern voice was back.

I remained facing away from him, fixing my eyes on the

shiny metal handle of the music room door. I was positive it would be the last time I ever saw it. "I was going to the main office to..."

"Class isn't over yet." He paused. "The boys offered to buy you an instrument, didn't they?"

I spun to face him. "How did you know?"

"But you refused?"

My finger found my lower lip. "They wanted to buy one for me. I told them not to. I couldn't ask them to do something for me when I couldn't be sure I could ever pay them back. They've done so much for me already." How did he find out about my contact with the boys? Didn't Kota say something about not letting Mr. Blackbourne know we knew each other? It was hinted at before. Did I make a mistake? Was it okay now?

He turned away from me. From behind the piano, he picked up a black case. I thought it was the same one from yesterday, but this one had a cloth material on the outside instead of a hard case. There was a strap along one edge for carrying it on your shoulder. "Should I give this back to them?"

My head tilted forward, an eyebrow going up. I recognized what he held in his hands for what it was, but my brain didn't want to make the connection as to why and how.

He brought the case to me, undoing the zipper as he walked. He balanced the case on one palm. He opened the lid.

Underneath was a violin. The wood was a rich brown, polished to a gleam. The fingerboard and chinrest were black. Delicate black pinstriping outlined the edge of the smooth curves.

"Where did you..." I breathed out.

"Victor brought it to me this morning."

I flushed. I blinked to get rid of the tears. "I can't, Mr. Blackbourne. They shouldn't have done it."

"You don't want it?" he asked in a quiet voice.

How could they? After I had told him not to, he went ahead and got one anyway and behind my back got Mr.

Blackbourne involved. The others had to have known about it. How could they not understand that I didn't want the burden of feeling like I owed them for this? I didn't want them to ever think I was friends with them for the things they bought for me. Guilt for their charity etched into me, prickling my skin.

Even as I thought these things, my fingers shook as my hand hovered above the wood of the violin in front of me. I was too afraid to touch it. I did want it. It warmed my heart that Victor went out of his way, after the day he had yesterday, and bought one for me.

"Miss Sorenson," he said. "I've known Kota and the others since they were ten years old. While it is true that they normally attend the Academy and they are nice people in general, they don't normally allow outsiders into their circle. Quite frankly, I'm not exactly sure how you managed to get involved with them so quickly. From what little Kota has shared about you to me, and with great reluctance on his part, you've only known each other for a couple of weeks."

I blushed. "I just bumped into him one day."

"And yet here they are buying you a violin."

"I told them not to."

"And they did it anyway."

"Yes."

"Do you understand what that means?"

I shook my head, unable to find my voice to reply.

"I'll show you." He closed the lid and tucked the violin case under one arm. He held his other arm out. "Come with me."

With trembling fingers, I touched the crook of his arm. He guided me over to the piano where he motioned for me to take a seat. I sat at the bench, crossing my legs at the ankles. He opened the new violin case again, freeing the instrument from the restraints. He held the violin to his neck, applying the bow.

He started playing a Chinese melody that I recognized, but didn't know the name of. The long, gentle notes vibrated at the smallest of changes his fingers made across the fingerboard. The music poured out from the violin like water, soothing, refreshing. It took only moments before I'd forgotten my predicament. I was entranced by his artistry.

After a few minutes, he stopped. The silence that filled the room felt like it had swallowed us both up.

"It's an exceptional violin," he said. He put the bow down and turned the violin over, tracing his hand over the wood.

"You play beautifully," I said softly. It was true. He was an excellent violinist.

His eyes drifted from the violin to my face. I wanted to look away, but the silent command from his gray eyes held me in check. He cradled the violin in the case and approached me. He bent over until his face was level with mine. "I'm going to ask you a few questions, Miss Sorenson, and I want you to answer me as honestly as you can. And believe me, I can tell if you lie." His eyes looked over my face, and his gaze landing on my lips. "Do you like the boys? I mean as friends?"

How else would he mean? I nodded.

"You should speak when you're answering my questions."

"Yes," I said clearly. "I want to be friends with them."

"And friends help each other," he said.

I blinked at him, not understanding if this was a question. "Yes."

"The boys have had an unusual lifestyle ever since they joined the Academy," he said. "Loyalty is a big part of our curriculum. Once you're a part of their team, anything you need, the Academy will provide it. It's the way we work. We don't have time to waste worrying about self-inflicted pride."

Hearing him talk about this mysterious Academy had me entranced. "I thought I wasn't supposed to know about the school."

He stood up and crossed the room, putting his hands behind his back and pacing in front of the piano. "Our work requires strict secrecy. We're exposing ourselves as it is being in this school. The school board and the principal only know we're a private school. There is a lot they don't know about it. We try to keep our students anonymous. I hope you'll keep our secret."

More than just a private school. What did that mean? So this was more than just a favor from a private school for the public school system or else they might have asked a less enigmatic school for help. If that was the case, what was in it for them to be here? "I've never told anyone," I said.

His eyes darkened, narrowing at me. "You have to understand," he said. "You can never talk about this. Not with family. Not with your friends. There's more at stake here than this school." He took a step toward me, motioning in my direction. "Kota's taken a big risk even mentioning it to you at all. I don't believe this is the best for the team, but I trust his judgment. However, I need your absolute word that you'll never mention anything you hear us say to anyone else. It doesn't matter how trivial you assume it might be. Lips closed."

I swallowed. This was more than I expected today, but I would never tell anyone. I had no one to talk to besides Kota and the others. Didn't he know that? Or was that why Kota felt he could trust me? Because I was friendless and wasn't close to my family? Did he not tell that to Mr. Blackbourne? I forced myself to look him in the eyes. I wanted him to believe this as I felt it was important to emphasize that I wanted to earn their trust. "I'll never say a word. Ever. If you want me to swear it to something, I will."

His eyes softened. He turned on his heels as he paced. "As I was saying, the Academy taught them to take care of one another."

"But I'm not in the Academy," I said.

"You are one of them now, though, or they consider you to be. That instinct to simply do what the other needs has been worked into them so fluidly. You'll have to forgive this flaw. They don't really think about what it means to someone like you, who may feel indebted to them. Trust me when I say you won't ever have to. They'll never ask." His eyes sparked. "It'll happen again. If you want to be friends with them, you'll have to let them do it. I don't think they'd understand if you rejected anything they give you. They possibly wouldn't allow it at all."

My heart skipped a beat. "But..."

"I hope you won't take advantage of their kindness."

"I've been trying not to,"

The corner of his mouth lifted a millimeter, softening his stern features. "If I had thought otherwise, I wouldn't have allowed this."

My breath caught. Was he pleased with me?

The door to the music room swung open. I peeled my eyes away from Mr. Blackbourne's face. He turned to address whoever it was, blocking my view. I stood up behind him.

"Mr. Blackbourne," called a familiar voice and I peered around Mr. Blackbourne's shoulder. Principal Hendricks stood on the other side of the music room. His large hands curled into almost-fists as he advanced toward us. "I've been trying to get a hold of you."

"I'm fairly busy," Mr. Blackbourne snapped at him. "I have a student."

Principal Hendricks's eyes popped open and he tilted his head, spotting me. "Hello again, Miss Sorenson."

Mr. Blackbourne stiffened. Did he think I was a troublemaker? Or did he think I was friendly with the Principal and would tell him things he'd just made me swear to keep private?

I managed to nod at Principal Hendricks. What was going on?

"I needed to talk to you about why the boys aren't wearing uniforms," Mr. Hendricks said.

Mr. Blackbourne frowned. "I emailed you that they don't have any. The Academy isn't..."

"You don't understand," Mr. Hendricks' voice deepened into a menacing tone. "The school board is after me to make sure the boys become the 'ideal' students for this school. If they're going to set the standard, they have to be the standard. I've already talked to the board and they agree. We have to show these kids what will be happening in the next couple of years. They can either stick with it or get out."

"You'll isolate my students, Mr. Hendricks," Mr. Blackborne replied. "There will be a lot more trouble if you insist on this."

"Isn't it your job to handle that?" Mr. Hendricks asked. "Didn't we hire you to..."

"I think we should discuss this somewhere else," Mr. Blackbourne retorted.

"Why?" he asked. "She's one of yours, isn't she?"

My head tilted back, an eyebrow going up. He still thought I was from the Academy?

Mr. Blackbourne shifted until he was standing completely in front of me, like a shield against the principal.

"I said just seven students," Mr. Hendricks said. "If you thought you could wriggle one past me..."

"I'll see what I can do about the required uniforms," Mr. Blackbourne said. "But I'm warning you. By separating my students like this, it makes them walking targets. They won't be responsible for what happens. They won't be the example you expect if they stand out."

Why didn't he say I wasn't his student? Was he going to let Mr. Hendricks continue to assume? Is that why Hendricks and McCoy seemed to be almost following me around school?

Mr. Hendricks rocked back on his heels a bit, looking satisfied. "I want to see uniforms on those kids by Friday. We've got the board members coming by to see this for themselves." I peeked around to watch as Mr. Hendricks nodded to Mr. Blackbourne and turned his eyes on me darkly. "Have a nice day, Miss Sorenson."

I swallowed as Mr. Hendricks turned and left the room. The air pressure in the room seemed to lift but only just.

"Miss Sorenson," Mr. Blackbourne said quietly, still looking at the door after Mr. Hendricks. "I trust you can keep what you've just heard to yourself?"

"Yes," I said quietly. Who would I tell? Did he mean Kota and the others, too? Would they be made to wear uniforms? How could the principal seem to want this so badly? If they're that different, Mr. Blackbourne was right. Other kids would pick on them. Fights may ensue. It was almost like Mr. Hendricks didn't care, or even wanted that to happen.

And why did Mr. Blackbourne not tell him who I really was?

"Good." Mr. Blackbourne turned slowly toward me, his eyes cool and calculating. "If he talks to you again, direct all questions to me. Just to me, not the others. Understand?"

I nodded. "I will."

He studied me for a moment and nodded. From under his breath, he whispered something. I don't think I was meant to hear it but in the quiet of the room, I heard every word. "Let's hope Kota knows what he's doing with you."

♥

NOTES AND PROPOSALS

*V*ictor was waiting for me outside of the music
room. His eyebrow rose when he spotted the
violin case. "Well?"

I blushed, shaking my head. I still wasn't sure if Mr.
Blackbourne meant I should keep secrets from them. Just in
case, I opted for silence. I would give Mr. Blackbourne
control of how much information he wanted to tell them
about what happened. "Someone did something when I told
him not to." I was trying to sound stern but I couldn't stop
the smile on my face. I knew that was what he was asking
about anyway.

Victor smirked. "Oh, you meant it?"

I rolled my eyes. "Thank you, Victor."

His hand found mine, giving it a small tug to indicate we
should get going. His thumb smoothed over my skin on the
back of my hand. It seemed to make him so happy that I
accepted his gift.

We rushed out to trailer 32 and slid inside. North was
waiting in a chair in the back, his arms crossed. His
shoulders relaxed when he spotted us. He didn't seem
surprised by the violin case.

When I slid into the seat in front of him, he leaned over
his desk and whispered to the back of my head. "Finish your
homework?"

"Uh huh," I said, unsure if I should turn, fearing I might
bump into his face. I twisted around slowly so I wouldn't
spook him.

He sat back a little, but his face was still close to mine
that it felt awkward. "Let me see it?"

I fished out my essay from my book bag and handed it over.

He scanned it and passed it back. "Good girl."

I pulled a face. "Checking for spelling errors?"

He turned for his satchel bag, picking out a notebook. "You didn't have any," he said.

I blinked at him. He only had my paper for a minute. How did he know so quickly?

Mr. Morris asked for our homework, but only half the class turned in anything. The papers were collected and Mr. Morris had us open our books, telling us to read the first chapter.

"I want eyes on pages, lips closed. You can take notes if you want. I recommend it. You're going to have a test next week on chapters one and two."

North and Victor grunted but neither said anything. I had to agree. Was he teaching the class or was he just going to have us read from the book and write essays?

Twenty minutes later, my eyes were glazing over the page. I wasn't tired, but it was a boring book and the first chapter was exactly what I had written about in my essay, so it felt repetitive. I spent most of the time writing down dates and details in my notebook just to keep myself awake.

I felt a nudge on my arm and turned, half expecting it was North. The girl next to me held a folded note out to me, looking annoyed that she was doing so. I glanced around. Mr. Morris was bent over his desk reading the essays.

Before I could reach out to take the note, North snatched it from the girl's hand. The note disappeared into his pocket. I glanced back at him, confused. His eyes darkened and he tilted his head at me, his expression telling me to never mind and to get back to reading. He could have been the teacher, his gaze was so demanding. I turned back in my seat, bending over my notebook and blushing. Was it meant for me or someone else and I was supposed to pass it on? I felt sorry for whomever it was meant and whoever wrote it.

When the class was over, I lingered back with North and Victor. Other students were almost running to get out the door and down the sidewalk toward the building. We trailed behind everyone else, including the teacher, on their way to lunch.

"North?" I asked him. He was walking to my left and so close that our arms were brushing. "What was the note?"

"Nothing for you to worry about," he said, his face transfixed ahead of us.

I slid a glance to Victor, who seemed distracted. He had his hands in his pockets. I had the urge to reach for his hand like he'd done so many times with me, but I couldn't get myself to do it.

♥♥♥

At lunch, I actually missed Nathan and was sorry that I had teased him about the taco soup. I felt like he was missing out, even though it was only school. I was probably the only one who felt the lack of him. I sat on the bench between Luke and Kota. At the bench facing us, Victor, Gabriel and Silas sat together. North sat cross-legged on the grass between us.

No one else said a word about the violin case. It was just like Mr. Blackbourne had said. It seemed they all expected me to have one. They got whatever they needed.

Kota opened his book bag, pulling out the thermos.

"So you did have leftovers," I said, smiling.

Kota nodded to me. "My mom said you're supposed to come over sometime this weekend if you can."

"Am I in trouble? Did I leave a mess?"

He laughed. "Nothing like that. She wants your recipe."

"What do you have?" Luke asked. He had bought a candy bar from the vending machine and was chewing on it.

The others perked up when Kota pulled out some plastic cups. I helped him as he poured out lukewarm taco soup and passed it around.

"Since when did you cook, Kota?" North asked, putting a plastic spoon into his soup and scooping out a little.

"It was Sang," Gabriel said. He had his hand out waiting

for me to pass one to him, looking anxious. "She made it last night. It's fucking good, too."

Silas grinned at me. North and Luke sniffed at their cups.

"It's not poison," I said.

"Not this time, huh?" North asked. He almost did a fraction of a smile. He dipped his spoon in and took a bite.

Luke nudged me with his elbow between bites. "Okay. You're cute and you can cook." He spoke up, looking at the others. "That's it. We're keeping her."

I beamed. After the highly emotional morning so far, this little bit of peace with the guys was just what I needed.

The taco soup was gone within moments. Silas was holding the thermos, looking longingly at the opening as he held it upside down over his cup. I kept my grin to minimal and got up, crossing to where he was sitting on the bench. I held out my half-finished cup of soup.

Silas glanced up at me. "You should eat," he said.

"I'm not really hungry." In truth, I really wasn't. I was too excited to eat. I held out the cup to him again. "Give me your empty one."

He smiled at me as he swapped his empty cup for mine. "Thank you."

I picked up his spoon from his cup. "Do you want your spoon?"

He shook his head, taking my spoon out of the cup and used it to take another bite. I tried to hide how it made my heart melt that he didn't mind using my spoon. I didn't quite understand why.

I held my hand out to North and Victor, who were still holding their empty cups. "I'll go toss them," I said.

Victor handed his over. North continued to sit but reached for the cups in my hands. "I'll do it," he said.

"It's okay," I said. "I've got it. The trash's right over there." I pointed to where there were two next to each door on either side of the courtyard. "I'm not going far." It surprised me that I was just assuming he meant he didn't want me going alone. I was getting too used to them following me. Was it really only the second day of school?

North smirked and handed over his cup. I collected everyone else's, too, as Kota reclaimed his thermos and the guys started talking about classes.

I crossed the courtyard with the cups in my hand, making a beeline for the trashcans. A shiver ran through me as I felt more eyes on me than just the boys'. When I dumped the cups and turned around, there was a group of guys laughing and walking toward the doors that I was standing near.

One of them spotted me, smiling. He was a big guy with red hair and broad shoulders. His freckled cheeks puffed out as he grinned. "Hey, pretty lady," he called.

I tried to ignore it, but walking around their group forced me to make a wide circle to avoid walking through them. The red-haired guy altered direction and moseyed toward me. He grabbed my hand, got on one knee and in a loud, but very sincere tone, he asked, "Hey sexy, will you marry me?"

I gasped and my head jerked back, positive he wasn't really asking me.

The boys around him started laughing. One of them shouted, "Mike, you scared her."

Mike earnestly looked up at me from his kneel. "Will you?" he asked. "Please?"

I came back from my disbelief and shook my head. "I'm sorry," I said.

What would he have done if I said yes? I knew for the most part he must have been teasing me.

"Damn," Mike said. He jumped up from the ground, releasing my hand and shrugged. "I've gotta find me a wife." He rushed by me, his friends following him and laughing.

I stared after him, speculating. I sensed someone behind me and turned, nearly bumping into Luke. He was close enough I could smell the sugar and vanilla of his cologne. He grinned and wriggled his eyebrows at me, his blond locks falling in his eyes.

"What?" I asked him. I hadn't gone far and he followed

me. I wondered how long he had been standing there. Would they always come after me?

"Never gone on a date and you've just been asked to get married," he said. "I think that's a first." He grabbed my hand, turning to walk back. "Let's go before he comes back with a ring."

My face was on fire when we got back to the others. Luke held on to my hand as we stood there. He did it so bluntly that my heart was thundering and I stood half behind him.

"What was that about?" North asked.

"Sang's just had her first marriage proposal," Luke said, chuckling. He squeezed my hand.

His laugh was infectious, so I started to relax. "He couldn't have been serious," I said. "He was just teasing me or something."

Victor's mouth hung open. Kota pushed his glasses up his nose, looking confused. Gabriel laughed. Silas and North twisted around, scanning the courtyard to where the guys had disappeared inside.

"Who was he?" North asked.

"I don't know," I said. "I've never seen him before. I think it was random."

He didn't look convinced. "What was his name?"

"The guys called him Mike."

Gabriel was still snickering. "We're going to have to keep a closer eye on you."

North dug into his pockets and pulled out a handful of folded notes in his pockets. He opened each of them on his lap, flattening the papers and checking the signatures. "Nope. No Mike."

"What are those?" Kota asked.

"Notes for Sang," North said. He crumpled them together and stuffed them back into his pocket.

My mouth slackened and my head cocked at an angle toward him. "Are you sure? What do they say?"

North shook his head. "Doesn't matter. If a guy can't say it to your face, he doesn't get to pass you notes."

I shared a glance with Luke. Luke smirked at his brother. "You mean she's getting notes in class from boys?"

"There's a particularly persistent one in our history class."

"Which one?" I asked. It made me uncomfortable that guys were passing me notes and I didn't know what was going on. Had North intercepted all of those for me and I just now noticed the one in class? Were there others? Was it that bad to get notes? I wondered if they all said bad things and he was protecting me from them.

"Doesn't matter," North said firmly.

I looked at Victor to see if he had some insight. His face was blank, and he only shrugged. "I didn't see it."

I wasn't quite convinced and thought maybe he did know and fibbed. Either he didn't want to get in the middle of this or he agreed with North. I couldn't be sure.

"Oy," Gabriel called out. "You can't just take her shit. Someone was giving that to her."

North tilted his head around until he was eyeing Gabriel. "Excuse me?"

Gabriel glowered at him. "Sang's never had notes passed to her in class and you're taking her first ones. That's like a fucking life experience or something."

I blushed. How would Gabriel know I'd never been passed notes in class? But then it must be obvious. Someone like me wouldn't get notes.

"Then you write her one," North said. "No face, no note. That's chicken shit. This isn't first grade where you're drawing boxes with the whole 'do you like me, check yes or no' choices."

Luke leaned into me, his lips nearly tracing my ear as he whispered, "I bet the girls checked the no boxes for him when he was in first grade."

"I can hear you," North said, leaning back on his hands to look up, his intense dark eyes fixing on my face. "Sang, do you want them?"

If it had been moments ago, before North had said anything at all, I might have said yes. He did have a point though. In a way it was kind of creepy to get a note passed to me from someone I didn't know. What would anyone have to say to me? "I guess not. Just let me know if they say anything like, 'I'm going to eat your liver'. I might want a heads up."

He smirked at me. Everyone laughed.

♥♥♥

In the middle of Japanese class with Victor, I was bent over a notebook, practicing some *hiragana* that we were supposed to be learning when the door opened.

"Hello Principal Hendricks," Dr. Green said. "Welcome."

Principal Hendricks entered the classroom. He smiled, his eyes swept over the room, singling me out and he gave me a wink before he crossed the short distance toward Dr. Green.

I snapped to attention in my chair, blushing. What now?

Victor's breath teased the hair at the back of my head. "Are we in trouble?"

"Maybe."

Victor grunted.

Principle Hendricks leaned in to Dr. Green to speak, but his voice was deep enough that we heard it from the back of the class. "I'm sorry to interrupt, but I wondered if I could borrow Victor Morgan for a moment?"

Dr. Green's eyes slipped to Victor. I caught that look he shared. He had that same silent communication ability. Dr. Green didn't miss a beat. He turned his head back to Hendricks. "Of course! By all means."

Victor stood up by his chair. I absentmindedly rubbed at the dip in my throat as he walked up to the front of the room, standing straight as an arrow and awaiting instructions.

When Hendricks took a look at him, he frowned. "What?" he chuffed. "Your face, son. You look terrible."

Was this about yesterday? Was he going to ask him questions about why he wasn't in school? Victor didn't look too bad. His make-up had held up. The bandage was still on his cheek.

Victor's eyes fixed on me for only the briefest moment, the fire lighting up, before turning back to him. "How can I help you, sir?" he asked in the smoothest way I've heard him speak yet.

Hendricks nodded his head toward the door and Victor followed. After they left, I caught Dr. Green's eyes. We exchanged bewildered looks. It didn't seem like any of us knew what this was about.

Victor was gone for the entire class. When the bell rang, I grabbed his bag, too. Dr. Green held up his hand as I came forward in class toward the door.

"Miss Sang," he said. "Can you stay for a minute?"

I sucked in a breath. His kind eyes were begging me without asking out loud.

I shuffled the book bags and the case in my hands as the others left the room. Dr. Green crossed his arms and leaned against the front desk. I liked his green striped tie and noticed the lean muscles of his forearms were tight against the rolled up sleeves of his shirt. There was the way the shirt fell against his torso, promising a fit body underneath. "How often have you seen Mr. Hendricks in the last week?"

I blinked at him and counted off the top of my head. "Maybe four or five times?"

"Is that normal for you? Does that happen around you often?"

I wasn't sure exactly what he was meaning. "I don't think so."

"I didn't think so, either."

The door swung open and Victor entered the classroom. His cheeks flushed as he looked at us standing together.

"Victor," Dr. Green said. "What happened?"

"He had me interviewed by some journalist for the newspaper," Victor said. "Victor Morgan now attends Ashley Waters. The press loves it." He crossed the room, taking his book bag from my hands. "But we don't have time right now. We've got to get to class. Come on, Sang."

I looked back at Dr. Green but he only smiled softly and nodded, flipping his hands at me as if I should hurry and follow.

I hurried so I could walk alongside Victor. He was frowning, pushing his hair away from his face as he walked.

"What did the reporter want?" I asked. I walked close to him in case he wanted to be quiet.

"They were doing a special report about the new kids in school in a 'special program'." He heaved a sigh. "It's bad, Sang. We weren't supposed to be caught out like this."

"Should we go talk to Mr. Blackbourne?"

"I'm going to go do that," he said. "I'm getting you to class first."

"I can go myself," I offered, "if you need to hurry and go talk to him?"

His fire eyes flickered at me. He grasped for my hand, tugging me along. "It's on the way."

♥

Tooth And Nail

*G*abriel and I were separated for all of gym class. The guys and girls were each taken to their designated locker rooms to try out our locker combinations. Since we didn't have anything else to do, the girls' coach had us wait in the locker room until the end of class.

I really couldn't focus on any conversation with the other girls. I sat away from them, my knees pulled up to my chest, drifting off. Victor was interviewed by the newspaper. Would there be an article about him tomorrow? Would all the boys be interviewed? Would Mr. Blackbourne allow it? I didn't understand what it meant, but if they needed to remain a secret, wouldn't that be the worst? Victor had said it was a bad thing. I rubbed at my forehead, wanting desperately to learn these secrets. How my world had turned over in a couple of days, I didn't understand. It was one thing to have brand new friends and a new school. It was another to have friends with secrets from an elite Academy no one was allowed to talk about. Further still was the fact that at nearly every turn, the boys were at risk and I was caught in the middle.

What could I do? Go back to being no one again? Sitting in the shadows? I knew other students weren't worrying about the things I was worrying about. How far did I want to take this? Inside of me, I knew that answer. I blamed my insatiable curiosity and my desire to please Kota and the others. I was hooked on their faces, their smells, and their touches, and the possibility of belonging with them. They'd said before I was one of them now. Was I really? Why didn't

I feel like I was? This felt like something bigger than the friendships I looked around myself at other students. Academy friends were stronger. Was it better?

When class was over, I wasn't sure if I should wait for Gabriel or walk on to the bus without him. I waited alone in the front hallway close to the gym doors and the entry way to the boys' locker room, searching out Gabriel. I didn't want to leave him behind just in case he was trying to get to me.

Minutes passed. I was about to give up and head to the bus by myself because I was afraid I would miss it.

"Hey, faggot," a loud voice reverberated from around the corner. "Where are you going in such a hurry?"

I turned the corner. There were a handful of guys standing around the far wall of the hallway, surrounding someone. I'd seen something like that a few times at my old school when fights were about to start. My first instinct was to run. Ducking your head is what everyone did. If it wasn't your business, you didn't get involved. What propelled me to remain and look, I don't know. I searched the faces of the ten or so boys.

Then I saw him: Gabriel was at the heart of the group , pressed up against the wall by a large guy who had forearms as big as his neck.

My fingers pressed into my palms. My heart stopped.

Gabriel murmured something to the guy holding him and I couldn't hear it.

"Shut the fuck up," the guy holding him by the shoulder pulled Gabriel away from the wall, only to slam him back into it. Gabriel's head rolled loosely, his eyes going up to the ceiling but he did nothing to stop it.

"Gabriel!" My lips moved and my voice called to him before I could stop myself.

Gabriel's crystal blue eyes flashed at me, focusing from across the hallway. Despite his silent warning, I dropped my things and strode forward. I wasn't going to leave him.

The guys turned and saw me coming. "Hey there," the guy holding Gabriel said. "Where'd you come from, sexy?" His short, curly brown hair looked greasy. Random pimples splattered his face.

My eyes flickered to Gabriel for only a moment. I looked back at the bully and I jerked my chin toward Gabriel. "What are you playing around with him for?"

"What? You mean gay 'tard, here?" the guy asked, pushing into Gabriel's shoulder.

Gabriel grunted.

My fingernails dug into my palms. My heart thundered to life in my chest. "What are you? Some kind of homophobe?"

The guy reeled his head back, letting go of Gabriel and pointing a pudgy finger at my face. "What did you say?"

"I just wondered why you were here playing with the boys instead of the girls."

"Sang," Gabriel called. He was on his feet, his back against the wall and breathing heavily. Did they hit him already? "Don't," he puffed out.

"Shut the fuck up," the guy said, and he jabbed his fist into Gabriel's gut.

Gabriel bent over, holding his abs. "Yeah, yeah, you've said that already," he quipped, sucking in a breath through his teeth.

The guy's hand moved into a fist again but my hand shot out, cupping around his knuckles. He paused, his eyes widening, confusion covering his face.

What was I doing? My mind blanked out. I wasn't about to let him hit Gabriel again. Where the new sense of bravery came from, I wasn't sure. All I knew was one of my friends was in trouble and I wasn't about to let him down. "Dude, seriously. Are you going to play with him or me?"

Feet shifted around me. Mumbling, laughing. Were people only going to watch? Did they think this was funny?

"Go home, Sang," Gabriel called to me.

"She doesn't want to talk to a fag," the bully spat at him. He turned to me. "You're Sang? I've heard about you."

My eyebrows shot up, shaking me out of my faux confidence. "What?"

"Greg said you were kinky shit." His lips pulled back,

revealing yellowed teeth as he grinned.

I bit my lower lip, losing the anger as the focus turned to me. Rumors were spreading about me. What did Greg tell them?

I took a step back, bumping into someone behind me. It forced me to stop. Hands grabbed my biceps, locking me in place against someone's chest. I yanked to free myself. The hands tightened. I twisted to check over my shoulder but he held me in place.

The crowed of guys started laughing, circling around me. The main bully let go of Gabriel and closed off the circle.

"Let her go," Gabriel warned. I couldn't see him around the bodies surrounding me.

My throat seized. I wanted to tell him to run like he did for me, but I couldn't find my voice. I'd taken this too far. I'd redirected attention as planned. Now what? He should go get the others. Go find a teacher to stop this.

The guy ignored him, his yellowed teeth parting. "What do you guys think?" he asked the group around us. "Do we want to see what kinky shit looks like?"

His hand shot out, his fingers hooked the collar of my shirt and wrenched. Two buttons broke, bouncing to the floor.

"Get your fucking hands off of her," Gabriel flew into the air, dropping hard on the back of the guy who'd yanked my shirt. His feet connected with the back of the bully's knees. His fist struck the side of the guy's neck.

The bully slumped to the floor. His voice erupted into a howl. He choked. His palms wrapped around his throat, and he sucked for air.

The guy who'd grabbed me pulled back, yanking me with him. The others started piling on top of Gabriel. I cried out Gabriel's name. Gabriel disappeared amid a pile of students, all swinging at his body.

I tugged, kicked and jerked myself to get free. The guy behind me gripped my arms tighter until my knees buckled at the pain.

A new body flew into the fight in a blur, landing on top of one of the students. My heart leapt that someone, anyone, was trying to help Gabriel. His head turned, looking my way.

My heart went from pounding a mile a minute, to dead still.

It was Kota. His glasses were gone, which was why I didn't recognize him sooner.

Victor sailed in behind him. They wrenched at the shoulders of guys piling on top of Gabriel.

Kota's fist connected with someone's abdomen. Victor lifted a foot, his heel making contact with someone's chest.

Shouting echoed to an all-encompassing thundering in the hallway. Most of the guys who had been watching and laughing fled. The handful that remained swung fists at the boys. Most flailed, trying to launch themselves at the Academy guys to knock them over.

Kota, Victor and Gabriel struck with precision. They waited, dodged and jabbed. Nathan was obviously not the only one who had training.

I was shoved aside like unwanted trash. I landed on my knees, and pain radiated from my bruises. It knocked the breath from my lungs.

The guy who had held me stepped over my body to join in. He seized Victor by his shirt, heaving him back.

I flew to my feet, wanting to help but not having a clue what to do. My hands found the guy's shirt, and I yanked as hard as I could.

The collar of his shirt jerked into the guy's neck hard. He let go of Victor, whirled with his hand out. It made contact with my face.

"Sang!" Victor's shout filled my ears.

My back rammed into the wall.

My feet slid out from under me on the tile and I fell to the floor. Tears filled my eyes at the sting at my cheek. My tongue shot out, tasting blood on my lip.

Victor's foot collided with the side of the guy's head. When the guy swung out again, Victor jabbed him with a fist into his face.

The guy reeled back, ducking away from Victor's oncoming foot. He backtracked and stumbled toward the exit.

Victor whirled on me, his fire eyes a roaring blaze. "Sang!" he called out, dropping to his knees next to me. His fingertips brushed against my forehead.

For the moment, all I could see were fire eyes.

Gabriel's cursing barked over the others. Kota shouted to people in the hallway to clear out, commanding anyone left to go home.

Victor took me in his arms. My body trembled. I wanted to be brave and stand up but my body wouldn't allow it. I swallowed back tears. I was ashamed. I'd been stupid. I couldn't help Gabriel even when I wanted to. I'd made it worse.

Victor pressed me close to his body, his cheek meeting mine.

"Victor," I whispered, my lips near his ear and tracing over his skin. I was unable to speak louder. Now that it was over, I was a wreck.

He shuddered against me. He bent down, his arm going under my thighs and picked me up off the floor. My face buried into his shoulder. I was worried about the others, but too afraid to look at them.

He held me, not asking, not judging. He simply held on. His cheek pressed to my forehead.

"Sang," Gabriel whispered. I opened my eyes and turned my face toward his voice. Blood trickled from his nose and his cheek was puffy. His hand sought out mine and he squeezed it.

Kota was next to him, looking over his shoulder. Blood stained his white shirt. His tie was flung over his shoulder. His lips taut, his eyes dark. "Let's get her to Dr. Green."

I wanted to tell them that I was fine, that I could walk and that I didn't need anything. Gabriel looked worse than me. My mouth wasn't working. My lips felt swollen shut. My cheek stung. My knees ached. I didn't want to let go of Victor. At the same time, I wanted to let go of him to hold

Gabriel because he looked terrible. I wanted Kota.

♥♥♥

Victor carried me through the now empty hallways. Trying to figure out where we were going made me dizzy. I forced my eyes closed, my forehead against his neck. His breathing was ragged. He gripped my back and thigh. He wasn't letting go.

Kota and Gabriel marched beside him, their three sets of footsteps the only sounds in the hallway. The continued silence had me trembling again. No one stopped us if they walked by.

Victor stopped. There was a gentle breeze of a door opening and then another. Victor drew me in closer as the new hallway was smaller. I curled into myself in an effort to make myself smaller.

Another door opened.

"What happened?" Dr. Green's voice floated to us.

Victor turned and I was perched on a hard surface. I forced my eyes open. Dr. Green's face swam into view.

I peeled my lips apart. "I'm fine," I whispered, swallowing to recover more of my voice. "I only got hit once."

"Sweetie, you look like shit," Gabriel quipped from somewhere out of my view.

"He backhanded her," Victor said. "He hit her in the face and she hit the wall."

Dr. Green opened a drawer, finding a flashlight. He clicked it on and hovered the light over my face. His eased his fingers over my eyelids and forced them apart. "I suppose you mean someone not Gabriel." He swung the light into my eye. I flinched at the brightness, but he held me in a way that forced me to keep still.

Gabriel snorted. "No, but I'm about to. What the fuck did you think you were doing, Sang? I told you to get out."

Spots of light hovered in my vision after Dr. Green checked my eyes. He poked my lip with a gentle finger, but I spoke around his prodding. "They were hitting you."

Gabriel laughed.

Dr. Green backed off and I was able to turn my head.

Gabriel was in Mr. Blackbourne's chair, his hands hanging over the armrests. "You should have seen her," he said, beaming and swinging from side to side in the chair. "Oh god, it was beautiful. She stormed down that hallway and I swear if it wasn't because she was so small, she'd have kicked their asses. If I wasn't so pissed off, I'd kiss her right now."

Dr. Green's lips twisted into a smile. "She doesn't have a concussion, but you should keep an eye on her." He fixed his gaze on me. "Anything hurt?"

I shook my head. Nothing outside of my lip and cheek and my own pride. "I'm fine."

He nodded and pulled away. Victor was against the wall behind Gabriel, his arms crossed, his eyes blazing on me. Kota was gone. Where was he?

"You're not fucking fine," Gabriel barked at me. "You're in a whole lot of trouble. You know what you are? You're fucking grounded."

Victor popped him on the head with an open palm. "Stop shouting at her."

"No. God damn it, she didn't listen to me. I told her to leave and she didn't do it."

"Maybe," Dr. Green said in a calming tone, a soft smile on his face, "she didn't listen because she was afraid you were hurt and she's not the type to back down." He flicked a wink at me. "Reminds me of some guys I know."

Victor crossed the room, giving Dr. Green some space to examine Gabriel. Gabriel whined as Dr. Green poked at his face. Victor searched drawers in Dr. Green's desk and came back with a first aid kit. He found some gauze and applied it to my lip. I flinched, pulling back as it stung.

Victor smirked, touching my chin gently and approaching my split lip at a different angle and with a delicate stroke. "Didn't think I'd be returning the favor so soon."

"Wasn't really planned," I breathed out.

Victor chuckled.

The door opened. Kota returned with a collection of book bags and the violin case. Behind him, Mr. Blackbourne appeared with two cold compresses. His steel gaze sought me out first, examining my face. He frowned, passing the compress to Victor. Victor took it from him and pushed it to my cheek and lip. With Victor hovering over me, his eyes a gentle smolder now, my shivering returned.

Victor squinted at me. "Cold? What's wrong?"

I shook my head. "Nerves," I said.

He smirked. "You know you're supposed to be nervous before you jump into a fight. Or at the very least during. I've never heard of anyone waiting to be nervous until after."

"Normalcy was never my strong suit," I confided. It was true. When we were forced into plays or speeches in school, before and during the event I was fine. Afterward, I was a jumble of shaking and twisted stomach. Right now if I wasn't forcing myself to keep upright, I would be crumbled on the floor. It was tempting, but I didn't want to scare them.

Mr. Blackbourne turned to Gabriel. "Start talking," he commanded.

Gabriel hovered the compress over his eye. "Typical homophobic goons. They took one look at me, made an assumption. They waited until the coach and most of the others were out of the locker room. They swarmed me when I was in the hallway. I was waiting for them to get bored when Miss Trouble herself showed up," he jerked his chin in my direction. "She opened her big mouth and got them to drop me and take her on instead."

Mr. Blackbourne twisted his head and his eyes widening with surprise. I shrunk into myself, quivering. His face was commanding me to speak but I couldn't find the words.

Victor rubbed a palm at my back. "One of them grabbed her and kept her out of it," he said. "There were at least ten on top of Gabriel. We were helping him when the guy who had her let go. When he came after me, she flung herself at him and he hit her."

"We took care of it," Kota said. "They're going to be reluctant to do it again if they think we'll be coming."

"They know her," Gabriel said. They all turned on him. "They knew her name. Now they know her face. Rumors are going around about her."

"What kind?" Kota demanded.

"I don't know," Gabriel said. "They called her kinky shit or something like that. No specifics."

Kota pressed a palm to his forehead, blowing out a puff of air.

"We need to find out," Victor said quietly. He shifted the compress, moving my hand up to hold it. When I had it pressed to my face, he turned to look at them. "A couple days in, and they've already started. If we let this go, they'll never stop. We need to divert, redirect attention from her."

"That coach deliberately disobeyed new security requirements," Mr. Blackbourne said. "I'll have to talk with him about leaving the area before students have cleared off." He turned to Kota, his hands on his hips. "I want a report tonight. Take Victor and Gabriel through records. Pick out the ones responsible. I want them wired before tomorrow."

Wired? My head was starting to throb. At the speed they were talking, I had no time to ask questions. Why are they taking over security for the high school? I shifted the compress against my face, applying it to my temple. My head hurt too much to think.

This brought attention back to me. Victor swept a finger across my cheek. Mr. Blackbourne caught this, the corner of his mouth dipping down into a frown. Victor was focused on my face and didn't notice. Did Mr. Blackbourne not like me now? Was he mad because I seemed to make things worse?

"We need to get her home," Kota said.

Mr. Blackbourne's frown softened. "Take her," he said in a quiet voice. "Reports on my desk and wires set up by start of school tomorrow." He turned, opening the office door, stepping through. The door slammed closed behind him.

I cringed.

Dr. Green moved around the desks toward me again. Victor stepped aside for him. Dr. Green checked my eyes again. "Head hurt?" he asked.

I nodded.

He smiled. "Shock is wearing off. That's good." He stood back and opened a drawer, fishing out a bottle of Tylenol and a bottle of water. "Someone deserves a night off and a hot bath at home. You should take it easy tonight. You're forgiven tonight's homework from my class and do the minimal required to do before tomorrow for everyone else. If you need an excuse, come see me tomorrow morning." He handed me two pills and opened the water before holding it out for me. I swallowed the pills, sipping the water to clear my throat.

"We'll take her home," Kota said.

Dr. Green nodded, standing back. Kota started collecting bags again. Victor fished out his keys and picked up the violin case.

Gabriel crossed the room, stopping in front of me. His face was wiped clean and he looked almost normal again except for some minor swelling at his nose and across his cheek. He hooked an arm under my thighs and around my back to pick me up.

"I can walk," I said.

"Like I give a shit," he said, his deep voice softening.

My arms threaded around his neck as he lifted me. His fingers gripped me tight to his body. My head sank into his shoulder. I breathed in musk and lavender.

Dr. Green held open the door for us. "I'll go find Mr. Blackbourne before we're one coach short tomorrow." He followed us out into the main hallway and seemed to disappear.

Gabriel, Kota and Victor marched together toward the parking lot. Gabriel carried me like a badge of honor, his arms tight around me. He pressed his cheek against the top of my head.

At the BMW, Victor held the back door open. Gabriel angled himself into the car, keeping me in his lap. The bags and the violin were dropped to the seat next to us. Kota slid into the passenger side and Victor started the car.

I wondered if my sister noticed I was missing. Would they say anything about my face? How would I hide it? I trembled.

"Okay, you need to stop shaking," Gabriel said against my forehead. He slipped fingers into the straps of my sandals, sliding them off of my feet and dropping them onto the floor. He tucked his arm over my thigh, pulling me to snuggle against him. "It's too hard to be mad at you when you're shaking."

"You're mad at me, too?" I asked. Now that we were away from school and he was holding on to me, I felt calmer. I wondered why I wasn't blushing from being in his lap, but in the moment, I didn't really care. It felt too good to have him touching me, enveloping me like a blanket. I felt I should be embarrassed. Kota and Victor didn't seem to blink an eye at this, so I could only assume it was okay to do.

"I told you. You're grounded." His jaw and his nose nuzzled against the side of my head by my ear. His lips curled up.

"For how long?"

"Until I'm done being mad at you. I don't know. A billion years. Fucking shit, Sang." He squeezed me to him, knocking my breath from my lungs. "Don't you ever jump in like that again. I don't care if my head is on fire. You ever see shit like that, you run."

"You didn't run," I said.

He released me and a chop fell on my shoulder. "Fuck you. I was saving your pretty ass."

"Stop yelling at her," Victor said, "or I'm kicking you from this car."

"See? Victor's mad at you, too. If you do it again, he'll kick your ass. And then Kota will, but then I'll do it again because Kota will probably be all soft and shit."

"Nope," Kota announced, turning in his seat to look back at us. He smiled at me, winking. "I'd have to beat her, too."

I chuffed, feeling the smirk on my face even though it hurt with my lip bruised.

"See?" Gabriel said. "And don't even get me started on Silas and North and Luke."

"And Mr. Blackbourne," I said. "He's mad at me, too."

"Girl, he's about to go murder some teenagers. I'm probably at the top of the list for letting those goons anywhere near you." He shifted. He pulled back to look down at my face, but he glanced down at my shirt, fingering the threads left from the missing buttons. "Aw, they ripped your shirt. Victor, we have to get her a new shirt."

I rolled my eyes, twisting my mouth awkwardly to grin and trying to do it without hurting.

"What's the plan?" Victor asked.

"We're taking Sang home," Kota said. "We need to cover her face."

"Have to do everything around here," Gabriel said. He pulled his book bag out of the bundle near us and started pilfering through pockets. "I might have something that's your color. You're lucky I brought this today."

"Sang," Kota said, his green eyes focusing on me, "when you get home, keep me in touch. Let me know if your family says anything. If they ask, tell them it was a crazy dodge ball in gym class."

I nodded. "What are you guys going to do?"

"We've got work," Kota said.

"Wiring those guys? What does that mean?"

Gabriel juggled compacts in his hands, looking at the back labels. "Stop asking questions."

"It means you're going to listen in on their conversations. You can't do that," I responded.

Gabriel popped a palm against my thigh. "I said shush."

"You said stop asking questions," I retorted. "I didn't ask. I answered."

"She already knows," Victor said. He turned down Sunnyvale Court. "It involves her now."

Kota grunted. "Let's just stop talking. We need to focus. We can have this discussion later."

"I just have one more question," I said.

Kota swung his eyes at me, his head tilting. "What?"

"So... Dr. Green is an actual doctor doctor?" I smirked because my question was ludicrous. It hadn't occurred to me until he was looking at my eyes earlier that his title might mean he was a medical doctor and not a doctorate in physics or something like that. I just wanted validation and to change the subject.

Gabriel snorted. Kota beamed, laughing. Victor chuckled.

"Fuck," Gabriel hooted, his eyes glossing with tears. He dropped his arms around my shoulder, hugging me. "Yes, okay. That's it. We're keeping her forever."

♥

SWINGING HAMMERS

When Gabriel finished applying makeup to my face, Kota dismissed me to my house. Gabriel and Victor wanted to walk me home, but Kota insisted I go it alone.

When I got in, the house was silent. Marie was gone. I suspected she ran off to Danielle's house. My mother was asleep. That was good news for me. I went unnoticed.

I sent a quick text to Kota to let him know I was in the clear for the moment at home.

Kota: *"Good. Now do your homework and relax. I'll call you later."*

I checked my face in the bathroom mirror. There was a dark spot on my lip if I pouted enough, but otherwise it was mostly just a little swollen. My cheek felt puffy. Any redness or bruising was masked by a thin veil of concealing foundation thanks to Gabriel.

I spent some time curled up in my bed. I kept trying to review what happened, analyzing my actions. How did I lose so much control like that? I imagined the warmth from Victor's arms around me. I missed the way Gabriel had held me in the car. I wondered why Kota was so quiet with me. He'd kept his distance the whole time and I wondered if he was angry, too. I worried how the others would react when they learned what had happened. What would happen tomorrow? Would those bullies see me in the hallway and try again?

And why were Academy students now in charge of

security at the school? Suddenly Nathan's and Victor's disappearance on the first day of school seemed obvious. There must have been another fight. Nathan got the brunt of it. Did Victor swoop in and help?

The speculation was annoying because I didn't have a method of figuring out what the truth was. I didn't think they would be honest with me.

I was finishing up homework when I heard the phone buzzing in its hidden spot in the attic.

Luke: *"Are you busy?"*
Sang: *"Not busy. Where are you?"*
Luke: *"At the diner. Can you come? And bring some water?"*

I put on a pair of shorts and brushed my hair. I checked in on my mom. Every once in a while, my mother got hit hard by the medication she took because she was sick. There were times when she would sleep for long hours, day and night. She was passed out now. I wondered if this was one of those cases or if it was just a nap. To test it, I made a little noise outside of her room, knocking the door into the wall.

Nothing.

She was out. If I was lucky, and I hated to think that because she was my mother and it was unhealthy, but I hoped she would be out for a while. The peace of mind of knowing she was asleep made it safer to venture out of the house for both Marie and I.

I wasn't quite sure where Marie kept running off to, but I was hoping this was a good sign. If she was with Danielle or anyone else, that meant I had more opportunities to get out of the house, too. We never had such a chance before. Would we finally get to here on this street? If our mother was kept in the dark about where we were, if Marie and I were careful, maybe being punished on our knees, or worse, wouldn't happen as often.

♥♥♥

The old church at the end of Sunnyvale Court had the cross removed now on the outside, though there was still a smudge outline over the top of the door. Otherwise, it looked like a big storage building.

There was a black truck parked in front of the doors I didn't recognize. When I got closer, I heard shouting inside. I paused, unsure if I should enter if they were fighting. I'd had enough of that today.

I opened the front door and followed the sound of voices and crashing until I found the kitchen. Silas and North were shirtless, causing me to do a double take. Their muscular chests were caked with dust in patches. Each held a sledgehammer.

Silas was standing back, wiping his brow. His broad shoulders and smooth chest had that exotic olive complexion. His muscles flexed as he caught his breath.

While North wasn't quite as tall or as broad as Silas, North's sculpted-muscled shoulders and long torso were just as exquisite.

I caught myself staring at their defined abs and the sweat that coursed over their skin. North had dark hair trailing from under the waistband of his jeans up to his belly button. Silas had something similar but it wasn't quite as thick as North's.

I pulled my focus away from the guys to look around. The kitchen was a disaster. The fridge and stove had been pulled out. Half the cabinets were demolished. It looked like they were working on the other half. There was a collection of broken wood and yellow Formica piled up by the door.

Silas spotted me first. He bent over until his hands were on his knees. He gasped and swallowed. "Please tell me you brought water."

I dropped my book bag and pulled out several large bottles I had brought from home.

They both grunted in what sounded like a positive way, and dropped their hammers onto the tile. They took the bottles from my hand.

"Thank god," North said. "We tell Kota we can handle it, and we forgot to bring everything."

"What else are you missing?" I asked, stepping around a broken piece of cabinet to put my bag out of the way.

"Luke, for one," North said. "He was supposed to be pulling the carpet in the chapel and check in every once in a while to help us haul out this shit. I haven't heard from him in a couple of hours."

"I'll go check on him," I said. "I brought crackers, too, if you guys are hungry. They're in the bag. Just dig in it." I picked up one of the water bottles to take to Luke.

"Thank you, *aggele mou*," Silas said. He leaned back against one of the few cabinets left. He opened his bottle of water, drinking heavily. Lines of water slipped past his mouth at the corners. The drips weaved across the muscles in his neck and along his chest. I forced myself to turn and walk toward the door, not wanting to get caught staring.

North flickered a half smile at me when I walked past him. He planted a hand on top of my head, his fingers massaging my scalp. "Keep my brother in line, will you?"

Nothing was said about the fight. Did they not know or were they trying to mask that they did know? I pursed my lips. I wasn't sure how to approach it now that I hadn't said anything. Maybe Kota didn't want to tell them.

♥♥♥

In the chapel, I found Luke on his back on the stage at the far side of the room. The floor had been cleared of debris, half the carpet was rolled up against the wall.

"Luke?" I called out. I had to climb over a roll of carpet that was blocking the door. "Did you need a hand?"

He sat up, smiling. Locks of his blond hair fell into his face, but most of it was held back with my clip. "I think we need twenty. Two will do for a start, though." His shirt was off, too. His leaner body glistened with sweat. He approached me, holding his hand out.

I was so caught up in watching his stomach and chest,

that at first I didn't understand what he was reaching for. I remembered the water bottle and handed it to him. "You're doing a good job."

He took the water, opening the top and slurping down a couple of gulps. He poured some out onto his hand and slapped it to his forehead and neck. "I think I'd rather be whacking down cabinets."

"They wanted help hauling."

"That's the boring part," he said.

"Let's go help them and maybe they'll let us swing the hammers," I said. The idea actually sounded like fun. It was better than being stuck at home or worrying about Kota or the others.

He smiled. "You're dressed kind of nice to be doing this."

I looked down at my shorts and blouse. I was still wearing the torn blouse with the missing buttons. He was worried about my clothes? His looked more expensive. "I'm just going to end up washing these, anyway."

He rubbed the back of his hand across his brow and crossed the room. He picked up his blue, button-up shirt and tossed it to me. "Put this on so you're not getting your stuff dirty."

I blushed, holding the shirt up and looking at the Calvin Klein logo. Wasn't that an expensive brand? "Over my own shirt?"

"Take that blouse off."

My eyes widened at him. "Luke..."

"Not right here, dummy." He smirked and landed a gentle chop on my head. "Not unless you want."

I blushed. He was such a tease! Why did they all enjoy picking on me so much?

He laughed, hooking his arm around my neck and pulling me around so we were heading back out of the chapel. "Sang, your face is priceless."

I found the restroom so I could put Luke's shirt on. The hem was long enough that it covered my shorts. It made it look like I wasn't wearing any at all. I rolled the sleeve cuffs up my arms. I folded my blouse and went to find the others in the kitchen.

Luke had taken up Silas's sledgehammer. Silas stood by the door, his arms folded over his broad chest. I walked up behind him, my hand reflexively touching his back so he knew I was there. As my fingers pressed to his smooth back, he jumped at my touch and spun on me.

"Shit," he said. "You're too quiet." He put a palm to his chest over his heart. "You can't sneak up on me like that."

North laughed. "You're scared of a little girl, Silas?"

I narrowed my eyes at North for calling me a little girl as if I were a child. I knew he didn't mean it like that, but it still stung a little that he would suggest it.

Silas only smirked at him. He reached out for me, putting an arm around my shoulders. His fingers closed over my collarbone. "Come on, Sang. We're going to watch Luke kill himself."

He pulled me forward until I was standing next to him. His body warmed me and he continued to hang his arm on me. My heart pounded. Was I back to being uncomfortable around touching again? Maybe it was because he had his shirt off and my mind kept thinking of his abdomen and chest. If I turned my face, I could get an up close and personal view.

"Ha," Luke said, his laugh definitive. He twisted his hands over the handle of the hammer. His eyes sought out mine and he winked at me.

"Don't get distracted," North warned. He was standing a couple of feet away from Luke, just out of reach of the swing of the hammer. His lips tightened and his eyes became stern, as if unhappy they had been interrupted.

Luke lifted the hammer slightly off of the floor, pulled back. He twisted his body, using the momentum to smack the hammer against the cabinet in front of him. The door broke off one of the hinges. A large crack splintered the center of the door with a large dent in the middle but the cabinet itself mostly remained intact.

The guys laughed. I couldn't help but smile. Luke pursed his lips. In a huff, he lifted the hammer again, swung it over his head and let it fall hard on top of the cabinet. The slam was deafening. It cracked the top in half but the cabinet still held.

"You're terrible," North said. "Sang could do better than that."

Luke blew out a heavy breath. "Let her."

Silas looked down at me. "Want to give it a try?"

I brightened, nodding. "Yes!" I had to admit, it looked like a lot of fun.

They all laughed. I wondered why it was funny.

Silas let go of my shoulder and nudged me forward. "I'd pay to see this."

"Come here," North said, curling his fingers at me. He had me stand beside him, holding his own hammer out to me. "Do you know how to use this?"

I locked eyes with him, hovering a finger to my lower lip but not touching, almost forgetting it was swollen. I shook my head. I'd swung a regular hammer before but I never even attempted to lift a sledge.

"You're right handed?" he asked.

"Yes."

He pointed to where I should stand. "Hold the bottom with your left hand." He held the end of the sledgehammer in an example. "Then near the head, hold it in your right."

My fingers tingled. I was nervous that the others were watching me.

North slipped behind me. His chin hovered over my head, his body pressing into my back. He wrapped his fingers around mine as he showed me how to hold the hammer.

"When you're ready," he said, moving his body in a motion like the swinging move he wanted me to do. As he was doing it, all I could feel and think was how his body flexed against me. The heat made my insides flutter. "All you have to do is lift it. Get it up over the top. Let gravity do the rest." His nose pressed to my hair and his breath tickled the back of my head. "And don't you dare hurt yourself."

He backed off. I couldn't see the guys behind me but I felt the weight of their eyes. I sucked in a breath, lifted with my legs and pulled the hammer around. I strained at first, trying to just pick the hammer head up off of the ground. I felt the weight of it. It slipped in my palms and fell back against the ground. It was heavier than I expected.

The others giggled behind me. I heard someone, North perhaps, moving forward as if he wanted to help.

Now or never.

I adjusted my hands on the hammer in a grip I knew would work. I heaved the hammer up. It sailed over my head. Momentum finished the swing.

The hammer slammed against the top of the cabinet, crushing through the surface. My bones rattled as the hammer crunched through the Formica. The head of the hammer dropped down into the bottom section of wood, disappearing among the debris.

Clapping and hooting startled me. I felt more embarrassed now than before I started when I thought I wouldn't be able to do it. I had my hand still on the hammer and tried to tug it out of the mess of wood but I couldn't get it to budge.

"Here, Sang baby," North said. He reached out and took the handle from me. He gently nudged me out of the way. He pulled once, noting how the hammer was hooked into the cabinet. He yanked hard again trying to get it loose. He huffed when it wasn't moving.

"I broke it," I said. My mind replayed the way he said my name. The tingling sensation returned. It made up for the fact that he called me a little girl before.

"Of course you would be the first girl on the planet to break a sledgehammer." North jerked on the handle and the hammer popped free. He dropped it near his feet. "But not today."

"She took out the cabinet," Silas said. "One Sang, zip

Luke."

"Hey," Luke said, making a face. "I started it for her."

"You two haul this stuff out," North said, hands on his hips and nodding to the pile of splintered wood they had collected by the door. "There's a wheelbarrow in the back of the truck. See if you can get it in here. Take it out to the Dumpster. And get her a pair of gloves."

"I want to do it again," Luke said.

"We've wasted enough time today," North said. "I want to get all this cleared out and you've still got homework."

Luke rolled his eyes. North responded with a grunt, picking up his sledgehammer and swinging it against the cabinet I had broken. With a few swings he had it cleared from the wall and was starting to move down the line.

Silas's face became granite as he hauled up his sledgehammer, and approached the cabinets. Luke and I stood by and watched the two of them working. They moved in a fluid motion. On occasion they glanced at one another as if they were watching out to make sure the other was okay. I was in awe of how their muscles moved as they were working and the way they seemed comfortable with their silent communication system.

Luke nudged my arm. I looked at him and he motioned to a large section of wood that we could haul out. I helped him wedge it through the door and we carried it together out of the building. No rest for the wicked.

♥

𝒢ROUNDED

𝓘t was dark when we pulled the last of the carpet into the rental Dumpster. I was sweating through Luke's shirt. My muscles ached. I leaned against the side of North's truck, trying to catch my breath.

It was hard for me to imagine the church as a diner before, but after the cabinets were cleared out of the kitchen and we finished rolling up the carpet in the chapel, it was looking less like a church, but even less like a diner.

Luke's chest was heaving. He bent over with his hands on his knees after hauling the carpet out. "Glad that's over."

Silas strolled toward us. He had my bag in his hands. He held it out to me. "You're not a bad little worker bee," he said, his eyes dancing. He poked a finger at my nose. "You're hired."

I stood up straight and smiled at him, feeling a second wind. I took my bag from him, letting it drop at my feet. "Will you guys be back tomorrow?"

"It depends on what happens tomorrow," North said, coming up next to Silas. "We'll see."

Were they ever not able to make too many plans ahead of time because of their obligations to the Academy? Or was it they liked to change things often enough and moved with how they were feeling? Things seemed to happen at such a fast pace with them.

North's face flickered and he reached into his back pocket, pulling out his cell phone and answering it. "Yeah? What? No, she's here."

Uh oh.

North's eyes widened and sought out mine. "What the fuck do you mean, she's grounded? What happened?"

I pursed my lips, avoiding Silas's and Luke's eyes on me by staring at North's feet instead. My shoulders hunched as I cowered where I stood.

"No, she's… yeah. She's going home now." North hung up, holding his phone out and pointing it at me as he came after me. "You're in big trouble, missy."

"What happened?" Silas asked, edging in front of me as if to shield me from North.

"I want to hear this, too." His eyes fired bullets at me. "Start talking."

I shivered and swallowed. "Gabriel got into a fight and I tried to help."

Silas smirked. Luke looked confused.

North shook his head. "Start at the top."

I started describing what had happened, from how I had been in the hallway when I heard shouts, to where I was in the office getting checked out by Dr. Green. "Gabriel said I was grounded, but I didn't know he was serious," I finished.

Luke rubbed the back of his head as if in disbelief. Silas's mouth was open.

North lunged for my arm. He half dragged me back to the church. I stumbled along the gravel drive until he stopped under the light near the doors.

"Easy on her," Silas barked at him.

North ignored him. He positioned me under the halo glow and examined my face. He licked his fingers and started smudging my lower lip and at my bruised cheek.

"Ouch," I said, backing my head away.

"Stay still." He cleaned the makeup off my face, observing the damage. He pulled my lip back with his thumb, checking the cut. "I thought something was wrong with your face, but I assumed it was just the bad lighting in the kitchen. God damn it Sang baby, why didn't you say anything?"

My lips twisted and I crossed my arms over my chest, feeling cornered and uncomfortable. "I don't know. I thought you guys already knew and weren't saying anything about it."

He pointed a finger at my nose. "What the hell made you think you could jump into a fight?"

"Gabriel was in trouble."

"Gabriel can handle himself. You, on the other hand, are in deep shit."

I backed away a half step, unsure of how to respond. My mouth seized. Wouldn't he have jumped in and helped, too?

Silas approached. He traced a broad finger across my chin, tilting it so he could examine the bruising. "Who did it?" he asked, his deep voice bubbling with subdued anger.

"I don't know who," I said. "Kota's got to, um..., wire the people who did it."

North chuffed. "Uh huh. Kota, Victor and Gabriel are out there working overtime because of you. You were supposed to stay home and out of trouble."

"But if I'm with you, I'm out of trouble, aren't I?"

North's mouth fell open but nothing came out. He grunted, threaded a finger through the dark hair on his head, and turned away to stare at the wall of the church.

Silas sighed. He bent over, wrapping his arms around my shoulders and hugging me. "Good one."

I wrapped my arms around his neck to return the hug. He dropped an arm down to scoop me up from my butt, picking me up off of the ground. He pressed me to his chest, hugging me closer so he could stand up straight. It was way too hot but I didn't care. His hug was amazing.

"Okay," he said, turning sideways to North as he hung on to me. This let me peek over his arm at North. "Sang didn't know. We can't blame her for sticking up for one of us if she didn't know. We'd do it for her."

"She was doing what we would do," Luke agreed, coming up from behind Silas. "What was she going to do? Run off? Are we going to ground her for that?"

"She's grounded for being reckless," North said, turning around again. He spotted me in Silas's arms and his shoulders dropped. "But I guess if she's here with us, it's better for her anyway."

"Right," Luke said. "But she can't stay out all night. I should take her back." He motioned to me. "Let's get going. You're already in trouble. Kota will probably skin us if we let you get caught again."

Silas lowered me to the ground until I was standing again. North spun me around and wrapped arms around my shoulders. His face pressed to my hair as he held on. "Next time, you better fucking say something. And no more fights."

I sighed, feeling better that he was done yelling. I wrapped my arms around his neck to hug back. "I'm sorry, North."

He stiffened against me as if surprised by this, but he embraced me tighter and then let go. "Get out of here before I ground you, too."

Luke had my book bag and handed it to me. I hauled it to my shoulders. I waved to Silas and North. Silas waved back. North only nodded, that half smile playing on the corner of his mouth. He shook his head at us and turned, heading back to the church.

Luke caught my hand and we walked together through the darkness toward the woods. We followed the short cut that led to my back yard. I was expecting him to let go of my hand at some point but he never did. His fingers intertwined with mine. I was grateful he was right there next to me. After the argument, I was worried as he'd been so quiet that maybe he was mad at me, too.

"We got a lot done today," he said. I couldn't make out the features in his face in the dark and it felt strange to be able to hear his voice but not see him. "We make a good team."

I smiled to myself that he'd changed the subject. I didn't want to talk about the fight any more. "I'm just happy I could keep up," I said, blowing out a breath. "You guys work hard."

"We do what we have to," he said.

We made it to my back yard. I expected him to leave me

there and walk back, but he held onto me as I moved forward in the yard.

"I don't think I should bring you to the door," I said, though I was sorry to have to say so.

"You were going to use the door?" he asked. "Maybe I should help you up." He tilted his head toward the second floor. "You can sneak in and pretend you've been there the whole time, right?"

I blushed. "Well, yes, but..."

He pulled at my hand and I stumbled after him. We slipped through the yard and toward the back porch. The back porch was screened in, and the roof was lower to the ground than anywhere else. He tilted his head, looking up at the ledge. "I'll boost you up."

"I don't know."

"Come on," he said. He moved forward, letting go of my hand so he could bend and interlace his hands together to make a spot for my foot. "You won't fall. I'm right here."

Even with my heart thumping and my legs shaking, he managed to push me up over his head until I could slide half of my body up and drag myself until I was completely on top of the roof. I turned around to look down at him, intending to wave and tell him I could make it from here.

Luke had stepped back. He dashed forward, grasped the edge of the roof and nearly bounced off the frame of the screens on the porch. He landed on his knees next to me. I caught the outline of his lips turning into a smile as he looked at me. "Don't tell anyone I know how to do that."

"What?" I asked. "Fly? I didn't even see you climb up."

He laughed. "I wish I could fly. Would make getting to school a breeze." He stood up on the roof and reached down to grab my arm and hauled me up next to him. "Let's get you inside."

I followed close to him as we crossed over the roof, climbing to where North and I had spread out a couple of nights ago. From there, I pointed to where I remembered North taking me. Luke led the way up over the apex and down the other side to my window.

I peeked in. My light was on but no one was inside and the door was closed. "I think we're good," I said to him. "I don't think anyone came to check on me."

He moved around on the roof, looking inside my room. He pressed his palms against the window and pushed it until it started to slide open. He grunted when it got stuck half way. "I need to fix your window," he said. "Remind me."

"You don't have to do that."

"We need to if this becomes a habit," he said, pushing at the window. It slowly shuddered up all the way. "And I think it will be."

I couldn't help but smile at the idea of him already thinking of next time.

He moved out of the way and held on to my hand as I angled myself into my room. I had expected him to say goodbye at the window but I turned in time to see him put a foot down on the carpet and slink into my room.

My breath caught in my throat. The moment he was inside, I grabbed his arm, putting a finger to my lips to motion to him to be quiet. I listened for noises. I heard my father downstairs talking in the kitchen. Music flowed from a radio in Marie's bedroom. I didn't hear my mother, but she could have still been passed out.

After a moment, I nodded to Luke. No one was paying attention to us. I crossed the room, turning the music on my stereo up a notch. It would drown out our noise but it wasn't loud enough that I couldn't still hear footsteps on the stairs or Marie coming from across the hall.

Luke was on his knees on the mauve carpet looking curiously at the half-sized door. "What's this?" he whispered.

"Attic space," I said.

He hooked his fingers on the handle and opened it. His eyes squinted as he gazed into the darkness. He stuck his head inside.

I moved behind him, putting my hand on his back before he disappeared too far. "It goes on for a little way and there's this platform at the end," I said. "When I call you guys, I'm usually back there."

"It's hot," he said. "Is there a light?"

"I use the phone's light."

"We could hook up something for you," he said. He backed himself out and shut the door. His head twisted toward the stereo. "What are you playing?"

My eyebrows shot up. My heart thundered. I wasn't sure how long he should stay. Here was a shirtless guy in my bedroom and snooping around. "Just a disc I burned from the computer, a mix of rock and classical and other things."

He stood up, starting to head toward the stereo. I wanted to say maybe he should go, but at the same time I didn't want to kick him out as I liked him being around. It was nerve-wracking.

Once he was further into my bedroom, he turned around again, considering everything else. I blushed as his eyes settled on the mostly-empty, small bookshelf and my bed pushed over to the side of the room. They were the only two real pieces of furniture.

"Where's all your stuff?" he asked. His eyes flicked to the trunk near my window. "What's in that?"

I shrugged. "Just some notebooks and some old things, clothes that don't really fit any more."

"Don't you have posters? Or magazines? Or you know...whatever girls have in their bedrooms?"

My cheeks warmed. I wasn't sure how to answer the question. I wasn't exactly sure what he expected me to have. I read books when I could get my hands on them. There wasn't much else I could think of to put in my room. What else was there?

He didn't seem to notice I hadn't responded. He headed to the closet, opening the door and peeking inside. His eyes flicked through my hanging clothes. "No dresser. No desk. You've only got like what, three pairs of shoes? What kind of girl are you?"

"I've got what I need."

He rolled his eyes and closed my closet door. He crossed to my bedroom door, unlocked it and peeked out into the hallway.

"Luke!" I gasped, going up behind him. "Don't..."

"Shhh," he whispered. He tilted his head toward the door across the hallway. "That's Marie's room, right?"

"Yes," I whispered back. I reached for his arm, tugging at him. "Don't get caught."

He stepped out into the hallway. I thought my heart was going to explode. He edged to the top of the stairwell that lead toward the front of the house. He looked down, angling his head to see as far as he could. He tiptoed across the hallway, checking the back stairwell. He opened the hall closet door. He opened the next door, the upstairs bathroom, looking inside quickly and closing again.

My fingers were over my mouth. I couldn't breathe. What in the world was he doing? If my mom could see this, I couldn't imagine what she would do to me.

He turned again and crossed the hall to my bedroom. I meant to step out of the way but his arm hooked around my waist and he pulled me back into the room, closing the door behind himself. Once he was inside, he let go and crossed the room to my bed. He sat on top of it, leaning back on his hands.

I sat down next to him, unsure of what else to do. It was a relief that he was back inside, but I was worried someone had heard him and would come up to check out what was going on. What was worse was my heart was beating so loud in my ears, I couldn't be sure I would hear footsteps.

Once I was sitting next to him though, I felt even more awkward. I rubbed my fingertips at the edge of his shirt that I was wearing. "I'll give this back," I said to him, mostly as a distraction for something to say.

"Keep it," he said. He relaxed back on the bed, looking up at the ceiling. "It looks good on you."

We fell into silence. Each movement, every creak of the house and I was panicking that it was someone on the stairs or out in the hallway. "Luke?" I whispered. I wanted to say something to remind him that Silas and his brother were probably waiting on him, but I wasn't sure how to put it.

He sighed and he got up, leaning his shoulder against mine. "Okay, I would die if I had to sit in here all day long. How are you still sane?"

I smiled, shaking my head. "Your diagnosis is questionable."

He laughed softly, reaching up to a stray lock of blond hair hanging in his face and pushing it behind his ear. He stood up, hit the eject button on my stereo and pulled the CD from the top. "I'm stealing this."

I blinked at him and stood to reach for the disc. I tried to remember if there was anything super girly or perhaps even embarrassing for anyone else to listen to. Would he think I was a nerd for liking some of the classical pieces or would he tease me about some of the lesser known bands I had put on it? "You're taking my stuff."

He held the disc over his head and out of my reach. "I said I was," he said, grinning. "You can't hold it against me if I tell you ahead of time."

"Sang!" my mother shouted from downstairs.

I gulped, blushing. Luke froze. I waved him toward the window. Time for him to go.

He started toward the window. He slipped the CD between his lips, swung his leg out and climbed onto the roof.

I stuck my head out. He knelt down until his face was close to mine.

"I'll see you tomorrow," he whispered to me.

"See you," I said.

He smiled to me, passed a finger across my cheek and stood up, slinking back the way we had come over the roof.

I took one more look around my room as if to reassure myself there wasn't another boy or something he left behind. I smoothed a palm over my hair and went for my bedroom door, opening it and dashed down the stairs.

My mother's bedroom was empty. I found her in the kitchen. She was bent over in the fridge, pulling out a package of grapes and a bottle of water. Her maroon robe was crumpled as if she'd been sleeping in it. I wondered where my father had gone, but a moment later I heard clacking at the keyboard at the computer in the family room. He was working.

"Yes?" I asked softly.

She spun, holding her food and water to her chest. "Where have you been?" Her lackluster blue gray eyes passed over me and she turned away to yank a paper towel from the holder against the wall.

I blinked at her. She didn't notice my shirt or the bruises on my face. "Upstairs."

"I called you for dinner. You were ignoring me."

"Oh," I said. "I had music on. I fell asleep for a while."

Her eyes fixed on the ceiling. Her cracked lips pursed. "Do you think I'm stupid? Why are you lying?"

I blinked at her. "I was just upstairs and came down."

Her eyes narrowed at me. She marched over to the hall closet and pulled out a wooden bar stool. She pulled it to the middle of the kitchen and pointed to it. "Sit," she commanded.

I swallowed. I hated the stool. I was sore already from the hours of working, too. I said nothing, moving across the floor to perch on the stool. The flat part bit into my butt as it was hard and uncomfortable. I put my feet on the cross slats between the legs.

"Stay right here," she said.

"It's late. I've got school," I said.

She ignored me and went back to her bedroom.

I sighed. It hurt but it wasn't kneeling in rice.

A footstep sounded behind me and I twisted in my seat. Luke stood in the living room archway. His head tilted, puzzled.

I gasped and covered my mouth with my fist. I silently yelled at him with a glare. *Get out! Are you crazy? What are you doing here?*

He put a fingertip to his lips, motioning to me to keep quiet.

Well no duh. I couldn't whisper. I couldn't think of how to tell him to get out of here. I tried spelling it with sign language, "Go! You'll get caught." He was a smart Academy student, he'd figure it out.

His eyebrows raised and he grinned. He flashed some sign language, but I didn't know any words.

I shook my head, spelling to him. "I only know the alphabet."

He spelled out, "Where did you learn?"

This wasn't the time to talk about it! I spelled, "You can't stay. She might come back."

He smirked at me, a blond lock falling away from his ear and hanging in his eyes. He stepped further into the kitchen. He was barefoot. He did a circle around me, tiptoeing and testing the floor for creaks. He started down the hallway toward my mom's bedroom and the staircase. I gulped, pushing my palms to my cheeks. He couldn't be serious thinking he was going to poke around. I swallowed, my heart thundering in my throat, listening for what I was sure was the inevitable discovery and the chaos that would happen when it did.

Luke returned via the living room again after making a full circle. He took a quick peek in at the family room. I waited for my father to see him but Luke pulled back. He seemed at ease with sneaking around. He tiptoed back into the kitchen and held out the pink cell phone to me. I blinked at him, confused and checked the phone for messages.

Luke: *"How long do you have to sit there for?"*

I sighed, pursing my lips and typing in a message for him.

Sang: *"Until she lets me go."*

He jumped up until he was sitting on top of the counter near the sink. He held his cell phone in his hands and typed in a message.

Luke: *"Why not get up now? She's not paying*

attention."

Sang: *"She could come back. If I'm not here, it'll be worse."*

Luke: *"Will she make you drink vinegar again?"*

Sang: *"Maybe. I don't know."*

He frowned. He typed something else into his phone and put it aside.

I twisted my lips, confused, frustrated, scared to death. Since my phone didn't rattle, the message wasn't for me. I typed into the phone.

Sang: *"Why aren't you leaving?"*

He checked the phone, smirked but put it down, not answering me.

I spelled with my fingers, "Stop sitting there. North is waiting for you."

Luke smirked at me, signing, "Not anymore."

No matter what I said, Luke refused to leave. He would sign or text me to say something or ask a question. He pawed through the cabinets for food. He brought me water and crackers and found an apple to eat for himself. On occasion, he'd slink away, as silent as a whisper, and trek into other parts of the house.

He was there for at least two hours. No matter how many times I begged, he refused to leave me behind.

Luke: *"You're one of us."*

He repeated it often. It became too frustrating to try to convince him to leave.

I got texts from some of the others, too.

North: *"I found your shirt. You left it in the kitchen."*

Sang: *"Hang on to it for me?"*

North: *"Will do."*

Nathan: *"I'm bored and my body hurts and I can't move and this sucks and my back hurts and I'm hungry."*

Sang: *"Get better. We'll hang out then."*

Nathan: *"I want taco soup. Come rub some of this lotion on my back again. I can't reach."*

Sang: *"Are you coming to school tomorrow?"*

Nathan: *"No promises."*

Gabriel: *"You weren't supposed to leave your house. I've been texting you all afternoon. I thought you were in trouble."*

Sang: *"I was with North and the others. I'm sorry I forgot my phone."*

Gabriel: *"How's your face?"*

Sang: *"Fine. How's your nose? Are you hurting?"*

Gabriel: *"I'm fucking peachy. Next time listen to me, will you?"*

Sang: *"Sorry."*

Gabriel: *"Stop apologizing. It makes it harder to be mad at you."*

Sang: *"I don't like it when you're mad at me. So I'm sorry."*

Gabriel: *"You're still grounded."*

Sang: *"Thanks again for the violin. It's beautiful."*

Victor: *"Get good at it and we'll play together sometime."*

Sang: *"I still haven't heard you play."*

Victor: *"Soon."*

After a few hours, I was rocking on the stool, sore, uncomfortable and embarrassed. I wanted to get my mother's attention and get this over with.

Steps echoed in the house. Someone was coming. My eyes shot to Luke, he nodded, slipped into the living room and disappeared.

My father came into the kitchen. His eyelids drooped. He'd finished up work and was heading to bed. When he spotted me on the stool, his head tilted at me in confusion. Did he get a haircut? I couldn't tell. There were more gray hairs at his temples, though. And what did I know? I never saw him.

"What happened?" he asked me.

"I came down when she called me," I said flatly. He'd been here the whole time and he now just noticed?

He raised an eyebrow. "Is that it?"

"She thought I was lying to her when I said I came from my bedroom."

He shrugged. "All right. Go to bed."

I jumped from the stool, taking the side hallway to avoid walking near him. I was too angry and didn't want to be anywhere near my parents. I was aching and exhausted. It was tempting to feign sick the next day and stay home. Maybe I'd sneak over to Nathan's house and spend the whole day with him.

Luke was sitting on the staircase when I approached. I reprimanded him with a glare. He hopped to his feet, leaned down to grab at my arm and pulled me up the stairs. He heaved me back into my bedroom, closing the door behind us.

I hit the stereo's volume up a little and stumbled over to the bed. I plopped onto it on my side.

Luke collapsed next to me, facing me. "I can't believe you stayed there for so long," he said."

I pouted. "What else was I going to do?"

He brushed a finger across my cheek. "She forgot about you," he said quietly.

"If she doesn't forget and comes back…" I pushed my hand over my heart and sighed.

His features softened, those brown eyes fixing over my face. "It's been a long day," he said.

I trembled, nodding, swallowing back my angry, tired tears. I didn't even care if he was there any more. I didn't care that we could get caught at any moment. Luke stayed with me the whole time. He didn't forget about me. He didn't abandon me, despite my asking. It was overwhelming how kind he was.

He leapt up, hitting the lights. In the dark, he pulled the blanket on the bed and slipped in next to me before covering us up. My heart thundered but as I continued to quake and with my willpower depleted, I was too weak to tell him to go home. I wasn't sure if he would listen to me, anyway.

His arms went around me and I sunk into his hug. His chin pressed to my forehead. I inhaled the vanilla scent. His fingers rubbed the muscles in my back along my spine. I pressed my cheek to his chest, listening to his breathing. My eyes fluttered shut, my lashes crossing against his skin.

I didn't care what happened to me. If there was another fight with Luke, or Gabriel, or any of the others, I would jump in. I knew it down to my bones.

Because I knew they'd do the same for me.

♥

THURSDAY

♥

♥

$\mathscr{I}$NAPPROPRIATE

I dreamed of holding the hand of a little boy, who was exhausted and wanted to stop running. We couldn't stop, though. The ground was falling out from under us. If we didn't keep moving, we would fall into the abyss.

$\mathscr{L}$uke was gone when I woke up the next morning. I smelled him in the sheets. It was the promise of seeing the guys again that had me moving, dragging myself into the shower and getting ready for another day.

Marie and I walked together to Kota's driveway. I was dying. My muscles ached to the point where I was in near tears carrying my book bag and the violin.

Kota took one look at me as I walked up and I could tell he was biting his tongue waiting for Marie to get out of earshot before he could start his reel of questions.

"What happened to you?" he asked. His green eyes narrowed at me.

I dropped my book bag on the ground at my feet, the violin joined it. "I'm all sore," I whined to him.

His eyes widened. "Why?"

He didn't know? "I was helping North and the others at the diner." I kept the other part to myself, about sitting in the kitchen for a couple of hours after. I didn't want him to worry about that.

He cracked a half smile, touching the bridge of his glasses. "You were helping?"

"We cleared out the counters in the kitchen and the carpet in the chapel."

173

He laughed. His eyes slid to Danielle and Derrick who were coming up the road. Marie was waving to them. Kota looked back at me. "Are you going to make it today?"

I let out a sigh. "Yes," I said. "I'm already here."

He pulled his cell phone out of his pocket, and punched something into a text message. "Wait until we get to school. I'll help."

Help with what?

He waited with his cell phone in his hands and it buzzed. He checked the message and nodded. "Good." He looked up expectantly toward Nathan's house.

I stood beside him, looking in the same direction. The front door opened and Nathan stepped out.

"Are you getting him to come along? I thought he was still hurt," I said.

"He can't miss any more school right now," Kota said. He turned to me. "Blackbourne's orders."

I pushed my finger to my lip as we watched Nathan stumbling up the street toward us. Nathan's eyes were dark, his lips in a grim twist. Even though it was warm, he wore a long-sleeve, collared shirt, open completely to reveal the white t-shirt underneath. He had doubled the layers to help hide the bruises still prominent on his body. His finger was still wrapped in the splint. As bad as I felt, he looked so much worse.

When he looked up, his eyes sought me out and he straightened as he walked. The corner of his mouth twisted up. Was he trying to put on a brave face for me?

The bus swung around the bend on our street as Nathan stepped up beside me. He sucked in a heavy breath as he clutched the straps to his book bag.

"Nathan?" I whispered to him. I was afraid of stressing him. Did he know about yesterday? Was he angry with me, too?

"Heard you missed me," he said, half turning and looking down at me. The smile on his lips broadened. "And that you're beating up the boys at school in protest to get me to come back. Couldn't let that happen."

My eyes slid to Kota behind us. He tilted his head, answering my silent question: Kota had lured Nathan out using me as bait.

I turned forward, my hand seeking out Nathan's forearm. I wrapped my fingers around it. "You better not die on me," I said softly.

I caught his grin as he moved toward the bus.

Kota picked up my things for me despite my small objection. Nathan fell into the seat first, I slid in next to him and Kota dropped our things at my feet before sitting next to me. I leaned against Nathan to give Kota room.

"What's up?" Nathan asked. "Why are we squished like this?"

I realized he'd missed a lot. Was he only gone for one day? "There's a lot more students that ride the bus compared to the first morning," I said.

"Last count I had was ninety-six students," Kota said. "I'm pretty sure there's more. This model was designed to hold maybe eighty."

Nathan huffed, tilting his body around until he had his back pressed up against the window and his arm wrapped around my shoulder. "Next project, figure out how Sang can ride in the car with us to school."

"We've got some other things to worry about right now," Kota said. "Where's it hurt, Sang?"

I blushed as Nathan's face fell on me. "What happened to her now?" he asked.

"Helping too long at the diner," Kota said. "Overworked her muscles."

"Shit," Nathan said.

"I'm not that bad," I insisted. Now that Nathan was there and I was sure he was in much worse pain, it seemed wrong to complain.

Kota eyeballed me.

I let out a puff of air but surrendered. "Okay, I'm a little sore." Mostly in places he couldn't imagine, like my butt and thighs.

When we finally got to school, Kota took my things

back as we walked out to the courtyard. The thought of sitting on the hard concrete benches wasn't tempting, so I opted to stand.

Kota and Nathan dropped onto the bench together. Nathan immediately fished out his cell phone and started messing with it.

Kota put our stuff down on the ground at his feet. He curled his fingers at me, and patted at his lap. "Come here, Sang," he commanded.

I tiptoed closer to him, unsure of what he was asking me to do. He placed his hands on my waist, pulling me down until I was sitting on his lap. He positioned me until my butt was out closer to his knees. From there, he pressed his fingertips and palms into my lower back, massaging in small circles along my spine.

It was magic. His fingers worked the soreness from my muscles. My eyes closed on their own as he massaged. My heart was thudding because I was sitting in his lap and from his touch, but I was powerless to stop him. I didn't want to, anyway.

I slid a glance at Nathan. He caught my eye and he grinned. "He's spoiling you," he said.

"We just need her to get through the day," Kota said. "She can go home right after school and rest."

"What she needs is a strength training schedule," Nathan said. "Build up some muscles."

I half smirked, rolling my eyes.

Kota was working my shoulders when Gabriel and Victor came through the doors to the courtyard. They gawked in our direction.

"What the fuck?" Gabriel called out as he got closer. "What the hell are you doing to her?"

"Her muscles were sore," Kota said, pushing his palm between my shoulder blades.

I was putty. My voice box refused to do much more than a soft moan at his touch.

Gabriel looked over at Nathan, his eyes squinting. "Your makeup is fucked up."

I hadn't even noticed Nathan wearing any. I glanced at him. There was a strange tint to the edge of his jaw where he had used concealer against his cheek.

Nathan shrugged. "It'll work," he said.

"Let me fix it," Gabriel said.

"I'm not getting it done here," Nathan said. "Forget it."

Gabriel rolled his eyes and focused on my face. He touched my chin, examining. "You're not too bad," he said. He felt into his pocket for a compact and passed it to me. "Brush this on."

I opened the compact with concealing powder and rubbed it in, using the mirror. When I tried to pass it back, Gabriel shook his head. "Keep it. Touch it up every once in a while."

Silas, North and Luke arrived. By then, Kota was done massaging. He positioned me until I was sitting sideways on his lap, his fingertips traced over my side.

North took one look at me in Kota's lap and grunted. "What's wrong with you?" he asked.

"*Someone* kept her out late working," Kota said in a suggestive tone.

North smirked at me. "Traitor. You told." He sank down next to Silas on the other bench. Luke sat on the grass in the middle.

"You need to be more careful," Kota demanded. "You should have known. I can't believe you kept her out for so long."

"It was fun," I said softly. "I don't mind helping."

Kota picked his legs up and brought them down sharply so I bounced in his lap. I leaned into him, wrapping arms around his shoulders, feeling like I was going to fall. "Shush," he told me. "I'm lecturing."

"Ouch," I pouted as a brief pain jabbed me in my butt. Luke's eyes widened at me but I pursed my lips, giving a slight shake of my head. I didn't want to talk about it right now. He seemed to understand. I was in enough trouble.

"Miss Sang Sorenson," called a sharp, bristly voice from across the courtyard.

A prickle started in my spine and I leapt from Kota's lap to address whoever had called to me.

Mr. McCoy stomped across the courtyard in our direction. His nostrils flared over his mustache. "You are coming with me to the office. Right now."

I bit my lower lip, blushing. I couldn't believe it. Had he been watching us? There was a glint in his eyes that betrayed the stern way he held his mouth. He was glad to have caught us out in something.

Kota stood up, his hands clenching. "What's this about?" His green eyes narrowed in on Mr. McCoy.

Mr. McCoy pointed a finger at him. "Inappropriate touching," he said. "And you, too, mister. Come with me."

I snapped myself together to collect my things. I felt the other guys watching us. North and Nathan both started to say something, but Kota shot them a look that I was sure meant they should hold back and let us go. We trailed behind Mr. McCoy toward the main office.

Kota walked alongside me through the hallway, his arm brushing mine as we moved together. I think he meant it to be reassuring but I couldn't look at him. I felt so guilty that we were both getting into trouble. This was my fault, I was sure. If I had only been insistent that I was fine.

Mr. McCoy held the office door open for us. We passed the front secretary's desk and down a hallway to an office at the end, right next to Principal Hendricks'. Hendricks' door was closed and no light shone from underneath. I wondered if he was in the building yet.

Mr. McCoy held open his door. "Miss Sang, first. I'll deal with you in a minute, son," he said to Kota.

Kota glanced at me but said nothing. What else could we do?

Mr. McCoy's office had one window looking out onto the front lawn of the school. The glass was frosted in a particular style, letting in light but not allowing anyone to see inside. I only caught the abstract brown-green blob of the school yard and the sky and the occasional blur of cars passing in the street in the distance.

The vice-principal waited for me to fully enter. I stepped around him, my sandals scuffling along the blue utility carpet. He shut the door, hitting the lock.

A prickling sensation swept over my skin. I'd been in closed rooms with the boys for a little while and I was still getting used to it. This felt completely different. I'd never been in trouble before with school administration, but I thought I would have rather gotten into trouble with any other teacher rather than McCoy.

Mr. McCoy pointed to a rigid wooden chair with a chubby finger. "Sit, Miss Sang."

His eyes locked on me as I crossed the room. I sat, carefully smoothing my skirt over my legs and crossing my ankles. His gaze never left me. I swept my eyes to his desk, and swallowed down a trembling shiver

He padded over to his chair at his desk. His lips frowned and he sat, unbuttoning his ugly brown blazer. His head tilted toward me. "Do you think it's appropriate to sit in a boy's lap on my campus?"

It was a strange question to ask. In the past couple of days, other students made out, groped, sat in laps and a variety of other things. Still, I knew the answer he wanted. "No, sir," I said in a soft voice.

"I may not know much about that Academy," he said, "but I know for sure they don't allow that kind of behavior in their school."

I didn't know how to respond to this. I didn't know anything about the Academy and I wasn't sure how much he was told about it. I swallowed back the urge to correct him.

"I find it sickening a girl like you would allow a boy to touch you like that," he said. His oversized desk chair creaked. I glanced up to see how he steepled his fingers under his chin. "I should call your mother."

I lowered my eyes again, trying to look compliant and apologetic. "I'm sorry," I whispered.

"Where did he touch you?" he asked.

My head shot up, unsure if I heard the question correctly. "Pardon?"

"Tell me every place that boy touched you," he said. His eyes pierced into me, stabbing unclear intentions at my face.

Was this necessary? "I... um..." My fingers found my bottom lip as I spoke. "He... I was sitting in his lap," I said. Wasn't that obvious? Didn't he see for himself? Why did he want me to say it out loud?

"He had his hands on your hips," he said flatly.

I blushed. Had he? I couldn't remember. My mind reeled while I tried to think of it. He did initially touch me there when he first placed me in his lap. How long had he been watching?

"Then he started rubbing your back," Mr. McCoy said. He smirked at me. "Did he touch your breasts?"

My eyes popped open and I started shaking my head. "No..." How could he say that? Just hearing him asking this of me made my insides quake. I felt ashamed of what I had done enough, and didn't want to let him assume Kota would do something like that. I was longing for Kota to be there at first, but now I was so glad he wasn't. He would know how to handle this but I couldn't imagine what would happen if he heard it from Mr. McCoy directly.

The vice-principal frowned at me. "You should address me as sir, Miss Sang."

"Sir," I repeated.

He twisted around in his chair to snatch a large black binder off the shelf next to him. He opened it and flipped through yellow carbon copy pages until he found an empty set of unused detention slips. "I expect you to behave better in the future." He bent over and started filling out the form.

This was bad. I was getting detention on the third day of school. My mother couldn't come get me. My father wasn't going to be able to pick me up until well after the school would be closed. I would be stuck there for hours.

He tore the slip from his book and he held it out to me. "You should thank me that it isn't an in-school suspension. Although next time it might be."

I wasn't sure what to say. With a shaking hand, I touched the slip, but as I tried to pull it away, he held on to it. I looked up at him, confused.

His watery eyes squinted at me. "Say thank you, sir," he commanded.

The bell rang for the start of our first class. I swallowed, my brain buzzing with fear. "Thank you, sir," I said quietly.

He made a sound from his throat that almost sounded like a grunt. "Tell that boy out in the hallway to get to class."

I fluttered where I stood, holding the detention slip in my hand. Was he not going to talk to him, too? What Silas said before to me about Mr. McCoy looking to give me detention the other day slipped into my mind. He had been right. He was waiting for this.

I stood, heading toward the door. A security system keypad was blinking to the left of the door and it caught my eye. Some of the numbers and other buttons had the words worn off. Did the vice-principal have a separate security system for just his office?

I opened the door. Kota was standing in the hallway, leaning with his back against the wall. I closed Mr. McCoy's office door behind me.

"What happened?" Kota asked.

I held out my detention slip. "We're supposed to go to class," I said.

He looked confused. "He doesn't want to see me?"

"No," I said. "He said you and I should go to class. That was it."

His eyes flitted to the door. I bent over to pick up my book bag and violin. Kota reached for my hand, holding it and tugged me along down the hallway. Neither of us spoke as he walked with me through the front office waiting room and back out into the school. We were both already late, so it didn't really matter if we hurried.

"What did he say to you?" Kota asked.

"He... he wanted to know where you touched me," I said. "He asked if you touched my hips and my breasts."

Kota stopped dead in the hallway, turning to me. His eyes widened. "He asked that? What did you say?"

"I denied that you did," I said. "And then he gave me the

detention slip and asked me to tell you to go to class."

Kota frowned. He tugged at my hand again and we walked across the school to my homeroom class.

"Sang," he said. "Did you get a good look at the inside of his office?"

It was the last thing I was thinking about. "Yes," I said. "Well, part of it."

"Can you remember what it looked like?" he asked. "Could you draw me a map?"

It was my turn to look confused at him. "What?"

His green eyes took on a strange glaze. "Do me a favor and write down everything you saw in his office, okay? Write out every detail." He squeezed my hand and let go. "Get in there. I'll catch up with you at English."

I turned to ask him why, but he was already in a sprint toward his own homeroom. I sighed, not understanding and wondering if this was something for the Academy or if this was his own desire. What would he want with a map of the vice-principal's office?

I thought about how Mr. Blackbourne commanded him to wire the boys who had caused the fighting yesterday. This was way more than figuring out rumors and preventing future fights. The Academy was infiltrating the entire school.

♥

$\mathscr{O}$NE $\mathscr{O}$F $\mathscr{U}$S

$\mathscr{N}$orth and Luke held my seat for me in homeroom. When the teacher asked where I had been, I revealed my detention slip to him. He looked it over, nodded to me and asked me to take a seat.

I fell into my chair, dropping my things at my feet. Luke turned in his desk and I felt North leaning over the top of his behind me.

"Sang baby," North started, "What--"

"I got detention," I said.

Luke did a half smirk. "Kota, too?"

I shook my head. It took me a moment to explain it to them. As I was talking, I pulled out a notebook and started scribbling notes to myself to remember what Kota had asked, giving him a detailed description of Mr. McCoy's office. When I was done with my story, I drew my best variation of a map on the side.

"What's the vice-principal got against you?" North asked. "I've seen kids nearly fucking in the hallways. No one stops them."

"I bumped into him a couple of times," I said, ignoring his last comment. Did he really see that? "He wasn't happy that Dr. Green helped me at the start of school and I'm pretty sure he and Mr. Hendricks thinks I'm part of your group."

I didn't have to look up to know they were exchanging glances above my head.

I was drawing out the keypad in the corner of my paper when the bell rang for the next class. Luke grabbed my violin for me and I picked up my book bag. I was going to get my violin from him but he reached for my hand, too and started tugging me toward the door.

When we were outside in the hallway, North put an arm around me, his fingers grasping my shoulder. We walked together like that, with Luke's hand in mine and North on the other side of me. A silence fell over us. I was almost grateful for it. This first week was the worst and needed to end. Feeling them around me, knowing they were there made it so much better. I don't know how I survived all my other schools alone. What would I have done without them at this one? It made me fearful of the future, of next year when I may not have them around when they went back to their Academy.

North didn't let go of me until we were standing outside of the trailer for our next class. Then, he walked off without looking back. Luke let go of my hand to hold open the door. I fell into my seat and Luke sat behind me. Kota filed in shortly after. Kota and Luke shared a silent look over my shoulder, checking in to make sure the other knew what was going on.

I had my notebook out and was finishing up the keypad. Kota studied what I was doing. He read what I'd written upside down, checking my work on the keypad.

"Why didn't you put numbers here?" he asked, pointing to the keys that were blank.

"There weren't any," I said. "It was smudged off. It looked like an old system." I sighed, looking over my paper one more time and ripped it from my notebook and handed it to him. "What's this for?"

He reviewed my work again, analyzing. "Do you remember the name of the security system?"

I thought about it. I held my hand out for the sheet of paper and wrote down the name: E&O Inc.

He nodded and took the paper from me again. "Thanks," he said.

I was about to ask him again what this was for when Gabriel burst in. He fell into his seat, breathing heavily as if he had been running to get there. "Okay," he said. "What happened?"

"I got detention," I said.

"What?" Gabriel asked. "You? Why?"

"Inappropriate touching," Kota said.

Gabriel blinked at him as the bell rang for the start of class. "Did you get detention?"

"Nope," Kota said.

"That's bullshit."

Kota shot him a look.

"Well, it is," Gabriel said. His crystal blue eyes danced around the room as if he was trying to come up with something.

Ms. Johnson stood at the front of the room. She barely finished roll call when Gabriel shot his hand in the air.

"Yes Mr. Coleman?" Ms. Johnson asked.

"I'm sorry to interrupt," he said. "What would it take to get a detention?"

Ms. Johnson pushed a finger to her eyebrow. "Pardon?"

"Gabriel," Kota commanded in a whisper.

Gabriel ignored him. "What would someone have to do to get a detention in this class?"

Ms. Johnson still looked confused. "I suppose if someone started cussing in class, but..."

"Goddamn-shit-motherfucker," Gabriel spat out. He pressed his index finger to his chin and looked apologetic. "Oh wait, is it one detention for each or can it just count as a group?"

The class roared with laughter. I pressed my hands to my face, smothering a giggle of my own. What was he doing?

Ms. Johnson's lips twisted into an almost smirk. "If you wanted a detention that badly, you could have just asked me after class."

"Oh," Gabriel said. "Then sorry. I'll ask you after class."

My shoulders shook as I giggled, and I folded my arms, pressing my forehead to the desk. I couldn't look at him. I couldn't look at any of them.

"Anyone else want detention?" Ms. Johnson asked.

I think she meant the question to be rhetorical as the

class was laughing. I popped my head up. Kota raised his hand expectantly. I looked back to see Luke nearly standing out of his chair and raising his hand.

"Just see me after class," she said. "No need to cuss." She looked bewildered, shaking her head as if her students had just gone insane.

"What are you doing?" I whispered to Kota. He ignored me though. I glanced over at Gabriel, who wore the biggest satisfied smirk. He winked at me.

I settled back into my seat, sighing.

I waited for the boys to get their detention slips at the end of class. Kota had to take off immediately after. I wanted to ask him more questions but he quietly shook his head at me. He couldn't answer me now.

Luke ran off to his next class and Gabriel waited with me for North.

Gabriel waved his detention slip in the air at North like a victory flag as he approached. "Oy," he said.

North grunted. "Not you, too."

"Not just me," Gabriel said. "Kota and Luke."

"Goddammit," North said. He sighed and gazed at me. "How could you let them do that?"

My eyes popped open and I held my hands up in the air in defeat. "I didn't let them. They wouldn't stop. I don't know what they're doing."

"We're not letting you go to detention alone, Trouble," Gabriel said. I shot him a look for the name he called me. I felt like trouble for them enough. He chopped me on the head and winked at me before running off to class.

North grumbled and hooked his arm around my shoulders, his fingers threaded through my hair to rub at my scalp.

"I don't get it, North," I said as we walked together to the main building. "Why are they getting detentions for me?"

"You're part of us now," he said. "Haven't you

noticed?"

I pushed a palm to my forehead. "I don't know what that means. Please don't tell me that you're going to try to get detention, too. I don't know if I can take this. You should tell Kota and the others to stop. I think the teacher would understand if they gave the detention slips back. They don't need to get into trouble with me."

He laughed softly, his deep voice seeming to reverberate in my bones. He pulled me closer and pushed his nose to my hair as he said, "Sang baby, you're beautiful."

His compliment had me floating all the way to our next class.

♥♥♥

Nathan was slumped over in his chair in geometry class when we walked in. I fell into the chair in front of him and North sat in front of me.

Nathan popped his head up. "Okay, what's going on?" He tugged a lock of my hair.

"Sang's got detention," North said.

"Fuck," Nathan said.

"So does Gabriel and Luke and Kota," I said. It felt good to tattle on them, even if it was only to Nathan.

"They're not the only ones," North said. He searched his pocket, pulling out a detention slip with his name scrawled on it.

My mouth popped open. "North!"

"Hey," he said. "I didn't think Kota and the others were going to do it. Besides, someone has to drive you home."

"What did you do?" I asked.

"I slept during class," North said. "I made sure to snore."

"Hell, I'll do that," Nathan said. He put his head to the desk.

I turned around in my chair to poke at his arm. "Nathan, don't you dare."

"You're not my boss," he said without lifting his head. "Kota is."

"Kota would tell you no," I said as the bell rang.

"No, he wouldn't," North said. He slapped me with a palm on my thigh. "Shush and get your homework out before the teacher gives you another one."

♥♥♥

Despite his best effort to sleep the entire time, Nathan didn't get a detention in geometry class. The geometry teacher seemed to have some sympathy since he did look tired and he'd been out 'sick' the day before.

Nathan walked beside me to my violin class.

"Don't get detention," I warned him as we got to the music room. "I'm telling you not to."

He waved me off dismissively as he held open the door. I groaned and stalked into class.

I swallowed hard as I spotted Mr. Blackbourne across the room. I wasn't sure what to say. Should I warn him what the others were doing? Would I have the nerve to tell him why this all started? So far every time I'd bumped into him, there was something new going on. He was going to think I was the troublemaker Gabriel claimed I was.

Mr. Blackbourne wore a dark gray suit, his red tie snug against his neck. Perfect. His steel eyes caught mine. "Miss Sorenson?" It wasn't the usual greeting, but a question inviting me to spill it.

"I got detention," I said. I thought it was best to get it out of the way. "And the boys are all now trying to get detention, too, so I won't have to do it alone." There. Maybe he'll give an order for them all to stop. I could spare Silas and Victor and maybe even catch Nathan before he got written up. If anyone could override the crazy hierarchy of these Academy students that I didn't understand, I was pretty sure Mr. Blackbourne could.

Mr. Blackbourne raised a dark eyebrow coolly, staring at me as if I were about to tell him I was just kidding. When I didn't, he sighed out loud. He held a hand out toward the bench of the piano, inviting me to sit. When I had crossed the room, he took my violin case and my book bag from my hands to put them in a chair nearby.

Mr. Blackbourne sat next to me on the bench, slightly turned so he could look down at me. I felt weak next to his powerful stature and under his steely gaze as he seemed to know everything before I even said it.

"Start at the beginning," he said softly.

My composure melted. My mouth opened and I told him everything, doing my best to explain sitting in Kota's lap, getting caught by Mr. McCoy.

When I finished, I was shaking. "And I can't let my mother find out," I slipped. It was what I was thinking, but hadn't meant to relay this to him.

"Why not?" he asked. He hadn't questioned the boys' participation or my own recklessness with Kota. Was he not angry that we were being so ridiculous? I was embarrassed for my own actions and for not putting more pressure on Kota and the others to stop.

I pushed a finger to my lower lip. "My mom is strict," I said. "If she hears I got detention because I was sitting in Kota's lap..." I didn't really know what would happen. What could she do? Maybe it would be enough reason for her to convince my father to pull me out of school. I shivered at the thought. It was the one place where I could get away from her without the overwhelming guilt I got when I ran away to be at Kota's or somewhere else. "But besides that, I thought maybe you could stop them. Silas and Victor might not know yet. Nathan's been trying to get detention by sleeping in class."

Mr. Blackbourne frowned. He took his glasses off and brought his fingers to his forehead, rubbing his eyebrows. "I've been working with the guys for six years and in less than a month you've got them wrapped around your finger."

My mouth fell open. "Mr. Blackbourne..."

He sighed, putting his glasses back on. "This is what you're going to do," he said. "Let the guys continue to get detentions if they want. More than likely they'll all have one by lunch time. Behave and avoid McCoy, if you can."

I blushed, feeling the strength in his gaze on me. "I'm trying."

"I know. Unfortunately it's our fault that you're getting into this," he said. "Meanwhile, don't tell the others you've talked to me yet."

I sucked in a deep breath. "I'm sorry for this. Did I mess everything up?"

His eyes softened. "No, Miss Sorenson. In reality, I think you've done us a huge favor."

♥♥♥

After class, I waited outside the door until Victor turned the corner. He slipped beside me quietly, reaching for my hand. He held it tightly as we walked to class. It was the way his thumb slipped over my skin between my thumb and forefinger that told me he knew what was going on. The fire blazing in his eyes told me he was doing the same thing as the others. I wouldn't dare tell him no.

In history, Victor answered a phone call in the middle of class to get detention. He even said thank you to Mr. Morris afterward.

North and Victor and I arrived at our spot in the courtyard for lunch. Silas was there, and he held up his own detention slip to me.

I smirked at him. "Silas," I said in a warning tone, though I couldn't help my smile. Since Mr. Blackbourne didn't flip out about the boys, I felt a little better about the situation. I was overwhelmed by how they were reacting to this. I think it was the first time that I felt we really were all in this together.

"What was I going to do? Walk home?" He grinned, reaching around my shoulders to give me a strong hug. I gasped, laughing a little and hugging him back.

"Watch out," Kota said, coming up behind us. "You'll both get another detention. I really don't want to have to ask Ms. Johnson for another."

Nathan walked past us, sinking to the ground on his knees and falling back on the grass. "I haven't been able to get detention yet," he complained. "I've been sleeping through all my classes. No one cares."

"All the kids sleep in class. You should curse," Gabriel said. "Just start cussing. They have to give you detention for that."

"You have to be careful with that," Kota said. "You might end up with in-school suspension instead."

We were sharing packages of chips and sandwiches we had made at home. I was picking pieces away from my sandwich to eat it a little at a time. They were talking about what detention might be like. I had to bite my tongue at thinking of Mr. Blackbourne and I was wondering if he was going to be able to get them all off the hook.

I also worried about what my mother would think when she found out. Could I get away with it not being mentioned to her at all? Would the school say why? Would they even call her? I wondered if Marie would notice. She hadn't said much to me since school started. I could only hope she wouldn't care today.

I sensed eyes on me and I caught Marie across the courtyard. She was walking alongside Danielle. Their eyes flicked my way. Marie said something to Danielle and Danielle laughed, looking at me again.

"Your sister is kind of stuck up," Gabriel said next to me on the bench.

"That's funny. She said the same thing about you guys."

Gabriel laughed. "I can see why she thinks so but doesn't she know pointing and laughing at people is really rude?"

I shrugged. "All the other students do it."

"You don't do it."

I blushed, being caught at being told I was different. "Should I start?"

"I'll shoot you if you do." He grinned at me. He took my hand that was holding my sandwich and brought it to his mouth so he could take a bite.

I laughed, rolled my eyes and handed him the rest of it. He took the sandwich from me and ate it. I stood up to brush crumbs from my skirt.

"Hey, sexy lady," called a voice behind me. I spun around as Mike, the red haired kid from the day before, crossed the courtyard. He was trailed by a couple of friends, shaking their heads. Mike stopped a few feet from me, and got on his knees. He knee walked until he could grasp my hand between his. His eyes settled on my face. "Hey there sexy. Will you marry me?"

"God damn it," North said. He crossed his arms over his chest, glaring at Mike. "She fucking said no already."

"Shut up, I'm not asking you," Mike barked back, though he was half smiling. He looked up at me again and his face became serious. "Please?"

I rolled my eyes, shaking my head. "No, sorry." I had too much to worry about to have to deal with crazy proposals. Now I knew he was teasing me.

"Damn," Mike said. He jumped up off the ground. "Maybe next time." He stalked off toward the door to the school. His friends were giggling behind him.

"What the hell was that?" Nathan asked from the grass. He had been on his back nearly the entire time but he was sitting up now.

"Second marriage proposal this week," Luke said, holding up two fingers. "Am I going to need to keep a scoreboard?"

"There might be another one in here somewhere," North said. He pulled out a handful of folded notes from his pockets, tossing them at his brother. "I didn't go through them yet."

My eyes widened, my hand going over my heart. Was this school so much different than my other one? "Who is it?" I asked. "Who keeps writing to me?"

"It's different boys," North said. "Homeroom, geometry and history now."

Kota pulled out two folded notes from his pocket. "English, too," he said, looking guiltily at me.

Victor pressed a palm to his eye. "God, I swear, I feel like we're back in elementary school."

"Why are they writing?" I asked, confused. "Are they being mean?"

They all blinked at me and started laughing.

"I don't talk to anyone but you guys," I said over their laughter, not really understanding. "No one ever talked to me at my old school."

"Sweetie," Luke said. He collected my hand and tugged me until I was sitting next to him on the bench. "What did you do at your old school?"

"Went to class, and went home. There wasn't much else I could do."

"Did you bother to try to talk to anyone?" he asked.

I blinked, and shook my head. "I never really had the opportunity or knew what to say. Most people ignore me."

Kota started to laugh. "Everyone probably thought you were stuck up. Since you're here and talking to us, everyone thinks you're open and popular so they're trying to climb the ranks."

"What are you talking about? I'm not popular."

They all laughed.

I groaned, putting my elbows on my knees to rest my face in my hands. "You're all crazy."

The other classes were quiet. I'd expected to see Mr. Hendricks or Mr. McCoy pop in, as I'd seen them so often that week. When I made it to gym class without incident, I was happy.

It was the first official day we were supposed to get dressed for gym. When I changed into the uniform, the shorts looked really short. I clapped my palms to my thighs. They were a few inches shorter than my longest fingers. Did the school check for this kind of thing? The t-shirt at least was normal, and perhaps a little big for my frame even though I'd ordered a small.

I'd brought another clip with me just for gym class. I twisted my hair, pulling it away from my face. Gabriel couldn't do anything about it now. At least I hoped he wouldn't.

I was walking with the other girls toward the gym when a hooting echoed through the hallway. The girls crowded at the door, peering out. A few of the girls had already entered the gym, crossing the room. The guys were sitting in formation and started hooting cat calls.

"What are we going to do?" one of the girls said, looking back at us. "They're being stupid."

The others were talking about taking the long way around so we had a shorter distance to walk.

"Let's just all go out together," I suggested. The others turned to me and I pushed my finger to my lip, unsure. It surprised me that I'd said anything. Maybe the boys were right. Maybe I needed to relax and open up more. "I mean, let's go and get it over with. Who cares what they do? We'll be doing this all year and we can't just avoid it. Just don't let them think we care. They'll get over it."

The other girls smirked. We waited until everyone was together and as a group, we moved into the gym. The guys started clapping and hooting again. The echo in the gym was deafening. I recognized a few of the boys from the fight yesterday. The one who started it wasn't among them. I wondered if he came to school at all or if Kota managed to wire him.

"Ignore it," I said to the group, quieter so the guys couldn't hear. "Just move to your seat and sit. If you look at them, they'll keep doing it." If I learned anything from my old schools, it was how to use being invisible as an advantage, especially when it came to avoiding contact with bullies until I was too boring to be any fun. Even I didn't want that kind of attention.

Focused, the girls moved toward the other end of the room. Some of them did glance up at the boys, but for the most part we all ignored the hollering. I caught Nathan and Gabriel sitting on the ground in their assigned spots, both of them watching but not participating. I was happy about that.

The other boys did manage to quiet down after we were

all sitting. The boys were rushed into what would be their warm up exercises. The girls' coach waited until the boys were done before she started talking. She spoke loudly, ordering us to stand up and stretch. She walked through our lines as she gave off commands, getting us to do push-ups and sit-ups and jumping jacks.

The boys took out basketballs and started playing. When the girls were done, we were told next week we would start with tennis. This week, since we only had one more day left, they would just let us do our warm up exercises and we could talk the rest of the time.

"Hey," one of the girls said. She was tall, lean, with pixie-styled brown hair and big brown eyes. "Don't we get to play basketball?"

The coach smiled at her. "Want to play?"

The girl nodded.

Coach blew the whistle at her neck, turning around. "Okay boys," she barked at them. "Play half court. The girls want to play."

The boys grunted. Nathan and Gabriel were the only two who seemed to perk up at the idea.

I stood up, not wanting to sit down since I'd been sitting all day. I was still sore and knew if I just warmed up my muscles, they'd feel a little better. I joined the brown-haired girl and three other girls followed. The others stayed on the floor so they could talk.

Since there were only five of us, we split up. I joined Karen, the tall one who had asked to play basketball first, and the other three were on the other team. Karen was competitive. She barked orders at me and constantly asked for the ball. I didn't mind. The action was getting me to stop thinking about detention that afternoon.

"Oy," Gabriel's voice called from the other side of the gym. He stood with his hands on his hips, watching us. Nathan stood beside him. "Let some of us join," Gabriel said. "It's too crowded on this side."

Karen held the basketball, rolling it in her hands. "Fine," she said.

Five boys joined us on our side. Gabriel flashed a grin at me and Nathan was beaming. He seemed to have forgotten he was hurt. Maybe he had the same idea about warming up muscles, or he'd taken some pain-killers and was feeling better.

The girls and the guys split up so it was five on each team. A couple of the other boys kept guarding Karen since she was the tallest and clearly the best out of us. For the most part, the boys had the advantage. The other girls were average sized and like me, simply outmatched.

I wasn't tall enough to attempt to cover Gabriel or Nathan. It didn't seem to matter. Both hovered over me more often than anyone else. I couldn't touch the ball before they managed to wrestle it away from me.

When the ball bounced out of bounds, Gabriel ran to fetch it. He caught it and dribbled it at the boundary, trying to figure out who to pass it to. An idea floated into my mind. I waited quietly in front of him as if I was tired and wasn't about to attempt to try to stop him. He bounced the ball a couple of times as Karen and the other girls were doing their best to guard everyone else. He focused on Nathan.

When he lifted the ball to pass, I jumped to life, running across in front of him to snatch it from the air. His eyes popped open in surprise and he ran after me. The others were preoccupied and I had no one to toss it to. In a desperate move, I spun, aimed for the basket from beyond the three point line and made a shot. The ball sank cleanly into the net. It was pure luck.

"Holy shit," Gabriel said, looking stunned. He laughed, came after me and hooked an arm around my waist, swinging me off the ground. "That was awesome."

"Hey, boys," called one of the female coaches. "Keep your hands off of my girls or I'll give you detention."

Gabriel smirked and let me go, a hand remained on my back until my knees stopped shaking.

"That's all it takes?" Nathan called out. He had the ball in his hands at that moment. He laughed, tossed the ball right at me.

Surprised, I took it back, not understanding what he meant. He raced across the court after me. I half cried out, trying to run and dribble at the same time. I couldn't get away from him. He hunched down, grabbed me by my thighs and hefted me up until I was sitting on his shoulder. He carried me that way until I was close enough to the basket and I could drop the ball inside easily to score.

"Hey!" The coach called. She pointed at Nathan. "That's it. I warned you. Detention. Put her down."

Nathan laughed, bending over and putting me down gently. He beamed. "I've got detention. I've got detention," he taunted at me, wiggling his fingers in the air. The silver brace on his right hand glinted under the gym lights.

I tucked a hand to my side, laughing. Gabriel laughed, too. The others in the group stood by, shaking their heads and trying to understand what was so funny.

♥

CHANGE OF PLANS

*A*fter gym was over, I changed quickly and waited in the hallway for the guys. Nathan and Gabriel came around the corner and I breathed in relief that they weren't held up by more taunting bullies.

Nathan brandished his detention slip, beaming.

"What do we do?" I asked. "I've never been in detention before."

Gabriel smirked. "And you assume we have?"

Nathan read his slip. "I don't know. It doesn't say where to go."

"Let's go to the main office," Gabriel said. "Someone there should know. Text Kota."

Nathan fished out his phone as we walked against the flow of students. He sent a message to all the other guys about where we were headed.

We gathered outside of the main office. Kota was the last to arrive. My heart started to thud. I would miss the bus. Marie would notice. What now?

Kota opened the main office door and motioned to North and then to me. "We'll go ask what to do," he said. "The rest of you stay out here until we figure it out."

While the others remained in the hall, I filed in behind Kota and North. We stood together in the main office waiting, as there were a couple of other students at the desk. The boys stood so close to me and they both had serious expressions on their faces. I wasn't sure what they were expecting, but I wondered if they were waiting for Mr. McCoy or Mr. Hendricks to appear at any moment.

We waited our turn to talk to the secretary, who informed us that detention was held in the auditorium. "I think you all are the first this year."

We left the office and told the other guys. We moved as a group to find the auditorium. When we were halfway down the main hallway, I realized the guys were surrounding me. Kota and North walked ahead, Gabriel and Nathan hovered close on either side of me, the other three trailed behind us. I was in the middle again. I didn't know if they realized they'd done it. Maybe they did. They seemed to do everything with purpose.

When we got to the right hallway, the doors to the auditorium were locked.

"Does this mean we can go home?" Gabriel asked. He hooked an arm around my neck, half hanging off of me. "If no one shows up, how will they know if we're here?"

"I think our bus is already gone," Nathan said. He leaned against the metal door, stuffing his hands into his pockets. "We can wait. If we don't do it today, we'll end up having to do it tomorrow anyway. I don't want to do this twice if we don't have to."

We all watched and waited next to the doors. I was starting to stare off at the wall when Kota cleared his throat. He tilted his head toward the end of the hallway to get us to look.

Mr. Blackbourne and Dr. Green marched down toward us. The guys straightened. Gabriel let go of me to stand tall. The others, while they weren't saluting, stood still, posture perfect. While I was confused, I followed their example, trying to look humble.

Mr. Blackbourne continued to walk past us. Dr. Green stopped in mid-step, motioning with his head at us. "Let's go," he said.

I pushed a finger to my lip, unsure if he meant me.

Dr. Green caught my hesitation. "You, too, Miss Sang," he said calmly.

What about detention? I glanced at Kota and the others, but their faces were all the same granite expression. Now I regretted telling Mr. Blackbourne. Were they displeased that he knew? Wouldn't he have found out anyway?

We collected our things and followed them outside. The temperature had changed from uncomfortable to broil, and the humidity was turned on maximum, sweat guaranteed. We were led out to the old wood bleachers at the abandoned baseball field. Mr. Blackbourne pointed at the seats and the others clustered together on various levels of the benches and faced Mr. Blackbourne and Dr. Green. I slipped onto the edge next to Victor, feeling the heat from the warm wood radiating through my skirt.

Mr. Blackbourne crossed his arms over his chest, standing in front of us with that steely gaze. Dr. Green stopped beside him. Dr. Green put his hands behind his back and his face became unreadable. This was business.

Mr. Blackbourne stared down Kota. "Start talking."

"Mr. McCoy isolated out Sang," he said. "We needed someone to go in with her. I think otherwise it would have been her and McCoy alone."

"It's not the first time," Silas spoke up. "He bumped into her the first day of school and started to blame her for it. He wanted to give her detention then, too."

All of the guys turned to me. My face was radiating as I kept my finger at my lip, pushing it to my teeth. "I don't know why," I said. "I've been trying to avoid him since the start of school."

"We'll have to figure out why later," Mr. Blackbourne said. He jabbed a finger in the air toward their faces. "We've got other things to do, and so far Sang is the one doing your job."

They had a job? What were they supposed to do other than be good students and set an example to the others? I was the worst example so far. Fighting. Detention on the first week! And I got all of them involved.

"Gabriel, Luke, I need you two to work out a uniform. Victor, make the calls to find out who will produce seven by tomorrow morning. Kota and Nathan, go tail McCoy and see if he's still here. Give me updates. North and Silas, you're with me." He pointed at Kota, and made a motion with his hands.

Kota pulled a folded piece of paper from his pocket. It looked like the notes I had written that morning about Mr. McCoy's office. Kota handed the paper off to Mr. Blackbourne. Kota and Nathan left their bags and started sprinting to the school again. North and Silas followed Mr. Blackbourne in the same direction.

I folded my arms around my knees as I watched Gabriel and Luke moving together to get started. Victor had his phone out and was thumbing through it. I felt useless. Were they going to go wire McCoy now? Could they get into trouble? This wasn't a student, it was the vice-principal.

Plus, Mr. Blackbourne had to deal with Mr. Hendricks' demands. With uniforms, they'd get into more fights. What was I going to do? I didn't know how to help or even if I should. It all felt like my fault. Maybe if I wasn't in the middle, Mr. Blackbourne would have stuck to his insistence that the guys couldn't wear uniforms.

"Miss Sang," Dr. Green called to me. He was still standing where he had been in front of the benches. "Would you like to take a walk with me?"

My eyebrows lifted. I glanced at Victor. He had the phone pressed to his ear but he nodded to me, silently confirming with me to do what I was told.

I left my things on the bench and stumbled down to Dr. Green. He smiled pleasantly and I felt a little better that I was being told to walk with him instead of Mr. Blackbourne. We started away from the others, walking around the rusted fence of the baseball field.

Dr. Green was quiet until we were out of earshot off the others. "I'm sorry," he said. "It looks like I might have made you a target."

"With the vice-principal?" I asked. "He was the one that started it at registration."

"Yes," Dr. Green said. Locks of his sandy hair fell into his eyes and he brushed them away. "But maybe if I hadn't intervened, he might not have been so determined to come after you." He dipped his hands into his pockets. "What do you know about us, Miss Sang? I believe they've mentioned the Academy, right?"

"It's a private school," I said. "They normally attend there and this year they're on loan to try to be an example. If you can help improve the grades, there will be some approval for more money to build a second school."

"Right," he said. He unlatched the gate of the baseball field. He held it ajar for me and I entered. He closed it behind himself and strolled toward the pitcher's mound. "Although I think we'll have to make a change of plans. Mr. Hendricks wasn't very happy that we stepped in. He would never admit he needed us. Since we're here, though, I believe he has developed a new idea on how to utilize us."

"And he wants uniforms to get other students to pick on them?" I asked. "I thought the point of the boys being here was to try to get the good students to do better. Like setting an example?"

"That's part of it," he said. He stepped onto the mound, drawing still and staring out toward the tree line. "A quick way to boost grades for school is figuring out the worst students and catching them out in something to legally expel them. We didn't like that idea. It's only depositing bad students into other schools or ensuring they drop out altogether. It displaces the burden instead of solving anything."

"But Mr. Hendricks wants quick results?"

He nodded. "The original plan was to only observe and only report on the most dangerous students, those who were leading fights or abusing the girls. I think Hendricks wants to perpetuate the fighting and kick out students who are going to be problems as soon as possible. Maybe he feels he can get rid of our students from his school if we do our job faster. Whatever the reasons, he seems determined to expose our team. First it was interviews. Now it's uniforms."

He was going to let me in on this? Was he going to tell me more about the Academy? Questions hung on the edge of my tongue to ask. "That's terrible," I said. I stood off to the side of the mound, feeling small. "They'll get into more fights."

Dr. Green smiled down at me. "I'm not really worried about that," he said. "The boys can take care of themselves. Haven't you noticed?"

I turned my head to look back at Luke, Gabriel, and Victor on the benches. Luke gazed back at us. Gabriel focused on his notebook paper. Victor was talking in his cell phone. The others hadn't blinked when they heard Mr. Blackbourne give the order. They weren't worried about what uniforms might mean for them, and didn't hesitate to make those preparations. They weren't afraid.

"Is that what happened on the first day?" I asked him. "Did Nathan get in a fight here?"

Dr. Green's eyes darkened. "Nathan barely managed to get a message to Victor before he was overwhelmed. As I mentioned, our original plan was to hang on the sidelines and see who was starting fights and figure out the worst offenders. Groups of students would lie, either for loyalty or self-protection. Nathan wasn't supposed to get involved but the fight started over a boy who wasn't able to defend himself. I fully believe Nathan saved his life. Victor needed to create a diversion so Nathan could get out from under it."

My heart started thudding. I had a vision of Nathan, as strong as he was, being kicked and beaten up as I'd seen in other fights at my old school. How many kids would it have taken for someone like Nathan, trained in jujitsu, to need help?

"Is this normal for the Academy?" I asked. "Is this what you do? Drop in on other schools and save them?"

Dr. Green laughed softly. "If only it were that simple." He sighed. "Miss Sang, I want to tell you about it but..."

"You can't tell me," I interrupted. "I know." I sighed. It was a strange school that needed students like Kota and Silas and the others so well trained and working together. That secret school with silent ninjas, that wired students and faculty, and bought each other what they needed without question, and stood up for each other.

How far did this go? Would I ever figure it out? I bit back the questions in my mind. I had promised I wouldn't try to ask too much about the Academy as no one could tell me. I would keep my promise. It would take time to be trusted with such secrets.

His eyes lit up again. "Kota was right about you."

I tilted my head at him. "What did he say?"

Dr. Green slowly reached out to me to catch a lock of my hair that had escaped my clip and tucked it behind my ear. I was looking into his eyes, still in awe that someone so young was a doctor and seemed to be in such control and so nice. "He said there's this beautiful angel who has her heart on her sleeve and we have to keep her safe."

My cheeks heated up. Was this more of the flirting that Victor told me about or was he being honest? It didn't seem like something Kota would say.

"I don't think telling you about your own school would be against our policy," he said, dropping his hand from my cheek. "Besides, you've been rather helpful. It seems the fights and grades aren't our only priority."

"Do you mean McCoy?"

He nodded. "We'll install cameras in McCoy's office and keep an eye on him. If he's interested in you, he might be interested in other young ladies. Kota seems to think there is a problem. I don't want to think so. I want to believe it is a rough first week and he's just getting back at us for upsetting him at registration."

I blew a breath out slowly. "What do you need me to do?"

His smile touched his lips again. He came down off the pitcher's mound and tucked his arm around my shoulders. He turned me around to walk back to the gate at the fence. "I'm afraid you're not going to like it. I hate to ask this, but I need you to test Mr. McCoy. I believe we need to figure out for certain if his interest is in you or if he's just trying to irritate us."

"How?" I asked. I shoved my fingers into my palms, pressing my knuckles against my thighs. The boys now regularly wrapped their arms around my shoulders in the same friendly gesture. With Dr. Green, I felt that same fluttering nervousness as when the others first started to touch me. I steeled myself from pulling away, wanting to prove that I wasn't as lacking in confidence as I felt.

"I think we need to get you to interact with other students. You've been close to the boys but we need to see if Mr. McCoy will lose interest in you if it looks like you've lost interest in us."

"You want me to back off," I said softly. "All the time?"

"Only during school hours," he said. He let go of me to open the gate again. "I know you've sat next to Victor in class. I'm going to assume you do the same with the rest of the guys. For the moment, try to vary it up. Sit next to other students. Make some new friends. Eat lunch with someone else."

Easier said than done. "For how long?" It was nerve-wracking to think of being alone again. He was probably right, though. I did need to make other friends if I wanted to be able to keep going to Ashley Waters after the boys returned to the Academy full time.

Dr. Green hesitated while we were still out of earshot of the others. Gabriel and Luke looked like they were arguing over something. Victor was leaning back on his elbows as he gazed out at us.

"Let's get the boys these ridiculous uniforms," Dr. Green said. "It'll be safer if you started separating from them anyway. The other students might not have noticed how tight you all have become and they won't be as quick to pinpoint you as one of us if you won't be wearing something similar."

"They'll be okay, won't they?" I asked, uncertain. How could I stand back and just watch as my friends were picked on and possibly getting into fights?

"Don't worry, Miss Sang," Dr. Green said. "This is a cakewalk. They're more worried about you than themselves." His gaze softened as he looked down at me. "Will you be okay?"

Being alone in school? No problem. Out of all the things

I thought I should do to help with the boys, becoming invisible again was something I thought I could realistically accomplish. "I've made it this far."

Dr. Green started forward again. "If you get into trouble, you come find me. I'll do whatever I can."

My heart warmed that he would say so. Out of all the boys, Dr. Green and Mr. Blackbourne had the least knowledge of who I was. They could have easily dismissed me and left me on my own. I was more than sure Mr. Blackbourne could have gotten the boys out of detention and left me alone with Mr. McCoy. He might not have said so out loud but he was watching out for me, too.

We approached the benches. I slid in next to Victor again. His concerned face relaxed when I drew near and he offered a small smile.

"Victor," Dr. Green said. "Sang and I agree that for now it might be best if she tries to go it alone while you all are getting situated with these new uniforms."

Victor frowned. "I don't think that should happen."

Gabriel and Luke turned their heads toward us and closed the space between us on benches. "Oy," Gabriel said. "What do you mean?"

Dr. Green cleared his throat. "She might not wear a uniform, but if you guys are the only ones she hangs out with, the other students will target her, too. I think it might be safer if you don't approach her in school anymore. For now."

Victor's fire eyes scorched. "She can't go out alone. Have you seen the trouble she's been in lately?"

"Did you stop to consider half of her problems are because of how you guys act around her?" he asked. He turned to me. "What happened to you in your old school, Miss Sang?"

My face was hot from the sun and from the conversation. I pushed a palm to my cheek to rub gently at the bruises. "Not a lot," I said. "No one ever talked to me."

Dr. Green tilted his head at me as if he were confused. Did he not know? Did Kota not tell him? "But you didn't get into this kind of trouble?" he asked.

"No," I said. "I was ignored for the most part."

"She's not ignored here," Victor said.

"Maybe not totally. Healthy student interaction will be adequate to what most of you will be experiencing. If there's fights around you, she'll be in the middle of it if she's right next to you."

The others frowned together as if this thought wasn't considered before.

"What about McCoy?" Luke asked.

Dr. Green rubbed at his forehead. "Can you guys keep an eye on her without walking next to her?"

The boys looked at each other, silently asking and figuring out the answer together. "I guess so," Victor said. "The hallways get crowded between classes and she's pretty small. It'll be more difficult."

Dr. Green's fingers at his forehead stopped. "I think we can make it easier. Can you bring your phone to me tomorrow?" he asked me. "We'll program it so you can reach us quickly. If something happens and we're not around, push a button and we'll find you."

I nodded. "I can do that."

Dr. Green smiled in a satisfied way. "Maybe we'll get lucky and things will settle down soon. If that happens, I don't see a problem with any of you hanging out together in school."

Victor darted his fire eyes away, looking out in the distance. Gabriel's lips were pursed, his crystal eyes dark. Luke was frowning. None of them seemed happy with this solution, but they didn't seem to have a better one.

"Well, here's what we've got for the uniforms," Gabriel said. He flipped over his notebook until it was pointed in our direction. There were a couple of styles put together in a quick sketch. The dark gray pants and dark shoes, white shirts and red ties would be quick enough to locate at the store. There were blazers in a dark blue. In the corner was a badge with wings, an A in the middle, with a key and an arrow below it. "It's probably generic but looks official, right?"

The others nodded. Victor made a comment in the positive that I didn't hear well.

I squinted at the badge. "Is that a heart?"

Gabriel lifted his eyebrows, taking his notebook back to look over his work. "What do you mean? What heart?"

"Let me see," I said. He flipped the notebook back at me. I took the pen from his hand and I scratched out two small embellishments to the bottom of his A just to show where I was seeing the heart at.

Gabriel smirked when I showed him. "Well hell," he said. "Random."

"A hidden heart," Luke said. He looked up at me, grinning. "Sang found it."

I blushed. Gabriel read enough of my poem and told Luke. Victor looked confused. Gabriel shot him a look that I understood. He'd tell him about it later.

Dr. Green's eyes focused on me so intently that I felt the air escape my lungs. He remained quiet, and I had no idea how to ask him if there was something wrong or if I did something silly. Maybe I was being too distracting.

From across the schoolyard, Silas, North, Kota, and Nathan appeared and headed for us.

"We're done," North said. He hopped up on the bench next to me, and leaned on the seat behind him to prop up on his elbows. The others sat on the benches again.

"Mr. Blackbourne's in the office now fixing the detentions," Kota said. "He's explaining to Hendricks that the school board won't like to see detentions on our records."

"What about Sang?" Victor asked. "What about her record?"

Kota frowned. "Well we can't ask special permission for her without making it look like she's with us, right? They already assume she's with us. We don't want to sway their judgment."

So they were still not outright saying I wasn't a part of their group. Why not? Wouldn't that be the fastest solution? "I don't mind," I said. "It's just one detention."

Dr. Green moved his hands behind his back. "Okay guys," he said. He glowered at us but his eyes held a glint of humor. "Do you think you've learned your lesson and won't misbehave in class again?"

They all diverted their eyes to me. I almost choked. "I didn't... I don't... I told you guys..."

They all laughed, including Dr. Green. "Sounds good to me," he said and winked at me. "Time to go home. Do your homework. Eat your vegetables. Get some good sleep. I'll go save Mr. Blackbourne before he ends up with detention from Mr. Hendricks."

I bent over to collect my things, but Kota picked up my violin case and Silas hefted my book bag on his back. I swallowed my protest. They still didn't know yet about how I needed to keep my distance while at school. For the moment, since everyone was mostly gone, I supposed it didn't matter. Gabriel caught me by the neck to tug me toward the parking lot. I looked back at Dr. Green, who was watching after us, that same soft and reassuring smile on his lips. It was like he didn't expect anything less of his own students.

How strange it felt now. I wasn't part of the Academy, but I was part of their plan. It amazed me how the others could focus on anything like school work when they had so many other things to worry about. How would I focus on another math assignment without thinking of the boys getting ready to get into fights and my own need to stay out of trouble? It was hard enough keeping an eye out for McCoy.

A tingling sensation swept through me. This was more than another day at high school. I was part of something so much bigger. Maybe what the Academy students did wasn't what other students did. The work was important. It excited me. Maybe I should have been afraid. Maybe any other girl would have bowed out rather than dealt with a mean vice-principal. Maybe most girls would have given up and left the guys entirely.

Maybe I was never meant to be normal.

$\mathcal{B}$AIT

*V*ictor, Luke and Gabriel needed to head out to get started on the uniforms, so they left in Victor's car together. I followed the others to a black Jeep Wrangler parked in the lot. North fished keys out of his pocket, hitting a button to unlock the doors. I wondered where North got so many vehicles. Maybe it was one of those necessities that the Academy provided. If so, why didn't Nathan have a car? What about Gabriel? Or did they have cars and I hadn't seen those yet?

Kota and the others piled our bags in the back. Nathan held open the rear side door, stepping back to look at me. I slid into the middle, with Kota and Nathan beside me. North started the car and Silas sat down in the passenger side next to him.

"Where are we going?" North asked as he started to back out of his spot. Instead of using the rearview mirror, he put a palm on Silas's seat and half-twisted to look out the back window. I ducked my head in case he was having trouble seeing. He grinned back at me. "Stop it, short stuff," he said. "If I need you to move, I'll tell you."

Nathan leaned against me in the seat as he pulled off the long sleeve shirt he was still wearing. "I am done," he said. "I'm going home for a hot shower and I'm going to sleep."

"Do your homework first," North said.

Nathan grumbled. He sat back in his seat, tossing the shirt at the floor. He wrapped an arm around my shoulders. My nose filled with the scent of cypress. My cheeks started to heat up again. Did it mean he liked me? No one else seemed to notice. I wasn't going to complain.

Kota was sitting so close, his leg was touching mine. He punched something into his phone. "First we have to make sure Sang isn't in trouble."

"Agreed," North said. He flicked his eyes to this rearview mirror as he pulled out into the lot. He caught my eye. "Can you go in the back door or roof or what?"

"No roof," Kota said. "Besides, it's broad daylight. They might not notice you monkeys at night but they'll for sure see you now."

"The side door should be fine," I said. "There's a chance no one's noticed I've been gone. Marie is the one I have to watch out for. If I'm lucky she went off to Danielle's right after school. If that's the case, I think we're good." And if that wasn't true, I'd end up on my knees or something similar again. Manageable as long as she never found out why I arrived late.

North hit the buttons on the dashboard and turned up the radio to some rock music. "Just say the word," he said. He glanced at Silas. "You want to be dropped off first?"

"I'll tag along," Silas said.

Now that we weren't on a bus, the drive to Sunnyvale Court was much shorter. North pulled into Kota's driveway. When Nathan hopped out, he held the door open for me. I climbed out and he shut the door and stretched. "Want me to walk with you?" Nathan asked.

"Nathan," I said. "Will you please go home and sleep? Let's just get through Friday and we'll all relax this weekend."

"You're getting as bad as Kota," he said.

"Hey," Kota said, but he smirked as he crossed his arms over his chest.

Nathan pulled his bag out of the back and hobbled down the road to his house.

"I'll walk Sang home," Silas said.

"I'll go," North said.

"We're going inside and starting homework," Kota said. "Sang goes home by herself. If her mom is watching out for her, the last thing she needs is to show up with someone."

Kota picked up my violin case for me. I put my book bag over my shoulder and took the case from him. He tucked his head closer to mine. "Call if you can't come out. If you can though, run back. We've got stuff to go over. Bring your homework."

"Yes, sir," I said, offering a short salute.

Silas and North laughed behind him.

Kota smirked. He stretched his arms around me, hugging me to him. "Be careful, will you?"

I hurried up the road, steeling myself against what might be waiting for me. I might need to go grab my phone and put it in my pocket before I faced off downstairs. If I ended up on my knees again, I'd need to reach Kota so he didn't worry. I crossed my fingers that I hadn't been missed.

When I got home, I opened the side door quietly and stood in the doorway to listen. The house was silent. I crept up the back staircase and padded down the hallway to my bedroom.

My door was open. I paused in the hallway, listening. There was a creak of the floor in my bedroom. I quietly slipped into the bathroom across the hall to hide myself, closing the door.

Inside the bathroom, I dropped my things into the tub to hide them. I checked myself in the mirror, rinsed my face with water and patted my cheeks dry. If it was my mother, I'd have the excuse that I was fresh from the bathroom. If it was Marie, I wasn't sure what would happen. I opened the door and tried to appear relaxed.

I stepped across the hall to peek through my open door at an angle. Marie was in there, her head and shoulders leaning into my closet.

"Need something?" I asked, trying to sound casual. I was peeved that she was digging through my things, but there were more important things to worry about at the moment.

Marie half jumped but when she spotted me, she frowned. "Where have you been?"

"A teacher held me back in class so long that I missed

the bus." Technically this was true.

Marie raised an eyebrow. "It's like five miles away."

"Yes." I realized I left her with the impression I'd walked home, but I didn't have another answer that was better. I was getting as bad as the guys, like how they let Hendricks and McCoy think I was from the Academy.

Marie seemed to consider this. "I was looking for clothes. Mine are all dirty."

"There's a washing machine downstairs."

"There's this one shirt I was looking for," she said. "A green one with buttons."

I thought about it. "That old thing? It's in my trunk. It doesn't fit me anymore."

Marie turned from the closet and headed to my trunk. I went back to the bathroom to grab my things. She might have believed me about the walk home, but I couldn't leave if she was still lingering in my room.

I returned to drop my book bag and the violin case on my bed while she spilled clothes out of the trunk, fingering around the clothes for the one she wanted. She pulled the green shirt out and held it up. She bent over to strip her t-shirt off in front of me. I turned, avoiding watching to give her some semblance of privacy even if she disregarded modesty around me. She slipped on the green shirt. The hem grazed her belly button and the sleeves were tight at her shoulders.

"It doesn't fit," I said. I noted the mess she left on the floor but didn't say anything. It wasn't the time for that fight.

"It does," she said. She smoothed out the fabric and stood up. "Are you going to that boy's house?"

I blinked at her. That was an opening line for negotiation. She wanted something so she was going to see if I was willing to play along. "Were you going to Danielle's?"

She nodded. Her brown eyes narrowed at me. "Mom's passed out still," she said. "I've been waiting for you to show up. If we're going to go out, we need a system."

"I agree." This was perfect. This was what we've needed to go over.

"Make sure the side door and the back door by the porch are unlocked all the time," she said. "Dad locks it at night. Check my room. If I'm not back at night, unlock it when he's clear. I'm thinking I might spend the weekend over there."

The entire weekend? She was crazy. Even I knew better. "You should show up on occasion," I said. "If you pop in and check on her, she's less likely to call after you during the day. Do it once and you should be good for the night." I thought about mentioning the roof but I didn't want to reveal that just now. Besides, unless someone was helping her, she might fall off. "Is there a house key somewhere around here?"

"Mom keeps one in her side table drawer."

I nodded, kicking my sandals off and putting them aside. "I'm going to get it. I'll make a copy. Do you have any money?"

Marie fished in her pocket and pulled out a ten dollar bill and slowly handed it off. "How are you making a copy?"

"I think I can ask Kota to make one. It'll be missing for the day. Cross your fingers that she won't notice," I said. I took the money from her, knowing this little amount was probably everything she had. We rarely got money. How would we spend it since we didn't go anywhere? "I'll see if I can get two and I'll bring you back change. If not, it'll be just one and we'll hide it in the garage or something."

Marie nodded.

I tilted my head toward the hallway. "Get out the door. I'll give you a head start before I go to mom's room. If I wake her up by accident, I'll tell her I saw you going for a walk or something."

Marie slipped off down the hallway and to the back stairs. I waited until I heard the side door shut. As long as Marie didn't get caught at anything, she didn't have a reason to tattle on me. However, even with a plan for a copy of a key and a new alliance, I had to be extra careful now. If she got caught, she had more evidence to take me down with her.

I quieted my thoughts to focus, listening to the empty

house. I probably should have sent a text to Kota, but I wanted to get that key and get out quickly. I grabbed the phone, stuffing it into the cup of my bra. I was going to take a big risk. For prisoners like us, a key would be like gold.

I used the back stairs, taking the long way across the house. I slipped past the kitchen and as soon as I was within earshot of my parents' bedroom, I started to creep along the edge of the hallway. From outside her open door, I peered in.

She was on her back, her mouth hanging open. Her hair was matted in the low ponytail at her neck. She breathed steadily. Her television was off. This would be trickier. I had no cover noise to mask me now.

I started by getting on my knees and crawling to the foot of her bed. It was a slow process as I didn't know her floor well enough to know where it creaked. I touched the surface of the beige carpet with my palm, putting pressure on it. When it felt like it wouldn't make a noise, I stretched a foot out to place next to my palm, in a crab walk motion. At the foot of her bed, I stretched out to see around the edge.

Her nightstand drawer was closed. The top of it was covered in a collection of orange prescription bottles, bottled water, and random notes she wrote to herself about doctor appointments. I swallowed and listened to her breathing. I counted off to three in my head to pressure myself into moving. I crawled closer, ducking my head low and pressing myself against the side of the bed and out of view as much as possible.

When I was close enough, I situated myself on my back so I could look at the underneath of the drawer. Drawer opening was complicated. There were only rare occasions that I ever needed to sneak into my parents' bedroom for things while they were there. Usually it was for money my sister and I needed for school and our parents had told us no. Most of the time it was Marie that needed it and I went to fetch it. I knew if they found out I was stealing a house key, there wouldn't be a reasonable excuse I could make up. They would know for certain I would be using it to sneak out of the house at late hours. On my back, I could look up at the drawer. I used my palms to press gently on either side. I waited, listened for my mom's breathing and tried sliding it out.

The slip of wood against wood squeaked through the silence. I froze, holding my breath.

When nothing happened, I tried again. It was a tricky balancing act. I couldn't let the wood rest on the rail of the drawer to pull it out and I couldn't lift too high to allow the wood to scrape against the top of the table. This time I did it slowly, and while my hands shook, I managed to half open the drawer without another sound.

I wanted to sigh, but held it in to keep the sound minimal. I slipped out from under the drawer and got on my knees. My eyes fell on my mom's face and her closed eyes. I wished she was breathing louder or even snoring right now. Snoring was good. It meant a deeper sleep.

The open drawer was in shadow, and at first there wasn't a sign of a key, only more orange prescription bottles and a packet of tissues and old batteries. I cursed to myself, wondering if Marie might have been mistaken and there might not have been a key here at all.

I started emptying the contents. It was always better to lift than to move things over. If I had been looking for prescription pills, I would have had an easier time. The empty ones I could easily place on the carpet. The ones with pills still inside required slow movements and careful placement.

The process was tedious. After the sixteenth bottle, I was about to give up and put it all back when I spotted the edge of teeth belonging to a silver house key closer to the back. I would have to empty out her entire drawer to get to it.

Something creaked in the house and there was whoosh of the air conditioner starting up. It spooked me so badly that I nearly dropped the half full bottle of pills I was holding. I grasped the bottle in my hands, trying to deaden the sound and held my breath.

My mother didn't stir. With the noise from the air conditioner, I couldn't hear her breathing, but I caught the way her chest moved, slight but steady.

I knew the air conditioner would run for a couple of minutes before shutting off again. I took advantage of the extra white noise and quickly pulled out enough bottles that I could ease my hand in and pick up the key. I slipped the key between my lips, tasting the sharp metal on my tongue. I managed to get all the bottles in and get on my back again to close the drawer before the air conditioner shut off.

I crawled back. In my hurry to escape, I accidentally stepped in a spot that squeaked. I froze, bending down on the floor farther and out of sight from the head of the bed.

My mother stirred. My heart thumped wildly and I held my breath again, hoping she was just turning over.

"Sang," my mother called out. "Sang!"

I paused, counting off the amount of seconds I suspected it would take me to come down the stairs if she called for me. I blew out a slow breath, forcing myself to calm and I stood up quickly, taking a large leap backward so I was closer to the door.

My mother was on her back with her eyes closed. I pushed a palm to my chest. I clasped the key in my other hand, tucking it behind my back. "Yes?" I said softly. I was hoping she had fallen asleep again.

My mother's eyelids dragged up. Her eyes focused on me. "Is your sister home?"

"Yes," I said.

"Is your room clean?"

I tried to hide my smile. "Almost."

"Don't leave your room until it's done."

I ran from her bedroom, and up the front stairs. I dumped books from my bag I didn't need, recollected the ones I had homework for and replaced my bag on my shoulders. I was shaking but my mother didn't call out again for Marie or for anything else.

I slipped out the back door and sprinted for Kota's.

I hit the doorbell at the door inside Kota's garage. I stood back to wait and was surprised to see Silas answer. His broad smile lit up as he saw me.

"Hey," he said. "You made it."

I nodded, smiling back to suppress my nervousness. I was so happy to see him, even though I'd seen him less than an hour ago. After sneaking around my mother's room and almost getting caught, I was on edge.

He stepped out of the way so I could get in. He closed the door and nudged me toward Kota's bedroom. I thudded my way up the stairs and he followed, closing Kota's door behind us and hitting the lock.

When I got to the top of the stairs, Kota looked over from his desk. He flashed a smile at me. North appeared half asleep on Kota's bed, the pillow stuffed between his arm and his forehead. I felt a wash of comfort being in the cozy security of this bedroom. The grave difference between my parents' house, where I walked on eggshells and kept secret diaries in code and didn't see my family for long periods of time, compared to Kota, North and the others made my heart trip. Why couldn't I feel this safe and wanted all the time?

"I was worried something happened," Kota said. He pushed his glasses up his nose.

"Got caught up," I said. I dropped my bag and pulled the key from its side pocket. "Do you know where I can get a key made?"

North yawned and turned, holding out a hand out for it. "What's it for?"

I crossed the room and placed it in his palm. "It's the house key." I pulled out the ten that Marie gave me and held it to him. "Marie wants a copy. I should get one, too. I didn't want to tell her about the roof thing."

Silas chuckled behind me. "She's getting as bad as you."

I held out the ten for North but he waved me off, shoving the key into his pocket. "When do you need it back?" he asked.

"It can wait overnight," I said. I crumpled the ten dollars at him and tossed it at his chest. "And you're not making keys out of thin air so I know it'll cost something to make."

He caught the bill and then tossed it back at my head. "Hang on to it. You might need it later. I can get you some damn keys."

I mustered up a glare for him and he glowered right back. My blood pumped in my veins. They had no idea what I'd had to go through to get that key and I was feeling clever and alive and in no need for charity. North was unrelenting

Silas grabbed my shoulders, pulling me back into him. "Easy, *aggele mou*," he said.

I sighed, stuffing the money into my palm.

"Was this part of the negotiations?" Kota asked me.

I nodded, pulling away from Silas to kneel on the floor. "As long as she doesn't slip up and get into trouble, it should be fine. Today wasn't a problem unless the school ends up calling."

"I think Mr. Blackbourne took care of that," Kota said.

Could Mr. Blackbourne do that for me without getting attention from Mr. Hendricks or Mr. McCoy?

Silas sat cross-legged on the floor next to me and leaned back on his hands. "What now?"

Kota touched a finger to the bridge of his glasses. "Unless we hear from Victor or the others, we get ready for Friday."

Silas nudged my arm. "Are you going to make something for tomorrow for lunch?"

I sucked in a breath, realizing they didn't know Dr. Green's plan yet. "I can make something," I said. "But I won't be around at lunch time. Dr. Green wants me to back off from hanging around you guys on campus."

North's eyes popped open. "What?"

I swallowed, glancing at Kota's curious face and over at Silas's. "Dr. Green wants to see if Mr. McCoy is going to come after me if I'm alone."

"No fucking way," North said. He glared at Kota. "He can't ask her to do that."

Kota frowned. He drew away from his computer desk to come sit on the floor across from me. "What did he say exactly?"

Silas's hand traced my back, warming and supportive. "He had to have a reason," he said.

I nodded. "A few things. He wants to draw out McCoy and see if he's interested in just trying to one up me because of what happened at registration or if this was a thing against you guys because he doesn't like you being there or something else. If I'm not hanging out with you guys, maybe McCoy might back off if he thinks I'm not as close to you all as he thought."

North's dark eyes flared, but he pressed his lips together.

Kota nodded to me. "What else?" he asked.

"There's the thing about the uniforms," I said. "He wants an adjustment period. If I'm walking next to you all the time, other students are going to assume I'm part of the same thing and I'll be another target. He wants me to back off until things settle down and the students get used to them."

"He wants her out of the way so we can do our job," North grumbled. He fell back onto the bed and rubbed a palm against his eye. "Christ, she's been the target all week and he wants us to back off."

"I don't think that's what he meant," Kota said.

"Fuck that shit," North barked at him. He sat up, swinging his legs over to put his feet on the carpet. "He's fucking using her as bait."

My heart thudded. This wasn't the reaction I was expecting. Victor and the others seemed better able to handle it. Maybe I should have made Dr. Green explain it to them.

Silas kept a quiet hand on my back, rubbing gently between my shoulder blades. I sensed he was waiting for North and Kota to make a decision.

"She's not bait," Kota said. "We'll be there. She can be nearby without it looking like she's right next to us. We're supposed to be the targets, not her, remember?"

"You've seen those monsters," North said. "She can't walk a few dozen feet away from us before they're on her. It's either Mike proposing to her, or that vice-principal, or fucking Greg feeling her up in the hallway."

Kota's eyes bulged open. "Greg?" He fired off a look at me. "Mall Greg? He goes to this school?"

I pushed a finger to my lower lip and nodded.

Silas grunted.

Kota fell back onto his butt. He took his glasses off, placing them up on his head and pressed both palms to his eyes. "Why didn't anyone tell us?"

"There's a lot going on," North said, seeming calmer now that everyone else was realizing the full impact he was trying to stress. He pulled from his pocket folded notes and tossed them at us on the floor. "I don't know what it is, but they're all crazy for her. You'd think she was the only girl at this school. I think the only thing holding them back from Sang is us. If we back off, there's no telling what they'll do."

"Maybe Dr. Green is right though," I said. "Maybe it's like Hendricks thinking I'm with your group. The others are only interested in me because of you all. Dr. Green wanted to set my phone up so I could reach you quickly if I need, and it won't be for forever. It's just until they check out McCoy and make sure you guys aren't getting into fights over uniforms."

"She might be right," Silas said. "McCoy's hot for her right now but it might be because he thinks she's the one that Blackbourne let slip in with us. If she can separate herself from us, they might turn their attention directly on us instead of her."

"I'm not leaving her alone," North said.

"I didn't say leave her alone," Silas replied. "We're still all in the same classes. I can keep an eye on her from across the classroom and walk behind her for a few weeks. We're still right there if something happens."

"What were we going to do if something did happen and she's around? That last fight started with us. What about the next one?" Kota asked. He pulled himself together, putting his glasses back on. The serene calmness of Kota was back. "Dr. Green is right. Are we going to be the hunted or the hunters? We need to focus on paying attention to the students. Mike seems harmless enough and the notes... well she can ignore those."

North frowned. "I'm worried about the attention she'll get when other students realize we're no longer watching over her. What if we get caught up and she's alone?"

"We'll train her," Silas said. He gazed down at me as his hand drifted up and held steady on my neck. "I've been meaning to do that, anyway."

My cheeks heated at his dark eyes full of concern.

"That'll work," Kota said, nodding. He glanced at me. "Can you make it out this weekend?"

"I can try."

"We'll take time for some self-defense lessons," Kota said. "We've got a busy weekend."

I fingered the folded notes on the ground. Some had my name spelled wrong. What could anyone possibly want with me? Right now, it seemed so trivial. I was with a group who were about to put themselves in one of the worst possible positions so they could save the students who got picked on and beaten up. They were working together to make the school safer. What were these other boys doing? Hiding behind a piece of paper.

Maybe over the years I would have gladly accepted such attention, but with the Academy changing my life, notes seemed so weak. I collected the notes and clutched them in my hands, crumpling the papers between my fingers. I passed them off to Kota dismissively. I may have been shy and could understand where the writers were coming from, but I didn't have time right now to play that game. "Maybe we should get homework out of the way," I said.

Kota took the notes and tossed them into the trash. North's eyes lit up. Silas's hand pressed lightly into my neck and he pulled me close to whisper in my ear, "Good girl."

♥

FRIDAY

♥

ALONE

I dreamed I was in a building, urging others around me to run. There was a bomb about to blow that would injure everyone. No one listened. The explosive detonated.

*T*he alarm woke me from a dead sleep the next morning. I stumbled around half awake to get ready. My muscles were stiff. I was more sore at that moment than I had been the day before. It was tempting to fall back into bed, but I forced myself to get up. Again, it was the thought of the guys needing my help today that got me moving.

I picked out a modest gray A-line skirt and put on Luke's blue button-up shirt that I had washed. If I was going to be alone today, I wanted to at least wear something that belonged to the boys. It felt important to me. I made sure to use a clip to put my hair up and out of my face. I didn't need to stand out with my hair down today.

I pulled out a textbook I wouldn't need for class and some paperwork that I didn't need any more, lightening the load. I left the bundle on the bed. My room was still a mess from Marie's meddling the other day, but I promised myself I'd clean it later when I got the chance. I just wanted to make it through Friday and finish this week.

I started out into the hallway at the same time Marie did. She wore her usual t-shirt and jeans. Her book bag looked like it carried only a couple of textbooks compared to my very full bag.

"Are you still going to... um, this weekend?" I asked, trying to keep my voice down. When I had gotten in last night, my mother was still dead asleep but that didn't mean she would stay that way. She could be listening to our conversation.

Marie nodded. "Do you have the key?"

"Come find me at lunch," I said. "Or wait until we're on the bus this afternoon. You'll have it then." I pulled out the ten dollars that I had kept for her and handed it over. "They're taking care of it. Keep the money."

She seemed relieved and pocketed the bill. "You'll be at that boy's house?"

"I should be," I said. "I'll try to pop in here. Don't forget to show up every once in a while."

She gave me a dismissive nod and headed down the stairs. I couldn't make her take my suggestion and I had a feeling she'd probably ignore it altogether. It was her risk to take. We were both taking big risks but maybe we had gotten used to getting put on our knees or sitting on hard stools for hours on end for things as ridiculous as a boy coming to the door and asking to play or for a bad grade. What could be worse? Take the punishment and move on. That's all we could do. Even with kneeling in rice, even with the lemon and vinegar and that I had experienced and she hadn't yet, it was still very much a possibility we could both have that happen to us again.

The guys were worth it.

We walked the distance to Kota's house. Marie immediately went to stand on the other side of the driveway.

Kota and Nathan were there waiting for me. They wore matching dark gray trousers, white button-up shirts and the blue blazers, almost identical to the sketches that Gabriel and Luke had put together. Nathan's shirt was unbuttoned all the way, revealing the white t-shirt underneath. Kota wore a red tie, shirt buttoned formally. Even wearing the same things, they still varied slightly to their personality.

The sight of them had me feeling better. It had been the longest week of school I had ever had to deal with and I was sure they felt the same after the craziness that happened. No wonder Gabriel and the others seemed to miss the Academy so much. I couldn't imagine doing this all year when something so much better was out there.

"Ready for this?" Nathan asked as I approached. He stuffed his hands into the pockets of his slacks. He looked a little better today. While he still had bruises, his eyes were alert and he stood straighter.

I nodded, dropping my bag and violin on the ground at my feet. "Let's hope today is quiet."

"Did you bring your phone?" Kota asked.

I glanced over at Marie, who was turned away and looking at Danielle and Derrick coming down the road. Nathan caught my gaze and he stepped in the way to provide a barrier. I reached into my bag for the phone, showing it to Kota.

"You don't have a pocket?" Kota asked. "You should keep it close."

I didn't think about that. I pursed my lips and then slipped the phone into the cup of my bra against my heart. I was blushing as I did it, as it felt almost like I was exposing something of myself even though they couldn't see anything. When it was in place, it was unnoticeable.

"Holy shit," Nathan said as he watched the phone disappear. "We need... no wait, I didn't say that."

Kota laughed. He reached out to plop a palm on my head and rub. "Girls do have a few tricks."

The embroidery on the pocket of the blazer caught my eye. I smoothed my fingers over Kota's patch. The two marks I had made on Gabriel's sketch were in place. I traced my finger over it.

Kota's eyes sought out mine. "What?" he asked.

"The hidden heart," I said. "He kept it."

He beamed. "Yeah."

"It's not too girly?" I asked. I shifted my eyes between Kota and Nathan.

Nathan shook his head. "Don't really care what anyone else thinks."

My heart continued to melt. "Can we still sit on the bus together?" I asked.

Kota nodded. "It should be okay. We'll let you get off the bus first, though. We'll follow you to Dr. Green's office and will wait in the hall."

The bus appeared around the bend. I picked up my book bag and Kota snatched up my violin for me. I shot him a look, but he didn't seem to notice. Maybe this had become a new habit. My heart warmed at the thought of it.

On the bus, I slid in next to Kota and his arm went around me. Nathan fell in on the other side, his palm seeking out mine to hold. I'd grown accustomed to their touches this week, they did it so often. This felt different, almost defiant.

Kota's fingers clutched my shoulder. Nathan's palm warmed mine. They were on this bus because of me. Marie wouldn't do the same if she had another opportunity to get to school. The boys and I were a team. Maybe over time, I'd accept it as easily as they seemed to do with each other every day.

I dreaded getting to school. It meant they would have to pull away and I would be without them for an entire day, at a place where I had thought I'd be able to have free access to them without the overhanging fear of my mother's wrath. Now that I knew how warming and addicting touching could be, I regretted agreeing to Dr. Green's plan so quickly.

When the bus pulled into the school lot, we waited until most of the kids had gotten off the bus. Nathan stood and backed up so I could get out. This time I did take my violin case and my book bag.

Off of the bus, I started out alone. I sensed Nathan and Kota behind me, at a distance but still within eyesight. Hunters and the hunted.

The hallways buzzed with activity. The majority of students hadn't arrived yet. I headed straight to the main office. The secretary at the desk gave me an eyeball, confused as to why I was there. I asked her for Dr. Green's office as I didn't want to assume I could go beyond the doors without permission. I took her directions and went down a hallway and knocked at the closed, unmarked door.

The door opened and Mr. Blackbourne's face appeared

in the doorway. His steel eyes looked over me once and he opened the door wider for me to enter. When I was inside, he closed the door and turned to me.

"Miss Sorenson," he said, nodding to me in greeting.

"Mr. Blackbourne," I replied.

Dr. Green was at his desk. His eyes lit up at seeing me. "Good morning," he said. "Did you bring your phone?"

My face started to heat up when I realized I should probably have taken it out of my bra before I entered. Unable to find a reason to leave and come back, I put down my things by the edge of his desk and reached in for it quickly, holding it out to him.

Mr. Blackbourne's eyes narrowed for a moment at me. "Could you find a more inconspicuous place to put it?"

"I needed one that was close by without being obvious," I said quietly. "I should only need it for an emergency. I won't use it otherwise."

His face softened. He seemed pleased with this.

Dr. Green pulled a laptop from his bag and he hooked it up to my phone. A loading bar popped up on the laptop screen. "Give this a minute," he said.

I stood uncomfortably in their office, unsure of what to say. I wished Kota or one of the others was there to intervene.

Mr. Blackbourne leaned against his desk, his arms folded across his chest. He gazed down at me. "I understand you'll be separating yourself from the boys today," he said.

I nodded. "I'll do what needs to be done."

"If Principal Hendricks or Mr. McCoy talks to you, have all questions redirected to me." He nodded to Dr. Green and the phone he was holding. "You'll be getting our numbers. I expect a call if they approach you at any time. Try to remember exactly what they ask you. I'll want to know everything."

"I understand."

"And come find me if some of the students are being a little too unkind," Dr. Green said. He unplugged my phone and pushed a button on the touch screen. He curled a finger at me to indicate that I should step closer. I hovered over him so he could show me the screen. "These apps reach each of us. Can you guess which ones?"

The phone screen had nine different apps added. It was obvious to me which ones belonged to who and I pointed them out. "The baseball is Silas, the violin, Mr. Blackbourne, music notes for Victor, the calculator for Kota, the paint brush for Gabriel, the hand weight for Nathan, Luke's pancakes, North's black car, and the Japanese word there is for you."

Dr. Green brightened. He poked a forefinger at my head in a tease. "I would have given you bonus points if you could have told me what the word means."

"What does it mean?"

"When you figure it out, I'll give you those points." He punched a finger at his icon on my phone and the application opened to reveal a panel of four different square buttons in the middle. "All you have to do is hit one of these. Red is emergency and it'll send me a text message with your approximate location. Green places a call that will cut you through an emergency line so even if my phone is on silent or if I'm on the line, it'll send your phone call through instantly. White is a quick text message that's not for a real emergency but that you're feeling uncomfortable and could use some help. The big black one will dial our numbers without using the emergency service." He closed the app and passed the phone to me. "I suppose I shouldn't have to tell you that those emergency buttons should be used very sparingly."

I nodded, nervous now that the phone could do something like that. I made sure to turn the screen off before putting it back into place in my bra. I didn't want to hit one accidentally. "What about the boys? Could they reach me?"

Dr. Green smiled softly. "I haven't added you. I don't think they'll be calling you in an emergency."

That was probably true, but it was disappointing. I liked to think I could help in some small way. I smiled at him and collected my things from the floor.

"Where are you going?" Dr. Green asked, looking curious.

"Kota and Nathan are waiting outside for me. I'm supposed to walk around the building a few times and find a place in the courtyard opposite of where they're sitting."

Mr. Blackbourne shook his head. "You should try talking to other people."

"I'm just trying to get through Friday without any more incidents," I said.

The corner of Mr. Blackbourne's mouth dipped. "Are you sure you can handle this?"

"I've managed this far," I promised.

That didn't seem to be the answer he was hoping for, but he nodded shortly at me. "Call if you need anything," he said. He opened the door for me.

I stepped out into the hallway, my heart pounding. The moment the door was closed behind me, it felt like the end. My hand fluttered to the base of my neck. I straightened and moved forward. Kota and the others would be nearby, I kept telling myself. I needed to think calmly and be aware of others and keep my head down.

Out in the hallway, I flitted my eyes around at the many faces but Kota and Nathan had disappeared into the crowd. I waited only for a moment to make sure they had noticed I was out. I picked a direction and headed through the throng of students.

I kept my eyes straight ahead, not looking right or left to avoid attention. I walked at a slower pace, too. I took a loop through the main hallway, and proceeded through side doors that lead down another hall toward the cafeteria. Chattering filled my ears. Was that my name being spoken? Were they watching me walking alone? Did they think something was out of place? Did anyone care at all?

The cafeteria was busy. The tables were full and I weaved my way through them. A couple of whistles sounded. I felt my heart racing, hoping they weren't aimed at me. I ignored it and no one stopped me. I did my best to look as if I was heading to somewhere specific and didn't have time to bother with them. At certain points I was worried I might lose Kota and Nathan as I was surrounded by people.

I made the turn around again to the main hallway and opened the door to the courtyard. I caught sight of Victor and Gabriel in the corner. I felt their gazes on me as I turned in the opposite direction toward a bench on the other side of the courtyard.

A thin boy with bad acne sat on one end, his head buried in a book, trying to look as small and inconspicuous as I was trying to go for. Perfect, I thought. It was where I would belong. The no-name, nobody-special spot.

I plopped my things down at the foot of the bench and pulled out the book we were supposed to be reading for English. I tried to appear focused on it but I couldn't help but glance up on occasion. I could easily see Kota and the others across the courtyard. I tried not to stare and draw attention.

I recognized a handful of the people that hung around the courtyard. There were some gamer geeks on the next bench over. The conversation revolved around Halo and other video games and some talk about weekend plans. There were a couple of hippy groups sitting together in the grass. For the most part they were quiet. One of the boys had his head in a girl's lap and appeared to be asleep.

Surprisingly, I felt jealous. I would give anything in that moment to feel the boys next to me. I missed Kota's lap, Gabriel's chop, and the others holding my hand and touching me. The morning bell seemed to take forever. I wanted to get into class, thinking the time would move by faster if I was busy with school work.

When the bell finally rang, I picked up my things and made a beeline for homeroom. Kota had made it clear to me that between classes, I was to do nothing but head straight to my next stop. The others would do the work of keeping up with me.

I blended into the crowd in the hallway. There was the usual amount of whistling and cat calls and random shouts. I ignored it all. At one point, the hallways were so crowded that I was forced to stop and wait as people sorted themselves out. I paused apprehensively, keeping an eye on the moods of everyone around me. Was this guy angry? Would that guy start picking on me? Was Mr. McCoy hiding around the corner and waiting for me to mess up?

In homeroom, I felt a little awkward for not picking the same spot I'd sat in all week next to the door with North and Luke. I picked another desk near the back. I kept my eyes on the door as others filed in. My heart lifted a little as North and Luke entered. They dropped into their seats and North pushed his bag into the middle seat between them. I hid my grin, wondering why he was saving my seat when I wouldn't be near them for a while. It was like some small amount of protest or like they wouldn't let anyone else sit there if I couldn't. Neither of them looked at me, but I felt so much better now that I could actually see them.

I admired how they looked in their new uniforms. North's blue blazer looked out of place on him since I was so used to his black clothes. The tie, however, looked striking on him. Luke's white shirt was half unbuttoned, no tie. His blond hair was tucked behind his head in my clip. They were always well dressed, but seeing them in the uniforms had my heart pounding. They were gorgeous.

Greg slipped into the classroom at the last minute. His eyes fell on the empty seat between North and Luke. He spotted me at the back. He flashed a grin. I tried to look bored and bent over to pretend to dig in my book bag for something.

"Hey there, Sang," Greg said. He snapped his fingers at the girl sitting to my left. She flinched. He jerked his thumb at her. "Move over there, bitch, that's my seat."

I shot the girl a sympathetic look, silently pleading with her to refuse. She frowned but moved to a seat closer to the front.

Greg slid into the chair and hung over the edge of it. He didn't have any books or notebooks with him. The scent of menthol cigarettes lingered like a cloud around him. "So did you break up with your boyfriends?" he asked.

I kept my lips glued together. I pulled a notebook and a

pen out of my bag and started writing random things just to appear busy.

"Hey," Greg said in a strong whisper as the teacher started calling roll. "Sang. Are you going to go out with me or what?"

I focused on the notebook.

"You mad at me?" he asked. "Am I not nice enough for you?"

I glanced up at Mr. Ferguson, watching his jowls wobble as he tripped over names. It was an excuse to slide a side glance at North, who was looking in our direction. His expression was stony, but I knew he was just waiting for me to tell him when he should intervene. I gave the slightest shake of my head to tell him to calm down. I could handle Greg.

Greg leaned over the front of his desk and he poked the guy in front of him. "Psst," he said. "Yo. Give me that."

I couldn't see what he was demanding but a moment later the guy in front of him handed back a brand new number two pencil. Greg snatched it from the guy and held it out for me in front of my face.

"Look," he said. "I got you a gift."

"You've got a stolen pencil," I said quietly. I had to back my head up as the pencil was right in front of my face. "I don't want it."

"Unappreciative bitch," he spat at me. His mouth twisted into a grin. "You playing hard to get, right? I like it. I like fighting for my girl."

I rolled my eyes, put my notebook away and sat back in my chair, crossing my arms over my chest, ready to stare ahead until he stopped talking.

Another one of the guys caught Greg's attention and he leaned over his chair on the other side to talk to him. I was grateful he had a distraction. I couldn't help but overhear the conversation.

"Yo," the guy said to Greg. "Friday Fall."

"I know, it's going to be sweet. We picked anyone out yet?" Greg asked. "My girlfriend and I are gonna be there to watch." He jerked his head in my direction.

I rolled my eyes.

"When is it?" The guy asked, seeming dismissive of me.

"Wait for the signal," Greg said.

What was Friday Fall? Some kind of school event?

Their conversation turned to what they were going to do that weekend, and that mostly consisted of boasts about how much they would sleep all day and stay up all night. Trivial. The conversation lasted until the bell for dismissal to the next class.

I picked up my things, crossing the room with my head down now, trying to escape without Greg coming after me.

North remained in his seat but as soon as I started to pass him, he held out something behind his back. I reached for it, taking what felt like a packet from his hands. The slight touch of his fingers sparked warmth that spilled through my body. I clasped the paper packet in my hand, feeling the keys inside as he had promised.

In English class, I slipped inside before any of the boys entered. I picked a seat at the far back near the door. I dropped my things under the desk. I checked the packet North gave me. It was a neatly folded piece of notebook paper with my name scrawled over the front. I opened it up to pull from it four keys, including the original. The inside of the paper had a note:

Do you like me? Yes [ ] No[ ]

My throat closed up and it took the strongest effort so far that morning to blink away the tears. I took out my pen, drew a heart over the *yes*, and below it I wrote:

Miss you all already. Do you like me?

As soon as I finished, I thought it was too much, but I had written it in pen so I couldn't take it back. I refolded the note and stuffed it into the pocket of my book bag.

Luke, Gabriel and Kota sat together on the other side of the room, with Gabriel taking my seat. Class started and we got back our graded poems. Ms. Johnson had us start on an essay project. I was focused on my notebook, willing time to tick by as I scribbled notes for the essay. I sensed motion around me and dismissed it at the sound of the pencil sharpener grinding a pencil.

I was adding another line to my essay when I felt a presence near my desk. I looked up in time to see Gabriel walking away with a freshly sharpened pencil and my finished poem that he had grabbed from my desk. The glint in his eyes betrayed his stony, disinterested mask. I smirked, looking back down, hiding my blush with a palm as I tried to remember the lines of my poem and if it sounded stupid.

Close to the end of class, the person in front of me dropped a folded note on my desk. I blinked at it, unsure what to do. Was it meant for me? I checked it quickly, looking at the handwriting. My name was spelled wrong. I stuffed it into the bottom of my bag quickly. The boys knew my name so it wasn't from them. Anyone watching and hoping for an answer might think I was going to read it later but would be sorely disappointed when I didn't reply.

When the bell rang, I was heading out the door and back outside toward the building. I felt something slip into my hand and I closed my fingers around a thickly folded note. I looked up in time to see Kota stepping double time ahead of me and disappearing into the crowd. I smiled, pushing the note into my palm. I'd read a note from Kota any time.

I was the second to get to geometry class. I knew North would be right behind me. Nathan sat in his spot keeping the seat in front free for North. I took the note out meant for North and dropped it on the desk before I passed around the back to sit on the other side of the room.

Nathan had grabbed the note and he was unfolding it when North walked in. He crossed the room quickly, snatching the paper out of Nathan's fingers. Nathan said something to him but North fell into his seat, looking at the page. His dark eyes softened and he pulled a pen and a notebook out of his bag, stuffing the note into his pocket.

From where I was sitting, I had an easier time glancing at North and Nathan casually without making it too obvious, or so I thought. I caught Nathan looking over at me on occasion. We'd share a look. He'd make a face. I'd wink at him. He'd grin and bend his head over his book again.

When I thought I could, I unfolded Kota's note.

I like your poem better.

I rolled my eyes, stuffing the note into my geometry book. I couldn't help the small smile on my face.

A couple of notes fell into my hands during class. I checked them just to see if they were from North. When I didn't recognize the names, I dropped them into my bag, unanswered.

No one seemed to notice the difference in where I was sitting in class. I thought that was a good sign. Maybe they thought the boys and I were casual friends, but we weren't joined at the hip. Maybe this plan would work out after all.

I did catch a whisper from two girls nearby.

"Watch out. It's Friday Fall."

A warning? Were the boys hearing this same thing? What was going on?

When the bell rang after class, I crossed the room. North was stretching in his seat and when I got close, he flipped a note in my direction. I caught it, holding it in my hand. Nathan had one too, and he quietly held it out for me. I smiled, pushing both of the notes into my palm as I walked out and headed to music class.

I read the notes on the way, knowing I wouldn't get a chance to read them with Mr. Blackbourne.

Nathan's note was complaining how bored he was in geometry and that I should come over that weekend. He wanted a promise that I would call him later.

North's had just one word:

Yes.

TROUBLE

r. Blackbourne was standing near the piano again when I entered. I stood quietly on the other side of the room, holding the violin case in my hands.

"Miss Sorenson."

"Mr. Blackbourne."

He nodded at me. "I trust everything is working out?"

"It's been a mostly quiet morning." I stepped forward, putting my bookbag and violin down in a chair nearby.

The slight lift in the corner of his mouth softened his stern face. "Maybe for once we can actually have a normal violin lesson."

I bent over to the violin case. I'd barely touched the thing since I'd gotten it. I'd looked at it, appreciating the beauty and thinking of Victor having bought it for me. I barely knew how to hold it let alone play it. It'd been a trinket I'd carried around.

A knock sounded at the door before I could lift the instrument from the case. I paused, turning toward the entryway.

Principal Hendricks stuck his head in and looked at us. "Mr. Blackbourne," he called. "Could I borrow Sang Sorenson for a moment, please?"

The air seemed to shift as the steel glare of Mr. Blackbourne landed on Mr. Hendricks. "Is this important?"

"I've got a reporter here who wants to talk to one of our special students," he said. His gaze slipped to me and he frowned. "Why isn't she in a uniform like the others?"

Mr. Blackbourne shook his head. He stepped forward, standing as a barrier between me and Mr. Hendricks. "This is inappropriate. Miss Sorenson declines being interviewed."

From around Mr. Blackbourne's shoulder, I could see Mr. Hendricks stepping further into the room and frowning. His bald head shimmered under the lights. His eyes narrowed at us. "We made an agreement."

"I agreed that the boys will do many things for this school," Mr. Blackbourne said sharply. "The boys only. Not her."

Mr. Hendricks jerked his head back, as if struck in the face. "You've slipped one of your little minions into my school without my approval and now when I've been gracious enough not to call it out, you're denying my request for something as insignificant as an interview?"

"You may isolate the boys by pointing them out as part of your special program," Mr. Blackbourne fired back. "You can ask them to wear uniforms, even at the risk of their safety. Miss Sorenson will not be part of it."

My heart thundered in my chest. Mr. Blackbourne's words were awkward. He wasn't flat out denying that I was one of his students. The way he was wording it made it sound like I was of the Academy, just under different circumstances. Why would he let Mr. Hendricks continue to assume I was a part of their team? I thought the whole point of separating myself was so someone like Mr. Hendricks would know I wasn't part of them. There must be something to this. Maybe they didn't really want to qualify their assumptions, but they didn't want to stop them entirely. What was the point?

Mr. Hendricks squared off his shoulders. "Should I call the school board?"

"You should," Mr. Blackbourne barked back. "And it won't change the situation. Miss Sorenson will not be giving interviews." He took in a deep breath and then spoke in a cold tone. "You might consider one of the others for this interview. Dakota Lee, perhaps. He should be in his physics class. Room 245."

Mr. Hendricks shot accusing glares at Mr. Blackbourne but pursed his lips and walked out.

I let out the breath I had been holding. My palm fluttered up, touching Mr. Blackbourne lightly on the shoulder.

When my palm pressed to him, Mr. Blackbourne spun around on me as if I had struck him. His eyes were fierce, as steely and sharp as a knife.

I don't know what had made me touch him; maybe so much time with the other boys and I simply associated him as one of them.

I cringed, drawing my hand back to flutter my fingers at the base of my throat. I'd gone too far.

When he saw my face, his eyes softened and he frowned. "I'm sorry," he whispered. He swallowed and his shoulders dropped a fraction. "I didn't mean to scare you."

"If you need me to be interviewed," I said softly, "I'll do it. I don't want you to get into trouble with the school board."

The corner of his mouth lifted a millimeter. "No, my dear Miss Sorenson. Mr. Hendricks assumes I would be in trouble with the school board. The only person he can damage here is himself. I have no problem with taking my boys right out of this school if it comes down to it. He can fight us if he wants, but we aren't here for him."

They could leave any time they wanted? That alone put me on edge. What would it take for them to leave? I knew they were only there for a year, but I didn't realize he could remove them now if he wanted. Could one day Mr. Blackbourne change his mind? "Who are you here for?"

His steel eyes found mine, his gaze sparkling. "For students like you."

♥♥♥

To calm my nerves, Mr. Blackbourne played a melody on his violin for the rest of class time. It was a Norwegian tune, he told me, and he promised one day he'd teach me how to play it. He also made me promise to use my phone in case Mr. Hendricks showed up in any other classes. I was to deny any questions or interviews and to notify Mr. Blackbourne at once if I were asked.

History class: Three unwanted notes from random students, one shared smile with North, four times caught staring at Victor. He looked so quiet and solemn on the other side of the room and his fire eyes lit up each time I looked over.

One whisper overheard about Friday Fall.

"Upstairs. Sometime after lunch. Friday Fall. Stay out of the hallways," warned a girl to the boy in front of me.

♥♥♥

Something was happening in the school. The rumors were crawling with Friday Fall updates. I couldn't get a clear picture of what anyone was talking about. All I knew was the whispers were warnings. Whatever it was, it was happening today, and it was going to happen in the upstairs hallway. Were the boys hearing the same thing? I wondered how many students they'd wired and if they were listening to them now. Or were they too busy watching over me?

Lunch was complicated. I brought nothing with me to eat as I'd known I would be too nervous to attempt it. I did one circle around campus, cutting through the cafeteria alone and around through the main hallway before changing direction into the courtyard. I knew North and Victor were tailing me since our last class. I tried to make it quick so they could relax and eat without worrying about me.

There was an empty bench across the courtyard. I wondered where the little thin boy with the book had gone off to. I sat down on the edge of the bench, hoping I wasn't going to distance him if he wanted a quiet space to read. I opened my book, intending to get through a couple of chapters.

About halfway through lunch time, a voice called out. "Hey there, sexy."

I couldn't help but smile. Mike might have been a flirt, but he seemed harmless.

I stood up as Mike came across the courtyard in my direction. I was ready to get this part out of the way. This time he had three friends with him tagging along. Mike waited until he was close to me before he got on his knees. "Hi," he said, a wide grin on his face.

"Hello Mike," I said softly.

His eyebrows shot up. I supposed he didn't think I knew his name. "Hi," he repeated. His freckled hands reached for mine and he held them together, close to his lips. "Will you marry me?"

I smiled apologetically and shook my head. "I can't marry someone I don't know."

"I'm Mike," he said, his chubby cheeks pushed out as he smiled. He jumped up from the ground.

"I know," I said.

The three friends behind him were giggling, but came forward. One of them, a tall boy with curly black hair and at least three days unshaven scruff spoke, "Mike, you've asked her already."

"I know," Mike said, waving a hand at him dismissively. "I keep hoping."

My eyes shot across the courtyard. Luke's hand shot into the air, holding up three fingers as he kept score. North popped him in the back of the head, a sour frown on his face. Luke dismissed it, saying something to North.

"You don't even know her name," the dark-haired guy said. He looked at me and held out a hand. "I'm Jer."

I sucked in a breath, unsure of how to handle this. It wasn't like Greg, I told myself. They were trying to be nice. Maybe North had been correct. The other students might have been more intimidated to approach since they hovered over me so much. I reached out to grasp Jer's hand, shaking. "I'm Sang."

He lifted an eyebrow. "Sang?"

I nodded.

"I like her name," Mike said. He held out a hand for me to shake. "I'm Mike."

I smiled, rolling my eyes. I reached out to shake his

hand, too. "I know."

In a quick motion, Mike gripped my hand and tucked his shoulder into my stomach. He lifted me off the ground and held me in the air, an arm going around my waist to hold me in place.

I choked back a screech. "Hey," I called out. "Mike, put me down." I wriggled, trying to get off of his shoulder. My heart leapt into my throat.

He popped me on the thigh with a palm. "Don't wriggle or I'll drop you." He turned slightly and started walking.

His friends were laughing. Jer chuckled. "Be careful."

I was dizzy being upside down and disoriented. I clenched my hands and started hitting him in the back. "Mike!" I lifted part of myself until I could look up. I caught North and Silas heading over, I saw Kota standing and walking this way, too. The others were standing, appearing unsure if they should approach.

In a desperate attempt, I put a hand out in a stop motion toward them. North and Silas halted, fists clenched and glaring but obeying. If they came after me now, I knew they might end up in a fight with Mike. I had to handle this alone.

"Mike," I said, trying to sound playful even though I was very embarrassed at hanging off of his shoulder. "I'm getting dizzy."

Mike laughed. He was parading me around the courtyard with his friends walking next to him. I wondered if Mr. McCoy was watching. Would he stop and give me a detention this time? Wasn't *this* inappropriate?

"Hey Mike," someone called out. Mike turned and I was unable to see who it was. "That's enough, dude. Come on, you'll hurt her."

"Aw," Mike said. He carefully grabbed me by the waist.

"Here," said the voice. I felt another pair of hands going around my legs and back and collecting me as Mike hefted me off of his shoulder. I tumbled into a pair of arms. My hands moved to the guy's shoulders to balance myself. A wash of colors swept over my eyes as the blood drained from my head. When it cleared, I was looking into a pair of blue-gray eyes.

"Hi," the guy said. He had soft brown hair cut cleanly around his ears. He was broad shouldered and had a handsome smile. While he was good-looking, the way he looked at me left my insides feeling like I was still hanging upside down.

I swallowed, blushing. "Um... thank you," I said.

He dropped the arm under my thighs, holding on to me with the other until I was on my feet. He kept his hand on my back as he stepped toward Mike. "You can't pick up Rocky's girl like that, okay Mike?"

"Oh, I didn't hurt her," Mike said.

The guy -- Rocky? -- shot Mike a warning look. "Just don't." His voice was deep but raspy, as if he had been talking a lot lately. I had the feeling that was simply the way his voice sounded.

Mike frowned. He waved to me. "See you later, Sang." He marched off in the other direction, heading toward the cafeteria doors. Jer and his friends followed.

"Sorry about that," Rocky said to me after Mike and his friends left. His hand was still on my back and I was uncomfortable. I was facing the wrong way to see if the guys were coming over. "You're okay, right?"

I nodded. "Yes."

"Rocky," someone said behind him.

Rocky let go of me and we both turned to see a tall guy behind him. His head was shaved clean and he was as broad as Silas. There was a wide scar on his left cheek and thick, dark eyebrows. Except for the scar, he reminded me of a younger Vin Diesel.

"We need to go," he said. "Coach wants to see us."

"Hang on, Jay," he said. Rocky turned to me again, flicking on a smile to show clean teeth. "You're a cheerleader right?"

I blinked at his question but shook my head, "No."

"You should be," he said. "Rocky's girl is always a cheerleader." He smirked. "And you're going to marry me instead of Mike?"

I didn't know how to answer him so I didn't. I shifted on my feet, feeling the incredible aggressiveness from him, even though he'd done hardly anything to me. This was different than the playful way Mike kept asking me. Rocky's eyes were intense. It was almost like he wasn't asking me at all, but expected it.

"Call me," he said. He winked at me and stepped away, following Jay through the doors.

I watched after him, knowing my mouth was open. How did he expect me to call him if I didn't have his number? Not that I was going to, but his assumption ground on me. What did he mean, claiming me as his girl? I blew out a slow breath, perplexed.

I turned, catching seven pairs of eyes bearing down at me from across the courtyard, each one asking a different question.

I slowly lifted my hand into the air, holding up four fingers. I blushed as I did it, turned and went back to my seat on the bench.

When I dared another glance back at the guys from over my book, none of them were laughing.

♥

$\mathscr{F}$RIDAY $\mathscr{F}$ALL

$\mathscr{W}$hile walking to my next class, I overheard more whispers about the Friday Fall. It was too much to keep to myself any more. I slipped a hand into my bra while everyone around me seemed distracted and sent a quick text to Kota.

Sang: *"Friday Fall."*
Kota: *"What's that?"*

They hadn't heard. I felt better that I'd taken the time to text him.

Sang: *"I don't know. But it's bad. Other students are talking about it. It's happening this afternoon. Second floor."*
Kota: *"I'll tell the others. Keep your head down. If you hear anything else, text me. If you see trouble, head straight to Blackbourne's office."*

The next few periods seemed to take eons. Silas sat next to me in class instead of behind me. He seemed unwilling to move any further, but minded to not talk to me at all. Victor only sat two chairs away and I felt his fire eyes on me the entire time. Dr. Green shot looks at me, too, wordlessly asking what was going on, but there was no way to explain it. I felt like I had failed at keeping myself indiscreet at lunch. I couldn't go one day without something happening.

Still, no McCoy. That was something.

Victor followed me to gym. I caught him watching and waiting at the end of the hall as I turned into the girls' locker room. I ached to run back to him and hug him or at least tell him it wouldn't be long and we'd hang out all weekend. His fire eyes were disturbingly subdued and he looked as lonely as I felt.

One more class, I kept telling myself, and we'll all go home. I touched the phone in my bra. I dressed in the red t-shirt and the short black shorts and my tennis shoes. I tucked the phone deeper into my bra, wondering if it would survive jumping jacks. I didn't want to let it go.

Inside the gym, however, the bleachers were pulled out and there were chairs and a podium in the middle of the basketball court.

"Sit on the bleachers," the girls' coach, Coach French, said. She waved to the seats and turned, walking off to talk with the other coaches.

I glanced at Karen, the tall girl who had played basketball with me the day before. It felt like a million years ago. She caught my eye and slid over to sit next to me. My heart raced and I swallowed back my fears. I needed to make friends, I reminded myself. I had to make an effort, like Kota said.

"What's going on?" I asked her, nodding to the podium.

Karen shrugged. "I don't know. Looks like an assembly. I heard there were some school board members here today."

An assembly? "Is this what the Friday Fall thing is about?" It didn't seem like an assembly was something to dramatize and avoid.

Karen's eyebrows lifted. "What? No. Friday Fall's a rumor."

"What is it, though?"

Karen shrugged, pushing her slim fingers through her brown pixie hair. "I think they push a bunch of students around until they fall over. I don't know. I heard about it last year as a freshman, but didn't see it then either. I don't really pay attention to that kind of stuff."

I slid a glance over to Nathan and Gabriel. Their eyes

locked on me. I didn't know how to reach them. It wasn't likely they had their phones on them. Did they get word about the Friday thing?

"You're name is Sang, right?" Karen asked.

I was grateful that she kept the conversation going. "Yeah," I said. "You're Karen."

She nodded, holding out a hand. I shook it. Touching was normal. Was making a new friend this easy? Was it like Kota said, that I just needed to open up more? Maybe there wasn't anything wrong with me. Maybe I just didn't understand. I felt awkward but I forced myself to smile pleasantly.

"Your friends keep staring at you," she said, jerking her chin to where the boys were sitting on the other side of the bleachers.

Her words forced me to glance over at Nathan and Gabriel. They were still watching us, curious. They made no attempt to look away now.

"They're being that obvious, huh?" I asked.

Karen smirked. "Why were they wearing those uniforms today?"

"There's some special school program," I said. "Those are the uniforms Ashley Waters wants everyone to wear maybe next year or the year after. Something about wanting the other students to get used to the idea."

"Is that why you're avoiding them? They seem mad about it."

Could I tell her? I remembered Mr. Blackbourne's words about revealing too much information about what the Academy did. Still, we were talking about what was right in front of us and about things that were happening to the school. Wasn't it important to gauge how other students were reacting?

"I'm supposed to avoid them," I said. "They were worried the other students would pick fights. I'm supposed to stay out of the way."

Karen laughed. "I saw Mike at lunch. They're all picking on you, instead."

I tilted my head to her. "So maybe this was a waste of time? Everyone knows we're friends?"

She laughed again, slipping fingers over her mouth. "Sweetie, you all stand in that courtyard by the windows of the cafeteria and the main hallway. Yes, everyone knows. They've been talking about why Sang isn't with her boyfriends today."

I blushed. "We're just friends," I said. I was being talked about? Why did they assume they were my boyfriends? Was it because I was sitting on Kota's lap the other day? Was it how they held my hand and sat next to me? Don't friends hold hands?

Karen's eyes sparked. "You're not dating any of them?"

I lifted my eyebrows, shaking my head. I glanced around, seeing if anyone else was paying attention. The only ones were Nathan and Gabriel and they were out of earshot. "I've never really dated anyone," I confided.

Karen's smirk softened. "You're kidding."

I shook my head. Why would she think I was kidding about it?

Karen opened her mouth to say something.

Bright flashes emanated above our heads and sirens begun to blare. I cringed, covering my ears at the onslaught of noise that echoed through the gym.

"Fire alarm," Coach French shouted to us. "Everyone outside."

A fire drill? Now? It was kind of early in the year for it. I sought out Gabriel and Nathan, but the male coaches were directing the boys out the side door toward the back of the school. The girls' coach pointed us toward the front doors to go in the opposite direction. It made sense since we were closer to that side, but I was reluctant to follow since the guys weren't able to stay close.

The girls filed into a line. Karen stood in front of me. The coach held the door open for us and we made our way out into the hallway. A mass of students from classes surrounding the gym flooded the hallway. Confusion set in, but most of the students started out toward the doors that led out to the parking lot.

A buzzing started in my chest. I fell back from the group. Karen turned, stopping when she realized I wasn't right behind her. We mixed in with other students. I pulled the phone out from my bra.

Kota: *"hey girl. cum upstars."*

My breath caught in my throat. Kota would never type like that.

"What's wrong?" Karen asked, a curious eyebrow going up.

It took me a moment to register what this message meant. Two thoughts struck me at once. Kota didn't have his phone. Upstairs.

Friday Fall.

Warnings flashed through my mind. They'd told me to stay away if there was trouble. I had no idea where Nathan and Gabriel were. Everyone should have been heading outside. Maybe this was a distraction for whatever was going to happen.

Kota was in trouble.

My fingers sought out Karen's arm. I fixed my eyes on hers. "Did you see where the guys went?"

She nodded. "Those two from gym?" she asked, catching on.

"Can you go find them? Tell them to meet me on the second floor." There was no other way to reach them. They wouldn't have their phones.

"Where are you going?" Karen asked, a puzzled expression on her face.

"The fall thing is happening. Say Kota's in trouble. Tell them that. Hurry," I said, turning away.

I tucked in against the flow of students headed toward the doors and sprinted for the main hallway. I was jostled and called after by teachers, but I ignored them all. I wasn't going to leave Kota alone. If Kota didn't have his phone, and he was in trouble, no one would know to reach him. In this mess for the fire drill, I had to find him. I'd risk another grounding from Gabriel, North and everyone one else if there was something I could do to help.

As I ran, I opened North's app, pushing the green button to call through. I held the phone to my head. The phone rang, but he didn't pick up. Did I push the wrong button? I tried Silas, but his did the same. Why weren't they answering? Couldn't they hear? Were they outside?

When I got to the main hallway, it had emptied. Echoes saturated the air around me. I glanced up at the balcony of the second floor, seeing heads of people clustered together. The stairwell was clear. What were they still doing inside? Why weren't teachers after them to go outside for the fire drill?

Something flew past my head, thrown from over the balcony of the second floor landing, crashing on the floor next to me. Books smacked against the ground. Papers fluttered across the floor.

Kota's green messenger bag feathered down next.

I charged the stairs, taking two at a time.

When I got close to the second floor, the shouting vibrated through my bones. I slowed, peeking around the corner at the top of the stairs.

Kota dangled up against the far wall. A tall kid grasped him by the throat while two others on either side held his arms to stop him from fighting. Clusters of other students surrounded him. Expectant. Cell phones were out, some filming the event.

Through the confusion, Kota's eyes met mine. His eyes widened in panic.

A shiver broke through me. My jaw tightened. My hands clenched into fists around my phone. I randomly opened any of the apps, one being Victor's. I hit the red button.

Kota wriggled and he tried to call out but a fist met his chest.

Where it came from, some deep survival instinct maybe, I wasn't sure. My feet moved. I sprinted across the hallway, shoving the phone into my pocket and cutting around people standing by. I leapt, my foot in the air, and aimed for the back of the guy holding Kota's throat. I kicked out. I had no idea if it would work, but I hoped it was enough to get him to loosen his grip on Kota so he could break free.

"Sang!" North bellowed nearby.

It was too late. I made contact against the guy's side. He called out in surprise, letting go of Kota's throat. Someone grabbed me from behind. I yanked myself away, spinning and flailing wildly out at whoever had touched me. More hands gripped me. I was dragged back. An arm shoved around my waist and held my arms to my sides. A hand seized my throat.

I was pressed against a large student, with my back across his stomach. I inhaled cigarette smoke and something sharp -- alcohol? I twisted my head and recognized the bully that had attacked Gabriel the day before. His chubby fingers pinched at the skin of my arms as he gripped me.

"Greg," he called out. "Got your girlfriend."

"Sang." Greg came into view. He smirked, his arms crossed over his thin chest. Students made a circle around us. Greg jerked his chin in my direction. "What the fuck are you doing with Eric?"

I struggled, but Eric kept his vice-like grip on my arms. I glared back at Greg. A commotion over his shoulder caught my eyes. Kota was hefted off the ground. He struggled, but more hands grabbed him. His blazer was stripped from his back.

Greg brought his face close to mine. "Come to watch?"

"Let her the fuck go," North called. I twisted my head, spotting North, Victor and Luke pressed up against the wall a short distance away. North was bucking against a group of guys restraining him. Silas was on the ground at their feet, moving, but with at least ten guys piled on top of him, throwing punches against his body.

I now knew why they couldn't respond to my calls. They'd been here the whole time. I swallowed a cry. Screaming at them wouldn't help. "What's going on?" I asked, facing off Greg.

"Someone goes over," Greg said. He tilted his head toward where the balcony overlooked the main hallway below.

"What? Why?" I asked.

"Someone always does."

Friday Fall. Someone gets thrown off of the second floor? Did it happen every Friday? How sick and twisted were these students? If Kota went over he might land on his back. He'd break his neck.

The group around Kota started moving in unison. Kota thrashed. His glasses were gone. His cheek was red and swelling. It took five of them to hang onto him and walk toward the balcony's edge. People were yelling, some cheering. Most were watching, phone cameras recording. The group had a hard time keeping Kota up off of the ground. He fought them every step and he was hard to hang on to.

"I'll go," I shouted. "I'll go over."

"Shut up," Greg said. "We can't throw a fucking girl over." Greg shot a hand out toward me, his fingers pushing against the middle of my chest, pressing my t-shirt up against my breasts.

"Sang!" Luke shouted.

North swung his body. Another student kicked him and jumped on his back. North went down next to Silas. Victor and Luke were thrown to the ground nearby.

Where were the teachers? Were they all outside? Why didn't anyone standing by stop this?

"We have to hurry," someone bellowed over the noise. "They'll let them back inside in a minute."

The group progressed, hoisting Kota above their heads again.

"Kota!" I called out. I elbowed Eric. He let go of one of my arms. His wrist crossed in front of my face.

I grabbed it with my free hand and clamped my mouth down on his arm. The taste of dirt and skin assaulted my tongue.

Eric cursed, dropping me to the floor. A kick landed on

my thigh, hurling me down to the floor.

North howled. Luke bellowed. Victor was screaming my name.

The pile on top of Silas shifted up. "Sang!" Silas called out. "Fuck... shit..." I knew he couldn't see what was going on but the hollering around him was enough to get him going.

It wasn't enough, the guys on top of him regrouped, sending him to the ground again.

Greg gripped me by the hair, pulling me to my feet. "Stop it, bitch," he said.

I crumbled under his grip, biting back a cry. I clawed at him, at his chest but he pulled tighter, swinging my head around.

He smirked, his menthol breath getting close. A hand pressed against my butt, pulling me closer to him, the grip pressing into my skin. His mouth hovered over mine. "I like a fighter."

I struck up against his jaw with my palm. I meant to slap him, but this was better.

His eyes widened in surprise. He pushed me away, dropping back. I didn't stop to see more. I flew across the hall toward the crowd, flinging myself against someone holding onto Kota. I jumped on his back, reaching for his grip on Kota's foot. I dug my nails into his arm. He let go of Kota long enough to turn around and push me away.

It was enough. Kota was fighting again. He kicked at the person who had his other leg. He disappeared into the group around him.

"Greg, hold that damn girlfriend of yours," Eric hollered.

I was grabbed again. I was hoisted up, pushed hard against the balcony, half of my body hanging over. A hand had me by the throat again.

"Sit still, bitch." Greg spat at me. He pressed me against the half wall. His hands caught both of my wrists and he held them away.

He dropped a hand down to my breast and squeezed. His

leg pressed up between my thighs against my crotch, he ground his knee into me hard.

Pain radiated through me, trailed heavily by disgust.

I wrestled with him, and pulled a wrist free. I flung a fist out blindly, striking against the center of his throat, knocking into his Adam's apple.

Greg screamed. He pushed me away and I was going over the balcony.

"Sang!" a chorus of male voices shouted at once.

In slow motion, I felt myself falling. I twisted, readying myself.

I knew before I hit the ground where I was going. The balcony wasn't that high up, not for someone like me. I struck it feet first, my right foot getting a sharp hit. I wasn't expecting how hard the floor of the hallway was. I sunk to my knees the moment I touched down, tucked my elbow in and forced myself into a roll, spilling out across the floor in front of a vending machine.

It took only a minute for me to recover and I was on my feet again. As I stepped forward, my right ankle bit back, letting me know it was probably sprained but, I ignored it. The landing shook me, but I was fine.

From the time I fell to when I spilled out on the floor, the hall seemed to be in a dead silence.

When I started limp-running back across the hall, shouts erupted around me. I became aware of the people closing in, including from the administration offices. Somewhere among the crowd I recognized Nathan's and Gabriel's voices calling my name.

I didn't stop. I zeroed in on the stairs again, leaping like a tiger up a hill against the steps to ease the bite in my foot. I was coming back for Kota and the others. No one could stop me.

A surge followed me. I sensed it like being chased in one of my dreams. Was the group chasing me going to try to stop me? I wouldn't let them. I'd already done the Friday Fall. No one else had to go over.

Upstairs, Kota was no longer in the air. More kids were

struggling against each other in the confusion, as if they were going to try to hurl anyone else over, the easiest one first.

Silas and the others were still on the ground. I jumped on one of the guys on top of Silas. I gripped at his shoulders, pushing my knees into his back to try to catch him off balance so he'd spill over. The boy pulled back off of Silas to push me away. This distracted a couple of the other guys around us and they struggled with me instead, trying to push me off.

It was all Silas needed. A foot flew out, followed by a fist. The guys on top of him started backing away. Silas was getting up.

Others that followed me from downstairs flooded around me. Fists flew. Kids holding camera phones, who were only there to watch, started running. The mob was cornered.

I struck out again at someone going after Silas. When I pushed him, he turned and hoisted me slightly as he pushed back, throwing me. I was flung across the floor. My phone sailed away from my pocket, disappearing amid the swarm. I tumbled, skidded, colliding with other students. The breath was knocked out of my lungs. I clutched at my chest, trying to will myself to breathe.

I was picked up. I struggled, clawing, biting.

The arms held strong around me. "Easy, girl," a voice called into my ear. "We're on your side."

The familiar voice was enough to get me to stop. Rocky held me, pressing me to his body. I coughed to get my lungs working again, sucking in air. He pulled me away from the crowd. He turned and I saw the group of students that had joined us from downstairs. All male. All angry.

Greg was on the ground, his hands covering his throat. I wasn't sure if he was breathing.

Kota was up on his feet. One of the students that had lifted him into the air was now swinging punches. Kota aimed a solid kick against the kid's chest. The student reeled back against the wall.

Nathan stood behind Kota, taking a defensive swing against someone else. Jay, Rocky's friend, stood beside them, pushing another guy away.

Silas and North were up off the ground. A group of large guys tried launching at them full force to knock them against the wall. Silas and North held them back. Silas swiped at their feet, knocking two guys down. North grabbed some guy's head and pulled him over his shoulder. The guy landed on his back at North's feet.

Mike, Jer and other students were fighting alongside Luke and Victor and Gabriel. Other angry guys were pushing students toward the stairs. The shouts were accusing.

"Who threw her?"

"Fucked up tradition."

"Chicken shit motherfuckers!"

I clutched at Rocky's arms, wanting to get in there with them. He held me back, pulling me against the wall. "Hang back," he commanded. I couldn't fight him as strongly since he didn't mean any harm.

The mob that started the mess receded. They were outnumbered now.

Kota and the others slowed as those left fighting started backing away. There were a handful of students knocked out on the ground, Greg was among them. Eric had disappeared.

"Let her go," Silas boomed. He surged toward us against the wall.

Rocky gripped me, not understanding why Silas was so angry and coming after us. I couldn't blame Rocky for being confused. He didn't know us. I wrestled with Rocky to get a hand out, I held up a palm toward Silas. "Wait," I called to him.

Silas stopped dead at my command. His fists still clenched, he gritted his teeth.

"Rocky," I said, "Let me go."

"You're not going to fight again," he said. He released me.

I dropped to my feet, stumbling toward Silas. The bite into my ankle was more painful than before.

Silas waited until I was halfway to him before he started forward again. He took me into his arms, pulling me up off the ground, hugging me to his body. I buried my head into his shoulder, inhaling in his ocean scent. I trembled at his touch.

Nerves caught up with me. Silas was okay. The others weren't knocked out. We were going to be okay.

More arms surrounded my waist. Hands rubbed against my scalp. Nathan's face swam into view, but I knew the other guys were there, too. I was being hugged and touched by familiar hands.

Kota voiced a command that I didn't catch. They shifted. Silas gently dropped me to the floor again. Backs were turned to me, all seven of them. They stood guard around me, challenging anyone to come closer. It was us against the school. Anyone that approached would get a kick or a shove back.

Mike, Jer, Rocky, Jay and others corralled students out toward the stairs. They cleared the halls.

When there was no one left to fight, teachers materialized from the side hallways. Mr. Blackbourne and Dr. Green marched up the stairs, followed by Mr. Hendricks and a handful of other teachers. They were clutching the shoulders of some of the students. Any student remaining was fleeing out of the building. Jer and Mike and some that had taken over the fight disappeared.

"Back off, guys," Dr. Green bellowed to us. "It's over."

The guys didn't move. They waited, instead, to make sure the other students were collected up.

♥

$\mathscr{D}$OUBLE $\mathscr{G}$ROUNDED

$\mathscr{D}$r. Green hovered over Greg and the other students who got the worst of it. Mr. Blackbourne led Rocky, Jay, us, and a handful of other students into one of the empty upstairs classrooms. Several of the other students had been hauled off to the main office downstairs.

Mr. Morris joined us in the classroom, too. He stood guard at the door, his arms folded over his chest, preventing anyone from leaving. Kota, North and the others quietly assembled near the back of the room to sit at the desks. Mr. Blackbourne shot looks at the guys and me, silently warning with a secret finger to his lips to keep quiet.

North had carried me into the room and I was put down onto a desk top. He tried to check me out for injuries, but with nothing obvious and with a warning look from Mr. Blackbourne, he couldn't do much. And I wondered how much he could see with his one eye so swollen, it was barely a slit. It made my heart ache that he'd gotten so hurt.

I drew my knees up to my chest, wrapping my arms around my legs and buried my head into my knees. It was the best I could do to stop the shaking. I sensed bodies crowding around me, and I breathed in Nathan's cypress and North's musk.

No one touched me, even as I yearned for it. Silence hung and I knew the only thing stopping Mr. Blackbourne from talking was Jay and the other students still lingering. The only thing that stopped the boys was Mr. Blackbourne's unspoken orders.

Secrets had to be maintained.

My lungs hurt. My ankle was aching. I had a throbbing headache and my mouth felt numb. Someone had punched me in the face again. My hair was mangled. I pulled my head up to collect the clip still snarled into my hair. I fingered combed it the best I could and re-clipped it into place. Keeping busy with straitening myself up kept my mind off of what just happened. I didn't want to think about it because it got me shaking all over again.

Silas leaned against the wall and fingered his swollen face, wincing. Gabriel's nose was bleeding again, but he held tissues to his face to try to contain the mess. Nathan clutched his hand to his chest, the metal cast on his finger was missing. North's left eye was now completely swollen shut.

Kota sat in a desk, his arms folded and his head down. Gabriel and Victor were slumped over in chairs. Luke was on his back on the floor, staring up at the ceiling. The tension was heavy with unspoken anger and questions.

I sensed a motion behind me and turned on the desk.

"You okay?" Rocky asked, his aggressive blue-gray eyes gazing at me. He hovered over me. He didn't look hurt. Forcing me out of the fight left him virtually untouched.

I nodded.

His hand shot out. His thumb traced over my lower lip, re-sparking a sharp pain.

North moved into action, grabbing Rocky's wrist.

Rocky turned, his head tilted. Confusion settling into his eyes.

"Don't touch her," North growled, positioning himself closer next to me. Nathan stepped closer on the other side, firing warning looks at Rocky.

Jay stood up next to Rocky. "Let him go," he said coldly, his deep voice a growl. I sensed movement behind me. The others were getting up to intervene.

"Stop it," I called out. "North, let go."

North hesitated, but slowly released Rocky's arm to gaze down at me.

I put a palm on North's arm. I didn't want to start another fight over something so inconsequential. I couldn't stand anymore fighting today. I stared down Rocky. "He helped us," I told the others.

North grunted. The others mumbled.

Rocky pulled his thumb away, drops of my blood and saliva shining under the light. With his eyes on me, he brought his thumb to his mouth, licking my blood clean from his finger.

"Why did you start fighting?" I asked him, ignoring the growling of the guys behind me.

"No one throws a girl from the balcony," Rocky said flatly.

"Did you know it was going to happen?"

Rocky nodded. "Happens every year. I don't know who started it and we don't participate. I'm fucking tired of it."

Who did he mean by we? "But you've never bothered to stop it before," I challenged.

His eyes narrowed at me, but I'd made my point. It wasn't a big deal until a girl got involved. How wrong was that?

The classroom door burst open. Mr. Hendricks stormed in, followed by a stout man wearing red Nike running pants and a zipped running jacket. A silver whistle hung off of a yellow cord around his neck. The guy pointed a finger at Jay and Rocky. "You two. And the rest of you. With me. Now."

"Yes, coach," Jay and Rocky said together. The other students stood up, crossing the room.

"Wait," Mr. Blackbourne said halfheartedly. "We need to ask them..."

"No one interrogates my team but me," the coach said.

Mr. Blackbourne backed off. He said what he was expected to say but he didn't really appear interested in keeping them around. Mr. Hendricks stood aside, saying nothing. Jay and Rocky didn't hesitate. They strolled out. Mr. Morris and the other students followed. Were they part of the team, too?

The moment the door closed, Mr. Hendricks spun on us. "What happened?"

Kota stepped up. His glasses were still missing. His

handsome face was swollen, bruised. Kota glanced at Mr. Blackbourne. Looks were exchanged. Mr. Blackbourne nodded in a silent command.

Kota started talking, his voice obstructed by a swollen lip, his throat hoarse. "It started right after the fire drill sounded. When most of the teachers and other students were on their way out, that's when Greg and his group started shoving students. I tried to stop them and Greg recognized me. When Silas and the others showed up, they isolated us. We became the target for the planned tossing of someone over the balcony."

Mr. Hendricks spun on me, an accusing finger pointed in my direction. "And what did you think you were doing?"

I hesitated, glancing at the others. Mr. Blackbourne inclined his head briefly – permission to speak granted. "Someone got Kota's phone," I said. "They recognized my name and texted me to come upstairs. I think it was Greg wanting me to come watch toss him over."

"Did you see her?" Mr. Hendricks said, turning on Mr. Blackbourne. "She launched herself over that balcony. She was up and running before we could get to her and heading back up the stairs. I never saw anything like it."

"She's had training," Kota said, smirking at me. "Elementary school, wasn't it?"

I nodded. All eyes in the room shifted to me. "I was taught how to fall. I knew I could make it. If they needed someone to go over, I was going to do it."

A palm slapped against the back of my head. I ducked after, looking back at Gabriel's outstretched hand nearby. "Don't you ever fucking do that again."

"She's what stopped it," Nathan said. "When she went over, the football team was standing downstairs with us. They followed her upstairs. It was fine if it was another guy. Since it was a girl, they got angry and stormed in to take them all out."

Mr. Hendricks barked at us, "We could have had all of them out of here if it was him and not her."

I felt the blood drain from my face. This was planned?

He knew it was going to happen? But it made sense. He had to have known. It happened every year. "I messed up?"

Mr. Hendricks turned on me. "Yeah, you messed up. One of them was supposed to go over unwillingly. Instead we got you practically jumping over. The school board didn't understand why everyone rushed up the stairs or why there was a fight. They're asking who the acrobat is."

Mr. Blackbourne frowned. He stepped in, standing between me and Mr. Hendricks. "That's enough," he commanded. "You made a circus out of this. You're lucky she knew what she was doing and landed on her feet. The other students believe she was pushed."

"That kid she punched is going to the hospital. She'll be lucky if his parents' don't press charges. This wasn't supposed to happen."

My throat closed in, my fingers hovering over the base of my neck. Someone wrapped an arm around my shoulders, a chest pressed against my back. I breathed in spice and relaxed back against Kota. Luke came up quietly next to me and took my other hand, squeezing it. If charges were pressed, there were plenty of witnesses to point out who did the damage. Would I be arrested?

"What you wanted," Mr. Blackbourne continued, "was for Kota to break his head and then charge the group of students to get them arrested or expelled? You deliberately set up my students, knowing this tradition was going to happen and being fully aware he could have broken his neck or worse."

"You agreed to this," Mr. Hendricks shouted at him. He pointed a finger at Mr. Blackbourne's nose. "I warned you this place was dangerous and not meant for prissy private school preps."

Mr. Blackbourne squared his shoulders. "These prissy students just brought to a halt a sick tradition in this school that should have been stopped a long time ago."

"That little girl..." Mr. Hendricks growled.

"*That* little girl," Mr. Blackbourne snapped back, "just got the entire football team and other students to step in and take over your job. She had more power than you did to encourage them to step up. If it wasn't for her, you would have had students trying again next year. Now they won't dare at the risk of angering half of the school. She's the martyr."

My body trembled. Kota squeezed me tighter to him. My head rested against his chest. What did I do? I didn't mean to do anything except to stop Kota from being flung over. If he had been pushed, he might have broken something or worse.

"What she is," Mr. Hendricks said in a low, menacing tone and pointing a finger at my face over Mr. Blackbourne's shoulder, "is fucking stupid. She should have stayed out of it. I should have her expelled for starting a riot."

A surge started around me. Silas and North moved in front of me and blocking my view of Mr. Hendricks. Kota pulled me away from the desk, his other arm wrapping around my waist as he drew me in. I quaked against his body. Victor, Gabriel, Luke and Nathan surrounded us.

Expelled! My poor mind couldn't comprehend the damage it would mean. It was more than getting kicked out of school. My mother may finally see fit to have me start home schooling, and I'd never be able to leave the house again. I'd possibly not be able to see the boys ever again.

Mr. Blackbourne headed off his students, standing in front of Silas and North. "You're going out there," he said, his tone cold. "You're going to talk to the police. You're going to say it was self-defense against that boy and we have many witnesses to prove it. Miss Sorenson stays here in school and you won't breathe a word about her to anyone."

"She should be calling a lawyer."

"The Academy's lawyers will be at her disposal," Mr. Blackbourne commanded, his tone rising. "But it doesn't have to come to that if you'll listen to me. I'll talk to the school board downstairs."

Mr. Hendricks growled. "You don't get to tell me what to do. This is my school."

"I talk to them or I'm sure they'd like to hear about how you've let people get tossed from balconies every year for who knows how long. Why was this never reported? Why was it allowed to continue? They might also like to know why you chose who was going to be thrown this year. Your teachers abandoned the area knowing this was going to happen. It was all a set-up. If Kota had gone over or if anyone had gotten hurt, you would have been at fault."

"You can't prove it."

"I've got eight witnesses," he said, gesturing behind himself toward us.

I stretched up on my left tiptoe to look over North's shoulder. Mr. Hendricks stared down Mr. Blackbourne. He glared over at me. I ducked my head behind North's shoulders again.

Mr. Hendricks started across the room, slamming the door behind himself as he left.

The air shifted around us.

My knees buckled. Kota caught me, catching under my thighs and picking me up, holding me against his chest. The others pulled back, stepping in a circle around us.

Victor approached, putting a hand on my forehead. "What's wrong?" he asked. His fire eyes searching mine.

"Sorry," I breathed. I trembled again against Kota. It felt good to be held. I couldn't stop shaking. "I can't believe I did that."

"Oh now you're nervous," Victor said, a gentle smirk appearing.

"She's in shock," Mr. Blackbourne said, his eyes softening, but his mouth was stern.

Luke removed his blazer and tossed it over me. "Can we take her home?"

"Not yet," Mr. Blackbourne said. "We need to talk to the police and figure out if that kid's parents are interested in pressing charges. We need to make sure Mr. Hendricks doesn't pin this whole mess on her."

"I'm sorry," I whispered.

Eight eyes narrowed on me. Mr. Blackbourne broke into a millimeter smile. "Why are you sorry?"

"I hurt a bunch of people." Now that it was over, I

worried I had gone too far. I'd never hit anyone before. I'd lost control and now I was sorry I got in the middle. I never wanted to hurt anyone. I would have done it again for Kota and the others, but it didn't make what I'd done any less appalling.

"Fucking shit," North bellowed. "Sang baby, you just sacrificed yourself for Kota and nearly killed yourself and you're sorry you hurt someone else."

I sunk my face into Kota's chest, trembling. I couldn't take fighting any more. I didn't want to appear to be so weak after they had been through so much, but I didn't have the strength to take them on, too.

"Oh god, I'm sorry," North said. A hand landed on top of my head. "Don't cry. God damn it, Kota."

"She'll be fine," Kota said. He pressed his cheek against my forehead. "But I owe her a beating."

I smirked, shaking my head against him. Did they have to do this now?

"Fuck yeah," Gabriel called out. "She's grounded."

"No," I said. "I'm already grounded."

"Fuck you," he said. "You're double grounded."

I started giggling. Why was this funny to me? "No," I half-whined again.

Kota's hand slipped away from my thighs and he held me steady as I stepped to the ground. I buried my head into his chest still, my shoulders shaking from giggling now.

"I mean it," Gabriel said. "Do you know that girl who came after us nearly gave me a heart attack? She said Trouble's in trouble. Again. Second time in a week. And what do I see when we get to the hallway? Trouble jumping from the fucking second floor, does a barrel roll and hobbles up to get back into the fight. And then I get up to that second floor and you're on top of some motherfucker on top of Silas. You took on the whole goddamn school. Fucking beautiful. So that's like quadruple grounding because you went in twice. I swear if you go over that balcony again, I'm going to break your damn feet so you can't go anywhere near it."

I peeked out at Gabriel, who was grinning.

"You should have seen her kick that guy who had Kota by the throat," Luke said, pushing his blond hair away from his eyes. "She's a secret ninja."

"You fucking ninja kicked?" Gabriel gasped at me. "I missed that? Someone go steal one of those phones that recorded everything. Did we get that on camera? Do we have cameras there? I need to see it."

"Stop," Victor said to him.

"No," Gabriel squared off his shoulders. He smirked. "And you owe Sang a beating, too."

That reminded me. "I think my phone is missing," I said quietly.

"Yeah, I found it," Victor said. He pulled it out of his back pocket. The front glass was smashed. The button on the front caved in. "I'll get you a new one."

"No…"

"Don't argue with me. You're grounded," Victor said. "You're not allowed to argue."

"How long am I grounded for?" I asked.

"Forever," Victor said before Gabriel could say it. His mouth twisted into a smile.

I pulled away from Kota to brush a palm across my eyes. "You all are so mean."

North started laughing. Silas grinned, his eyes twinkling. The others chuckled.

Mr. Blackbourne shook his head at us. "We've got work to do, gang," he said. He turned to me. "I'm sorry," he said. "Can you hang on for a while longer?"

I nodded, swallowing back nerves. "I've made it this far."

Mr. Blackbourne tilted his head at me, seeming confused by my words. "You're a crazy little girl," he said.

"Yeah," Kota said, beaming. He rubbed my scalp. "She belongs with us."

Nathan wrapped an arm around my shoulders. Luke's hand found mine again. For the first time, I think, I didn't blink that they were touching me or that we were holding hands. In that moment, it felt like it was us against a school that didn't want us there. I had been completely unprepared for Ashley Waters. If it wasn't for the boys, I don't think I could have gotten away with being the empty, invisible person I had expected to be. Around Kota and the others from the Academy, I was becoming a part of something. We were a team. I didn't understand exactly what I was doing. What I did know was how desperately I needed them.

And as I met their eyes, shining, looking back at me, I understood. They needed me, too.

There was a lot more to do.

We were doing it together.

♥

r. Blackbourne's encoded GPS unit guided him to the jam-packed restaurant in downtown Charleston. He was early, and waited the thirty minutes inside his car, wondering about the background check he'd requested for Sang Sorenson. His Academy contact had insisted on meeting him in person. That alone told him there was something important to say. He hated for his team to get their hopes up about a girl they might have to keep at a distance, or worse, avoid completely. They didn't know enough about her to make such a decision, but tonight's report should tell him everything he needed to know.

He was pessimistic. Academy contacts didn't call you out in the open for good news.

He slipped his glasses up the bridge of his nose while watching a familiar, nondescript black sedan park across the lot. Mr. Blackbourne held back, waiting for the older gentleman getting out of his car to enter the restaurant. Mr. Blackbourne left his car, hitting the button on his key fob, knowing his contact would hear the distinct beep of his car locks.

The restaurant was an average burger and fries shack, but it served the purpose they needed: neither of them had been there in a while so they would be unfamiliar and forgettable faces, it was overcrowded already, and they'd had Kota there earlier sweeping for bugs before the evening started. It was highly unlikely their random meeting was going to be contaminated with recording devices of any kind, but Kota also ensured security cameras wouldn't be recording that evening.

He'd broken the computer's hard drives that stored the data and cut the feeds that linked to televisions.

It was overkill for their needs, but the Academy preferred it that way. Students of the Academy knew to always be ready and never expose yourself unless you had to. Security redundancies gave them their advantage in everything they did.

Mr. Blackbourne joined his companion at a booth near the back. They were crowded in but the more people, the better.

"How's it going?" the man said, standing up with a friendly smile warming his face, revealing his familiarity with Mr. Blackbourne. His eyes were blue, and gentle age spots kissed the thinning skin over his cheekbones. His white hair was thinning on top. He held out a hand toward Mr. Blackbourne. "Nice to see you, Owen."

The sound of his first name being spoken nearly made Mr. Blackbourne flinch. He'd had his own team call him Mr. Blackbourne for years for the sake of establishing the sense of respect and seniority – difficult to do at nineteen when his team members were only three years younger than himself. Other Academy members called him the same, even Dr. Green. He didn't need to be so formal with anyone they worked with, but he preferred formality. "It's a pleasure to see you again, Dr. Roberts."

"Will you please just call me Phil? You make me sound old," the man said, his wrinkly grin betraying his age further. He nodded to Mr. Blackbourne and slid down into the booth's seat. "I like this place. The food is excellent. I wish I could come here more often."

"It's interesting," Mr. Blackbourne said, sitting across from his companion. "I prefer quieter places."

"Of course." Phil settled back into his seat, crossing his arms over his chest and grinning. "A friend of mine told me you were interested in acquiring a little bird. I thought you were strictly a dog person, myself."

This was code. Dogs were males. Mr. Blackbourne's mind flashed images of Sang Sorenson at the mention of a bird. "There's a particularly remarkable one I hear is in need of adoption, and has a fondness for other animals."

"Has she been trained?"

"We've just been introduced, although she shows potential."

Phil's eyes focused on the menu splayed out in front of him. "Does she know?"

Mr. Blackbourne was hoping this wasn't going to be asked. He opened his menu, holding it up to mask his mouth. It was probably overkill for such a place, but he wanted to be extra careful when dealing with anything that involved Sang. "She knows we exist. She knows our cover story at the public school. She doesn't know the full story, but it won't take her long. She's clever."

Phil nodded, smiling wide. "I didn't think you'd consider someone who wasn't. Is she cute?"

Mr. Blackbourne tried to mask his displeasure at Phil's attempt at teasing. Yes, Sang Sorenson was cute. That was half of his problem with her right now. He knew what this could lead to. His carefully chosen Academy family could be torn apart by Sang. She had the power to bring everything he'd worked for down with a single look if she desired. Only she didn't know she had that ability, and that made her even more dangerous.

The Academy disliked the thought of a bird joining an all dog team for that very reason. Disliked, but didn't forbid it entirely. It had happened successfully before. It'd been an unusual team, but it worked. Sang was unexpected, and Mr. Blackbourne at first doubted she would have stuck around.

But wild circumstances, and Kota's insistence, pushed her onto their Academy family. When the guys had accepted her, she dismissed their curious behavior and stuck by them. She'd taken every blow his team had received at that school and bounced back, standing strong beside them at every turn.

It surprised him the first time when he learned Sang had jumped into the fight to save Gabriel. She didn't know Gabriel could defend himself, so he hadn't berated her for it, and actually admired her courage.

At Friday Fall, however, everything changed in his perspective. After hearing the reports and analyzing the recorded videos collected by cell phones, Sang Sorenson displayed a backbone and loyalty she'd kept suppressed in her timid, outward appearance. He couldn't erase the image of her beautifully exotic face, her trembling body wrapped up in Kota's arms after the fight. If it hadn't been inappropriate, he would have held her himself.

Her allure had not gone unnoticed by anyone on his team. He saw it in their eyes.

He almost wanted to say this out loud in an effort to ask for advice from a senior member, but was saved by the waitress coming over to take their order. Her interruption gave him enough time to realize he could easily lose Sang to another team. He recanted his idea for advice, as he didn't want to talk up Sang.

Adoption into the Academy family wasn't the same as being accepted into the Academy as an official member. Any official Academy member could formally adopt anyone they wished. Adopted family of the Academy meant protection and financial security for life. It relieves the burden of having to handle personal family problems on a singular team member, and shifts it to the entire Academy and their expansive teams of various levels of expertise. Lawyers, doctors, scientists, even construction workers and private investigators were the staple of what was the Academy.

They kept their circles tight; usually blood relations and close friends were restricted to the family member who had adopted them.

Potential future official members, those not related to any team member, could be adopted by anyone. He didn't want anyone else learning too much about her and possibly luring her onto their teams instead.

Adopting a bird or dog meant your team became the lead team. Any further Academy interaction with the adopted had to be directed through the lead team. It'd make it harder for another section of the Academy to try to talk Sang into joining them. Harder, but not impossible.

It was selfish, but he was allowed to be selfish about his own team.

They ordered uninteresting burgers, fries and sodas. The waitress glazed her eyes over them with a tired smile and disappeared again.

"Owen," Phil said, "You've got to be careful with these things. Birds are very delicate creatures. It's not easy to adopt one, given your situation."

"I've considered that," Mr. Blackbourne said, knowing he meant all the dogs on his own team.

Phil waved a finger in the air. "Who instigated?"

"Mr. Lee."

"And the team?"

"All approved."

Phil sighed, running his fingers through the white hair above his ear. "Then I hate to bring this up."

Mr. Blackbourne jerked his head back. "What?"

Phil twisted his lips, as if hesitating to respond. "You asked for a background."

"Yes?" Mr. Blackbourne said, not wanting to sound so anxious, but after letting Sang get so close, he'd hate to learn she was disqualified. It didn't seem likely. She attracted trouble but she didn't seem to be an initiator.

Phil grinned. "It's not that bad. Relax."

Mr. Blackbourne bit back a grumble at Phil's hesitation, wanting to tell him to start talking as he so easily told his team to do. "What is it?"

Phil glanced around the room, as if checking for anyone that could be listening in. He leaned over the table. "She's clean."

Mr. Blackbourne scrunched his eyebrows. Why was this bad? Clean, for Academy purposes, meant no criminal history and no bad record at school. Phil still frowned in a way that made Mr. Blackbourne's body rattle unwillingly. "Explain."

"I mean she's absolutely clean. We've got a birth certificate and a social security card, and even those are sketchy. That's it."

That didn't sound right. "Medical records?"

"None. Not one. She's got a shot record on file with the schools she's been with, but the corresponding doctors don't have her on file. She's not on health insurance. They don't claim her on their taxes. She's even missed every school photo day since kindergarten."

Mr. Blackbourne's lips parted. "Do you mean--?"

"She's a ghost," he said. "We're double checking on the birth certificate, but our first answer on that has come back as negative. It's a fake. Your bird doesn't exist."

Mr. Blackbourne fell back against the booth seat, his palms resting on the table top and his eyes wide. "Could she be... I mean, could she have been kidnapped?"

"We want to check DNA from the family and find out. I'd like to know before conducting a goose chase. But if the DNA checks out and she's theirs, then..."

"I know," Mr. Blackbourne said. He didn't like to interrupt someone older than himself but he couldn't help it. It was too much to say it out loud. A ghost bird was rare among the Academy.

Ghost birds, or dogs, were kids without much history to their names. It wouldn't take much to erase their existence completely. A slipped fold of bills across a school secretary's desk could erase a transcript. Medical records and federal records were complicated. Without a medical history, a dental record, or a police record, it wouldn't take much to make Sang Sorenson completely invisible.

She was priceless.

Which also meant that if she qualified, Academy teams would be hounding her to join them. This is what Phil meant when he said he hated to bring this up. He wouldn't want to see Kota's or the others' hopes for Sang dashed when another team swooped in and took her.

C. L. Stone

They were already at a disadvantage for being an all dog team. The Academy rarely gave outright orders to any team families, mostly only strong suggestions. To go against a strong suggestion though, like not letting a girl into an all-male team, often meant adding heavily to a team's financial and favor debt.

"Does anyone else know?" Phil asked.

Mr. Blackbourne was about to answer, but their food arrived. This meant following decorum and eating in silence as if they were hungry. The anticipation of countless questions etched in their faces as they forced themselves to swallow fries and burgers.

"No," Mr. Blackbourne admitted finally when he'd cleared a reasonable half of his plate. "There's no one else working with our team right now. No contractors, either. Your team and mine only."

The older man nodded. "That'll keep her a secret for now, but only for so long. This recent incident didn't help."

Mr. Blackbourne nodded. Sang's involvement in the fight nearly risked her Academy career before she knew it existed, including her severe advantage they'd just discovered. Luckily he had been able to talk Greg's family out of a lawsuit or pressing charges, but only with the promise that Sang could also press charges for sexual assault and attempted murder. The fall over the balcony could have killed her if she hadn't been trained, and most of the witnesses said Greg had pushed her over confirming the incriminating phone and security video evidence. With the new information, he'd have to destroy them permanently now. It was a risk if Greg's parents changed their minds. They'd have no video proof.

"Which reminds me," Phil said. "She was taken to one of our hospital wings. X-rays, you know…"

"I will incur," he said absently, reciting the familiar line for taking on Academy family members' financial and favor debts. Only official Academy members could incur. He knew if he didn't, his other team members would have done so later. He simply wanted the matter closed now.

276

Phil nodded, as if expecting this. "You haven't taken a debt personally since you started with us. You and Sean Green, the youngest ever to pay off both financial and favor debt. Our youngest graduates ever, for that matter."

"I'm still in the positive," Mr. Blackbourne said. Academy debt meant little to him. He could easily refill his accounts on his own. He would ensure his foothold in the positive side for several years, possibly his entire life, by the end of this school term. That is if he managed to get his team through this year at public school without too many more incidents.

"You'll have to be more careful."

Mr. Blackbourne nodded, pushing his plate away. "I trust we can keep this between our families?"

"You have my word," Phil said. "I can't promise she won't go unnoticed. Your team is observed carefully, especially now that they're readily exposed. She's bound to be detected by the others."

"It's a risk we'll take," Mr. Blackbourne said. He didn't begrudge anyone wanting to take on Sang for their team. He still knew little about the girl himself. What he had to go on was Kota and the others, who seemed determined to include her as part of their family. He knew with their particular team, it was probably because of her private family life. Their team was built on broken family problems. He suspected Sang was the same, thus why Kota was desperate to include her. He wanted to save her from something. If they fully adopted her, they would have to find out what the problems were and eliminate them.

Mr. Blackbourne wasn't sure if they realized she was also a potential future candidate for official Academy membership.

And if that was true, and she was qualified, he had to review the case of that other team that had a group of dogs and a singular bird. He made a mental note to give the team a call, but he wasn't sure how to approach the group without alerting others about Sang's existence. He didn't know them personally. Any Academy team would be curious about a single bird a team didn't want to share.

Phil picked up the check, pulling out cash and dropping the price of the meal, plus a reasonable tip. The Academy was normally very generous, except when they were trying to be forgettable. "I don't suppose you'll consider a merger."

Mr. Blackbourne's eyebrows scrunched together. Merging teams? "You're kidding."

Phil chuckled as he shoved the receipt into his wallet. "Don't dismiss us old dogs. Ours might be a little outdated but we're a lot like your team. We already work together. I think we'd get along well."

"I'll bring it up at family meeting," Mr. Blackbourne said, but he was pretty sure Kota and the others would decline. They appreciated the Academy for what they could do for them, and the promise that it held over their heads, but they were close-knit, like many of the individual teams. They wouldn't like to merge without a good reason. Larger groups meant it was harder for personalities to get along with each other. Working indirectly with other teams on occasion wasn't bad, as both teams could go home at the end of the day. A true team was around each other constantly, and you needed to be able to not just tolerate, but appreciate your entire team's company. "But to be honest, you'll likely just have to find your own ghost bird."

Phil laughed. Mr. Blackbourne knew it was highly unlikely someone Phil's age would be a ghost. Most men and women, by the time they were adults, got stuck with college transcripts, marriage certificates and a number of federal incidences, if not records. Tax records alone were nearly impossible to eliminate. The work simply wasn't worth it.

Phil got up from the table and Mr. Blackbourne followed him out the front door. They stood together, looking out into the parking lot, and beyond to the downtown Charleston streets. Traffic was subdued. The ocean breeze picked up around them, stirring fallen leaves to dance in the street.

"So," Phil said as he fished his keys from his pocket. "Are you adopting this little bird into your family now?"

Mr. Blackbourne had a lot to bring back to his team members, but he considered also not telling them as well. He'd tell Sean Green, of course. He told him everything. Together they would make a decision for the whole group.

But should they expose Sang as a jewel, possibly to be negotiated with? He wondered how close Kota, North and the others were to her. With Sang, they could eliminate all their debts right now, including Kota's and Gabriel's, whose debts were the most severe.

He had a feeling, though, that Kota would resist this, and he was pretty sure the others would, too. He recalled the way Kota held her after the fight, how the others gazed at her during classes when they temporarily forgot they were being watched. He knew they held hands through the hallway. He'd caught himself gazing at her in that same way on occasion. Three years' age difference wasn't much, but right now, it was two years too many for him to ever consider trying to get close.

At least for now.

No. It was too late. Sang's allure had already won them over. Sang was growing on his family. If they wanted to keep her, they'd have to win her over, too. The Academy was a choice. Your team was a choice. You could always leave, always choose another team, or work alone at will.

If they wanted to keep her, they'd have to earn her trust and loyalty. Mr. Blackbourne knew the answer to whether they would try.

He could already hear the resounding voices of his eight companions if he tried to ask what he should do.

"I am willing," he told Dr. Roberts, repeating the lines that made her adoption official. "And my team will incur."

For new release and exclusive Academy and
C. L. Stone information sign up here:
http://eepurl.com/zuIDj

Connect with C. L. Stone online
Twitter: https://twitter.com/CLStoneX
Facebook: https://www.facebook.com/clstonex

If you enjoyed reading *The Academy First Days*, let me know.

Review it: at your favorite retailer
and/or Goodreads

Books by C. L. Stone

The Academy Ghost Bird Series:
Introductions
First Days
Friends vs. Family
Forgiveness and Permission
Drop of Doubt
Push and Shove
House of Korba (October 2014)

The Academy Scarab Beetle Series
Thief
Liar (August 2014)

Other C. L. Stone Books:
Spice God
Smoking Gun

READ AN EXCERPT FROM THE NEXT
BOOK IN THE ACADEMY SERIES

The Academy

The Ghost Bird Series

Friends

vs.

Family

Book Three

Written by C. L. Stone
Published by
Arcato Publishing

♥

$\mathscr{S}$ECRET $\mathscr{L}$IVES

I dreamed a wind swept through, laced with fire and blinding anyone that it came across. I was tied to a tree, unable to dodge it no matter how I struggled. All I could do was wait what was coming for me.

Part of me felt like I deserved it.

$\mathscr{S}$ang?" a voice woke me from my dream.

I sat up in bed, shivering, confused. It was dawn. My alarm hadn't gone off yet.

A knock sounded at the door. "Sang?" my father called. "Are you awake?"

My father never came to my door unless something was wrong. Was he going to the hospital with my mother? I kicked back my blankets, my heart rattling hard in my half-asleep body. I swallowed back my fears, smoothing my t-shirt on my body as it had crept up my stomach while I was sleeping. When I was decent, I opened my bedroom door, peeking out.

My father loomed in the hallway, dressed in dark slacks, white collared shirt and tie. A suit coat hung over his arm. If he was going to the hospital, he wasn't going to be wearing that. He peered in at me with his dark eyes.

I opened the door more, tilting my head. "What's wrong?" I asked.

"I'm going on a business trip," he said. He nodded toward the stairwell, to the direction of his bedroom, where my mother was likely still sleeping. "I won't be back for a couple of days. I need to make sure you get your mother to eat something while I'm gone. You know how she gets when she doesn't eat."

I nodded. Since I was about nine years old, my mother had been sick. She first went in for a sinus infection but came back weeks later with bottles of morphine for an illness I wasn't told about. She'd never been the same since, in and out of hospitals almost as often as I went to school.

Her illness was bad enough as it was. The drugs, however, made her paranoid. My sister and I spent most of our childhood and early teenage years at her mercy, isolated in our rooms. She told us that men would rape us; monsters would kidnap and kill us. If we disobeyed, if we left the house and she found out we'd talked to anyone outside the family, she punished us by getting us to kneel in rice or sit on a stool for hours at a time. If she didn't eat, didn't take her medicine, the punishments got worse.

"Where are you going?" I asked. It was Friday, and not only did I have school, but I also had something secret to do with the Academy. I'd have to hope it wouldn't take all day.

"Mexico," he said. "I'll be back soon. Tell your sister."

Marie, my older sister, was probably still asleep across the hall. I wondered why he told me and not her. I couldn't remember the last time he went on a business trip. I usually didn't notice until he was already gone. I hardly saw him anyway, he was always working. It had me wondering why he mentioned it this time. Maybe he expected to be gone longer.

He marched down the stairs, turned the corner and was gone. A moment later, the sound of his car starting echoed through the house. His suitcase must have already been in the car. Telling me he was leaving was like an afterthought. No goodbyes. No promises to call.

A hollow household with hollow people. We did what we had to do.

♥♥♥

The shower that morning was almost too chill for my liking. No matter how much I twisted the hot water handle, I couldn't get the heat. It was perfect timing, since my father had already left. I wasn't sure how to fix it. I thought of mention it to the guys later. Kota, North or one of the others might know.

I got dressed for school in shorts and a blouse. When I was ready, I went to the kitchen downstairs. I found some crackers in the cabinet and grabbed a yogurt cup and a spoon, along with a bottle of water. I tiptoed through the quiet house toward my parents' bedroom.

My mother was slumped over her pillow, her mouth open and she was snoring. Her mostly graying hair was pulled back in a ponytail, recently brushed out and fixed up. If I didn't know any better, she looked almost normal, peaceful.

I didn't want to wake her. I dropped the crackers and everything onto her bedside table. I hoped it would be enough if she woke up and was hungry.

Something glinting under the bed caught my eye. I checked her again to make sure she wasn't going to wake up and then dropped to my knees next to the bed, ducking my head.

There was an open shoebox on its side under her bed. I recognized her handwriting on some of the notes that spilled out. The silver metal glint was a picture frame. The picture was a little faded, and it took a moment for me to realize it was her. She had to have been no more than twenty or so at the time the picture was taken. Her hair was longer then, and her eyes clearer, sharper than I'd ever remembered.

It was in that moment I couldn't recall ever seeing a picture of anyone in my family. I didn't think she owned a camera. Why hadn't it occurred to me before? It was a small thing, but something that never crossed my mind.

This photograph, as far as I knew, was the only one of

any of us in the entire house. She'd kept it hidden.

The sight of this had my heart thundering in my chest. Why was it under her bed? Did she not like it? She didn't want anyone knowing she had it. Did my dad know?

There were other objects in the box as well, needles and old bottles of prescription medication, some dating back to before I was born.

I didn't want to go through her private things or get caught doing so. I closed the lid for her, slipping the box back underneath the bed again. I scrambled to get out of her room.

I would let her keep her secrets. I had my own to deal with. Adding hers to mine right now was too much. I needed to get to school.

That afternoon, I was flat on my back in a thin, pale green hospital gown as I waited for the MRI machine to start. The guys had taken me to this nondescript medical building in downtown Charleston with the promise that my parents wouldn't learn about where I was or why. I'd skipped my last three periods of class to get here, with Mr. Blackbourne covering for me. I wasn't sure how late it was. I was worried we were running short on time for me to get back into my neighborhood, preferably before my mother noticed I was late from school.

"Just lay still for a second, Miss Sang," Dr. Green's voice filtered through to me from overhead speakers.

It was difficult to be still. The room was cold and the table I was on rattled with the movement of the MRI machine. I was naked, except for the thin gown around me. I knew Luke, Gabriel, Victor, Nathan, and Kota were probably watching from the same room Dr. Green was sitting in.

I shifted my head to the side, trying to glimpse through the glass window where I knew they were standing, but from my position, and the glare of the fluorescent lights overhead, I couldn't see their faces.

"I said be still, Miss Sang. You can talk if you want, but don't move."

"You might want to listen to him, Miss Sorenson," said the disembodied voice of Dr. Philip Roberts. I'd met him briefly before they chased me into the MRI room. He was from the Academy, I knew, with white hair and age-spotted cheeks. He was Dr. Green's mentor and residency supervisor. I liked him immediately. "If you move, it takes longer. We might have to start over."

"It's cold," I said, shivering.

Kota's voice cut through. "Didn't you wear shorts and that pink shirt to school today?"

I blinked and worried if blinking counted as moving. "Yes."

"Why'd you take those off? They didn't have any metal. You could have worn them. It probably would have been a little warmer than the gown."

My mouth popped open. "Luke!"

There was snickering in the background from both Luke and Gabriel.

"I hate you both right now," I said.

"Oy, Trouble. You've got to have the full hospital experience."

"Yeah, Sang," Luke said. "Rite of passage."

I grumbled. Earlier, it had sounded reasonable when they told me I *just had* to put the gown on. After all, I was in a hospital and about to go into a very large machine. Medical dramas on television always showed people in the gowns. I'd never been to the doctor before. How was I supposed to know?

Victor's sweet baritone voice sounded through the speakers. "Do you want a blanket?"

"She can't have one now," Kota said. "She's in the middle of the MRI."

"We can start it over," Victor said. "She said she's cold."

"She's tough. She can take it. Can't you, Sang?"

I sighed. "Maybe." I knew I could, I just wanted to

grumble. It distracted me from the loud machine and moving parts around me. They were kind of scary.

"This machine costs an arm and a leg just to push the 'go' button," Dr. Roberts said.

"I'll pay for it," Victor said.

"We're already started," Kota said. "Let her finish. She'll be fine."

There was a softly spoken protest from Victor but he quieted.

I swallowed back my complaints. I thought of North and Silas, who were probably getting ready for football practice out in ninety degree weather. They'd probably love to relax in a cool room right now.

Nathan spoke, "Your ankle doesn't hurt, does it?"

"No worse than usual," I said, although his question caused me to focus on my foot. After Friday Fall and I'd jumped from the second floor to the first, I'd ended up with what Dr. Green thought at first was a sprained ankle. It's been a couple of weeks and I was still limping, despite applying ice packs and the boys' berating me to sit down and rest it. I couldn't hide my pain walking through school and Dr. Green insisted on bringing me in for an MRI, since the first X-ray didn't show a broken bone.

"Give me a few more minutes," Dr. Roberts said. "We'll find out what's bothering you."

"It's probably nothing," I insisted, like I'd done for weeks. "If it isn't broken, there isn't much else that will fix it besides resting it, right?"

"Will you let us doctors do the doctoring here, please?" Dr. Roberts said. "She's a miss smarty-pants, isn't she?"

Gabriel chuckled. "If I hadn't already nicknamed her Trouble, I probably would have gone with Smart Ass. Or Pretty Ass. I can't decide."

"Ugh," I said, grateful the MRI machine was hiding my blushing.

.

The Academy

The Ghost Bird Series

Friends

vs.

Family

Book Three

Written by C. L. Stone
Published by
Arcato Publishing

ABOUT C. L. STONE

Certification

- Marvelour of Wonder

- Active Participant of Scary Situations

- Official Member of F.A.M.E.

Experience

Spent an extraordinary number of years with absolutely no control over the capping of imagination, fun, and curiosity. Willingly takes part in impossible problems only to come up with the most ludicrous solution. Due to unfortunate circumstances, will no longer experience feeling on a small spot on my left calf.

Skills

Secret Keeper | Occasion Riser | Barefoot Walker Strange Acceptance | Magic Maker | Restless Reckless | Gravity Defiant | Fairy Tale Reader
Story Maker-Upper | Amusingly Baffled Comprehensive Curiousness | Usually Unbelievable

Website: http://www.clstonebooks.com/
Twitter: http://twitter.com/CLStoneX
Facebook: http://www.facebook.com/clstonex